That old gang of mine

Leslie Thomas was born in South Wales in 1931 and, when his parents died, he and his younger brother were brought up in an orphanage. His first book, *This Time Next Week*, is the autobiography of a happy orphan. At sixteen he became a reporter on a weekly newspaper in Essex and then did his National Service in Malaya during the Communist bandit war. *The Virgin Soldiers* tells of these days; it was an immediate bestseller and has been made into a film with Lynn Redgrave and Hywel Bennett.

Returning to civilian life, Leslie Thomas joined the staff of the *Evening News* becoming a top feature writer and travelling a great deal. His second novel, *Orange Wednesday*, was published in 1967. For nine months during 1967 he travelled around ten islands off the coast of Britain, the result of which was a lyrical travelogue, *Some Lovely Islands*, from which the BBC did a television series. He has continued to travel a great deal and has also written several television plays. He is a director of a London publishing house. His hobbies include golf, antiques and Queen's Park Rangers Football Club.

His other books include *Come to the War, His Lordship, Arthur McCann and all his Women, The Man with the Power, Onward Virgin Soldiers, Stand Up Virgin Soldiers, Tropic of Ruislip, Dangerous Davies: The Last Detective, Bare Nell* and *Ormerod's Landing* – all of them published in Pan.

Leslie Thomas

That old gang of mine

Pan Books London and Sydney

First published 1979 by Eyre Methuen Ltd
This edition published 1980 by Pan Books Ltd,
Cavaye Place, London SW10 9PG
© New Lion Dealings Ltd 1979
ISBN 0 330 26118 5
Printed and bound in Great Britain by
Richard Clay (The Chaucer Press) Ltd, Bungay, Suffolk

one

'This is Station WAIA, Miami, a bee ... utiful morning,
people. We expect a high of seventy-eight degrees today, a
low of sixty-two tonight, with a twenty per cent chance of
rain. It's real good to be alive ... Station WAIA, your music
way, serving the Golden Coast from the Palm Beaches to Key
West.'

The pelican cruising down from Palm Beach, Florida, towards the islands of the Keys that January day had fine flying
weather. A gentle wind sniffed from the south-west but there
were few clouds and the long golden arm of Miami Beach was
in good shape. A remote storm in the night had disturbed
the sea and there were surfers at Pompano; at Fort Lauderdale
basking ranks of vacationing college students, boys and girls,
blew bubble gum. Rich old widows in bikinis and pastel pink
knee boots, which hid their varicose veins, sunbathed at the
Fontainbleu Hotel and many blocks down, along Ocean Drive,
South Miami, two thousand elderly folk sat on small chairs
beneath the sea-grape trees.

The Golden Coast to which radio station WAIA, Miami,
refers in its call sign stretches for two hundred miles from
Palm Beach on the Atlantic seaboard of Florida, through
Boca Raton, Pompano, Fort Lauderdale, Hollywood, and a
dozen other seaside conurbations, through Miami Beach, separated from Miami proper by fine lakes and lagoons, and then
south to the curving small islands of the Florida Keys which
terminate in the city of Key West, the most southerly in the
United States.

South Miami Beach lies roughly halfway down the distance,
an area gradually diminishing to squalor, in contrast to the
expensive real estate only a couple of miles to the north. Once
it was *the* Miami Beach, but now it slips a little with each
season. It has become a museum of art deco buildings of the
nineteen twenties, inhabited by a tribe of old people, ninety
per cent of them Jewish, many impoverished. They have
colonized it with that special talent they have for colonizing;

5

it has kosher shops and kosher hotels, synagogues, talking places like salt beef bars and selected shady trees and Jewish social centres. The accents and dialogue of twenty old countries can be heard on Washington Avenue or Ocean Drive. For these are the people who once arrived in America for a new life. Now they have almost had that life and they sit in their collapsible canvas chairs and watch the sail boats and the automobiles of the new generations.

There is not much money about, the people do not live or eat extravagantly, but they stick together beneath the Florida sun. They believe that it lengthens their days, days spent in inactivity or in pseudo pastimes. The people are no longer useful. Frequently they have been sent to South Miami Beach by families who have ceased to have time or space for them. A cynic has called the place God's Waiting Room.

As the ungainly pelican creaked on his journey that morning he might have spotted on the South Beach a solitary figure in red vest and shorts, running steadily with the shore line, a man known as Ari the Greek, sixty years of age. Although at that moment he was unaware of it, he was about to become involved in one of the most bizarre series of crimes in the history of the state of Florida.

He ran every day on the beach. Most of his fellow pensioners sat where the grass was clean and cool beneath the sea-grape trees, but there were a few who were on the sand and they exchanged waves and words as he jogged by.

'Hiya Ari! Still running?'

'If I'm running I'm living!' the Greek called back, hardly panting. He had a strong Mediterranean face although he had lived in Jacksonville, Florida most of his life. In Prohibition days he had been a bootlegger, then he had operated a pancake house and later branched out into hotdogs. His hair was just a memory and his large nose seemed to have features all its own, like a second face. He drew abreast of a barefoot woman in a red dress, plump as a strawberry. They called her Molly Mandy and she was searching for treasure with a metal detector. She saw Ari call to her but she did not hear because of the dishes clamped over her ears. She obligingly pulled one of the dishes away and extended the exposed ear towards Ari.

6

'What d'yer say, Ari?'

'I said have you found something? Like treasure?'

'Jeez, I swear this machine makes you deaf.' She switched off the detector. 'Now what d'yer say?'

Ari jogged on the spot as though fearful of letting his momentum run down. A dollop of sweat careered down his nose and hit the sand at his feet making a hole like a bullet. 'Molly, I said have you found anything?' he repeated patiently. 'Like treasure?'

'Sure, sure,' Molly nodded. She had serene Jewish features, deep, dark eyes, broad forehead, hair grey but neat. She should have been sitting in the comfortable house of her elder son in White Plains, New York, where he was important with the telephone company, but his wife did not like her being around there. They had told her she would like it better down on Miami Beach in the sun. She had innocently believed them. 'Yesterday I found gold like Fort Knox never had, Ari,' she joked. 'Ten million dollars in gold! How about that! But I figured I just couldn't give up looking. Like it's a hobby.'

'I know just how you feel,' nodded Ari understandingly. 'Like I'm in the American Olympics team. It provides some-, thing to do.'

He slipped into gear and started off again. ''Bye now, take care,' Molly called automatically after him. She clamped the dogs around her ears and returned to searching the empty sand. Half an hour later she found a nickel and a dime.

Ari habitually terminated the beach section of his run by the comfort station coyly labelled 'Boys' and 'Girls', near the place where the City of Miami, with a stroke of tactless genius, had erected a large concrete calendar recording the time, date, day and year. If there was anything the many people in that region did not need it was a calendar. Had they been more militant they might have blown it up. As it was Ari projected a spirited raspberry at the object's timeful face which brought a wry laugh from some old men playing dominoes in the shade. Ari did that every day. It was not much of a defiance, but it was something.

The Greek crossed Ocean Drive, the street running parallel with the sea, but divided from the beach by the grass and the sea-grape trees. He went up Eighth Street on to Washington Avenue. It was hot now and his padding feet made prints in the sidewalk dust. There was a kosher shop advertising guaranteed clean water at twenty-five cents a jug, bring your own jug. He curled his lip because he did not go along with all these Jewish precautions, but it made him feel thirsty and he began to look forward to the lime juice he always drank after his exercise.

There was a small funeral on Washington. They never had big funerals in those parts because, in general, people did not enjoy attending them. This was just two cars, one with the coffin and the other with a clutch of bland and blank mourners. The cortège had halted at the traffic signals and the driver leaned out and mopped his brow with an appropriately black handkerchief. Ari, as if he were a motor vehicle, pulled up and ticked over also, his old but muscled legs slowing carefully like pistons. He knew the hearse driver, a violently cheerful young man who also drove a truck for an anti-bug, delousing company doing business with the small hotels. They often joked about the young man scratching a living.

'Who's travelling?' asked Ari, watching the traffic lights. He nodded casually back towards the coffin.

'Guy called Sylvester, I think,' replied the driver. 'Resident at the Beau Park.'

'Don't remember him,' shrugged Ari.

'Not many do,' said Herbie casually. 'There was no interest. He left ten dollars each to pay for some mourners.'

'If it's gonna be like that I ain't going.' Ari snorted like a horse through his nose.

'Maybe you'll be next, Ari,' warned Herbie cheerfully. 'All that running could kill you, man.'

'If I'm running I'm living,' recited the dogged Greek. The lights changed and he went into gear and got away ahead of the funeral. 'Goddamn you,' he said over his shoulder.

The conversation had worried him, so he went to the Kress Bargain Store and paid the man a dollar to test his blood pressure. The man sat all day at a small table at the entrance and tested many people's blood pressures. Some came back every day, some twice a day. A doctor would have charged ten dollars. At a dollar a pressure, it was a giveaway.

The man, who wore a proper white coat, wound the tourniquet around Ari's arm, pumped on a rubber globe, while Ari watched both his arm and the registering arrow anxiously.

'It's okay, Ari,' said the pressureman. 'Same as before. You ain't going nowhere yet.'

'I get these headaches ...' Ari began hopefully.

The man pointed sternly to the notice which said: 'Please do not ask for medical advice.' He said: 'If I knew about headaches, Ari, I'd be a doctor now, wouldn't I? Not a gas pump attendant for humans. That'll be a dollar.'

Loose Bruce got off the Greyhound bus at the depot just across the street from the Shelbourne Hotel where beauty queens used to imprint their feet in wet concrete on the forecourt. He was twenty-five years old, tall, stringy, with a casual face and a sloppy way of walking. He had been a car washer and a waiter in various parts of New York State and then had taken a job as an usher in a pornographic movie theatre off Times Square, but had been fired after being found asleep during working hours. He had taken the bus to Miami Beach because it was January in New York and he understood they had a different January in Florida. As he sloped from the bus depot with his canvas bag and his scarred jeans he was grateful to feel the sun on his face.

Walking across the street he stood on the sidewalk examining the feet of Miss Americas and Miss Universes, immortalized in concrete. Ari the Greek, who was passing by at the end of his run, loitered too. The footprints had stopped when the district began to fade, when they started to build Miami again, forty blocks north.

'Sure had big feet some of them beauties,' observed Ari. Loose Bruce nodded. The inhabitants of the district made a habit of talking to young people whenever they were available. They believed it kept them in touch.

'Not many girls around here now, huh?' said Bruce, looking at the big toe of Barbara Ann Morley, of Gary, Indiana. A family of busy blank ants had gathered in its depression.

'You have to look real hard,' admitted Ari. 'But we

some real nice *old* ladies. The young girls, they're all up at Fort Lauderdale and so's the young fellas.'

'So I'm too far south,' nodded Loose Bruce. 'That figures. Know anywhere I can stay?'

The Greek squinted at him with amazement. 'You want to *stay*?' he said. 'A young guy like you and you want to stay? Here?'

Bruce chewed on imaginary gum. 'Don't they allow anybody under eighty?' he asked.

'Eighty? Jeez. How old d'you think I am? Come on, take a guess.' Ari did a little trot on the spot and showed his teeth.

'Oh, man, I don't know. I really couldn't tell at all,' replied Bruce cautiously. 'I guess about seventy.'

Fury gathered like a cloud around Ari's great nose. 'Seventy! Goddamn you, you're ten years out! Ten whole years!'

Bruce looked at him again. 'Mister,' he said admiringly, 'you sure look great for eighty.'

'I'm *sixty*! You blind young bastard!' retorted Ari. 'Get a load of those legs, son.' He displayed the gnarled calves hanging from his running shorts. 'Take a look. They ain't no old man's legs.'

'Sorry,' said Bruce genuinely. 'I mean I can never tell the ages of older folks – or babies either. I guess you look fine for sixty. I hope I look like you when I'm sixty. I hope I can still run.'

'If I'm running I'm living,' recited Ari a little mollified. He seemed to be measuring Bruce. 'You could try where I live,' he said. 'I reckon they'll have a bed to fit you. Sunny Gables Hotel, on the ocean. It's real nice. They have a guy comes and plays the banjo in the evening.'

'Sounds the place I could be looking for,' said Bruce doubtfully. 'What's the rate?'

'Forty-five dollars a week, but maybe if the boss-woman likes you she'll give you a reduction. There's a vacancy right now because a guy fell out of bed last week and they took him to the hospital. I don't figure he'll be back.'

They began to walk towards the beach, Loose Bruce tall, with his bag on his shoulder like a sailor, Ari, almost a foot shorter, loping at his side, pausing every twenty yards for a spell of frenzied running on the spot.

'They got a burlesque up the street,' he said informatively. 'I took a look at it on my birthday. Jesus, the girls sure have got boobs these days. I figure it's the good food, the nutrition, that does that. In my day the young girls didn't get that sort of eating. Some of the older women around here ain't too bad. In fact some of them's real comfortable. But the routine takes so long you kinda lose interest. Your mind wanders. Know what I mean? And if you do anything to them – any little thing – it's a bet they start crying and thinking about their husbands, who are dead years ago. In the main it's no good. Not for women.'

Bruce took the information in. 'Well,' he said, 'that don't worry me. I'm not planning too much in that way right now. I just feel I'll stick around and get the feel of the place. Forty dollars you calculate?'

'Maybe less. Mrs Nissenbaum maybe would like a young face about the joint. And she's a widow too. South Miami Beach is kinda hung with widows.'

'That's just the room, forty dollars,' said Bruce thoughtfully. He only had seventy in the world. 'For a week.'

'It ain't for a year,' said Ari. 'That's for your room. Right. I got an efficiency, that's a room with a cooking pot. There's a stove to put it on, but mine don't work. The pot leaks anyway. It's a non-efficient efficiency, you could say. So I got it reduced. Maybe you could get a job.'

'I'll sure need one,' admitted Bruce.

'Mortician, that's a good deal around these parts,' said Ari sombrely. 'Busy, busy. Never out of work.'

'Black never suited me,' said Bruce, shaking his head. 'Maybe I could be a swimming instructor.'

'You a good swimmer then?'

'No, I can't swim. But maybe around here they wouldn't notice.'

'They wouldn't,' agreed Ari.

As though coming as a comment on their words they walked out on to Ocean Drive and Bruce saw what it was like. The beach and the sea were empty, just touching each other as if for company. But on the grass between the sand and the street there were hundreds and hundreds of old folk.

11

They massed like many-coloured penguins along a lonely shore, moving, still, chattering, silent, all bunched together beneath the fanned branches of the trees. Jazzy shirts and pants, bright hats above sunburned faces, extravagant robes and dresses. Bruce stopped in astonishment. They were around tables playing chess and cards and dominoes; they sang and danced in groups to the accompaniment of ancient violins and desperately blown trumpets; they wrote letters to remote loved ones who only occasionally replied, and read out extracts to their uninterested neighbours. They sat singly, a transistor radio clamped to the ear, they fed the seabirds and the sparrows, or they merely sat dozing or awake and staring at the enormous shining sea as if wondering what the hell it was.

'Jesus Christ,' breathed Bruce.

'Not too loud. He may arrive,' mentioned Ari. 'You get the feeling down here that he's kinda loitering. Eighty-five per cent of the people here are Jewish and they worry in case they did the wrong thing by Jesus, if you get me. When you get older you get things like that on your mind. I'm Greek Orthodox so He don't bother me.'

'I just never saw so many old folks,' said Bruce.

'They clear them out of the rest of the country,' said Ari. 'They get swept down here, like a corner. God's Waiting Room they call this place.'

They walked south on Ocean Drive. A frail couple went in the opposite direction between them wheeling a supermarket basket trolley. It contained their suitcases and other worldly belongings.

'Moving,' said Ari, giving a brief nod towards the pair.

'Very moving,' agreed Bruce. 'Real sad. Have they had to quit where they lived?'

'That's what I said, didn't I? They're *moving*. I don't know where. Maybe they're going to the penthouse at the Fontainbleu.' The commonplace sight had evoked no sympathy in him. He stopped on the sidewalk. 'Listen, kid,' he said. 'Let me go ahead and do some negotiating for you. Mrs Nissenbaum, she respects me because I'm not Jewish, see? Maybe I can get you a good deal for your room. Okay?'

'Okay,' said Bruce. 'That sure is nice of you.'

'To the Greek, kindness is only second to avarice,' said Ari baring his teeth. 'Stick around. Go and see the ocean, it's real neat. I'll be back.'

He loped away, still pausing every so often to perform his strange running-on-the-spot routine. He threw out a few ghostly punches too before continuing on his way to the Sunny Gables Hotel. Loose Bruce watched him go, shrugged and grinned and, throwing his bag over his shoulder again, walked through the people and the sea-grape trees towards the beach.

In contrast to the market-place atmosphere of the Ocean Drive lawns, the beach was almost deserted. The sea was clear, long indolent waves curling towards Florida, still echoing the storm of the night before. There was a lookout watchtower with a man gazing out over the empty waves to sky where the pelicans and the seagulls flew. Bruce sat idly on a low wall and watched the lookout. He could only see half his head, chopped grey hair under a ragged, dirty white tugboat cap.

The half a head nodded rhythmically as though the man was talking or singing to himself. Bruce wondered what was the age limit for lifeguards. Not that there seemed to be any risk of ever having to make a rescue. The ocean at South Beach was empty.

At that moment a fat woman in a rainbow bathing suit waddled on to the beach near where Bruce was standing and proceeded towards the shoreline. The lifeguard seemed to have been waiting for her.

'Mrs Blum,' he called in a friendly way through his loud-hailer. The voice was firm, not old. '*Not* today, Mrs Blum, you promised.'

The rainbow woman half turned and waved a dismissive hand towards him. She shouted something that Bruce did not catch.

'Mrs Blum, come on back right now. *Please, Mrs Blum!*' called the guard.

Bruce turned and saw the numerous old folk now gathering by the parapet of the wall behind him, watching the developing scene with keen interest. 'This time she'll do it,' forecast a tiny bald man. 'You just see. This time she'll do it.'

'Mrs BLUM!' echoed the despairing shout from the lookout

tower. 'YOU COME BACK HERE THIS MINUTE! MRS BLUM ... !'

She had now reached the fringe of the ocean and, after pausing, then stepping with fat daintiness over the first waves, she strode boldly into the rollers advancing on her. Bruce heard the lifeguard mutter, 'Shit, Mrs Blum,' as he slid down the ladder. Below the prematurely grey hair the rest of him was about thirty-five years of age. He was wearing a sun-faded track suit and he ran across the sand in athletic fashion. Bruce h   y risen to his feet and now began to saunter, th   *got*   him. Mrs Blum had become like a multi-
       9   all in the great green sea.

          rd plunged into the waves. A mutter of surprised
            me from the spectators on the parapet. 'There, Thel   told you he could swim. He wasn't kidding,' said the tiny man with the bald head.

'The water ain't very deep there,' answered Thelma in a flat tone, pleasurably anticipating tragedy. 'You wait till that guy has to get into *deep* water. Or wait till there's a killer shark. He won't go, no sir, he won't go.'

The bald man had a lifetime's experience of not arguing with Thelma beyond a sentence or so. They watched the life-guard wrestling with slippery Mrs Blum. Her ringed colours spun in the waves. Twice she knocked the man backwards with powerful dorsal sweeps of her fat forearm. Bravely he struggled from the water and tried to get his arms fixed about her. He could not get a hold. He had salt in his eyes and brine in his throat. He was not, he repeated to himself, a very good life-guard. He had a nasty vision of Mrs Blum eventually rescuing him. 'Please, Mrs Blum, cooperate,' he pleaded. Then Loose Bruce arrived and the lifeguard saw him gratefully.

The two men closed on her, but Mrs Blum was not finished. She began to howl the name of her late husband whom, she bellowed defiantly, she intended to join. 'Arnie!' she cried above the rollers. 'Arnie, come and get me Arnie!'

She turned and brilliantly knocked Bruce backwards into the waves. The lifeguard had to help him to his feet, letting go of Mrs Blum who made a final suicide bid, lying face down in the water, her multi-coloured backside rolling like some

Walt Disney whale in the swell. This time the two men managed to turn her over and tow her towards the beach. The final effort had exhausted the old lady and now she was a dead weight in their arms as they struggled for the sand. Her eyes were closed and her mouth hung open like a large cave. But she was breathing.

'I ain't doing no resuscitation,' said Bruce as he looked down at the mouth. 'It ain't my responsibility.'

'Don't put ideas into Mrs Blum's head,' whispered the lifeguard urgently. He looked down at the large coloured expanse. 'Resuscitation could take six months.'

Mrs Blum unhinged one eyelid to get a look at Bruce and closed it quickly again.

'She does this often?' said Bruce.

'Twice a week. At least twice,' nodded the lifeguard. 'It's her only contact with a man.' He looked expectantly up the beach and waved. Two men with a stretcher were coming towards them but with no urgency. They had obviously seen it all before. They even paused while one of them bent to pick up an unusual shell from the sand. 'That's the first time she's got that far out,' continued the lifeguard. 'Maybe she's been practising. One day I'm going to wake up on this sand with her blowing into *my* mouth.' He closed his eyes and shuddered briefly. Then he leaned gratefully across the coloured satin mountain that was Mrs Blum. 'My name's Oswald,' he said. 'I like to be called Ossie.'

'I don't blame you,' said Bruce reaching across. 'I'm Bruce. I just got here.'

'Glad you arrived in time,' said Ossie. The two shook hands across the meridian of Mrs Blum. It was the beginning of a partnership.

'What I gotta tell you,' said Ari the Greek loping along beside the wet Bruce, 'is that there's two hotels. The Sunny Gables and the Waving Palms, one right next to the other, if you get me. There's Mrs Nissenbaum, she runs Sunny Gables, and Miss Nissenbaum runs the Waving Palms. Like they're sisters-in-law. One is uglier than the other, but I don't know which.'

'She don't have to be Miss America,' shrugged Bruce. 'Just so I can get a room and get dry. Life-saving is very wet.'

'It's no problem, not as I see it,' Ari assured him seriously. They had walked three blocks along Ocean Drive. Some people looked at Bruce with curiosity but not many. They were mostly elderly and they walked with their own enclosing thoughts, not taking much notice of anything else. Eventually the two men stopped short of a tired building that managed to reach eight floors. It looked as though it had hunched shoulders in the way of a tall, old man. Across the front were letters tipped at various angles with the words Sunny Gables Hotel and beneath that the inducement: COME SWING WITH US.

Three old ladies nodded approvingly at Bruce from their seats on the narrow porch. They could have been operated by clockwork. Bruce nodded back and nervously tried to wipe some of the wet from his shirt.

Immediately next door was a similarly weary building. One letter of its name had vanished so that it announced itself as Waving –alms Hotel. It boasted WE SWING MORE, apparently as a taunt to the hotel next door, and added PULLMANETTES and CONDOS.

'Who are they?' asked Bruce.

'You sleep in a pullmanette and you sleep in a condo, which is a condominium,' said Ari. 'There ain't a lot of room. It's good practice for when you're dead and in your grave.'

Bruce saw the Greek's expression alter. He followed his eyes and saw an almost fearsome woman arrive on the top step of the Sunny Gables Hotel. Another lady of comparable aspect came out on to the porch of the adjoining hotel.

'Mrs Nissenbaum of the Sunny Gables and Miss Nissenbaum of the Waving Palms,' whispered Ari. 'Get what I mean?'

Bruce could. Dark, ugly and truculent, they stood on their separate doorsteps. The Sunny Gables Nissenbaum was the shorter of the two, so there was less of her to be ugly. But it was the only thing in her favour. He looked up like some boy slave put forward for auction.

'Too late, Sadie, he's coming in here,' said the Sunny Gables Nissenbaum nastily to her sister-in-law. She pointed an enormous finger towards Bruce.

'And plenty you'll charge him,' said the Waving Palms Nissenbaum. 'And goddamn little he'll get for it.'

Bruce stared up one to the other. Two grey men came out on to the porch of the Waving Palms and nodded in support of their landlady. The three women on the front of Sunny Gables had never stopped nodding.

'You'll be happy here,' Sunny Gables Nissenbaum promised, waving Bruce towards the steps. 'We could do with a young face.'

'You sure could,' said her sister-in-law coarsely. She put in a rival bid. 'Here, my boy, you pay two dollars less than you pay there. How much she charges, we charge two dollars less. You got a deal.'

Bewildered, Bruce looked at Ari. The indecision brought Mrs Nissenbaum heavily down the steps of Sunny Gables and she caught him by the wet arm and hurried him into the house. 'He'll be sorry,' shouted the Waving Palms Nissenbaum after them.

'That woman,' sneered her sister-in-law once they were in the lobby. 'Haggling. She's so Jewish.' She noticed Bruce's state apparently for the first time. 'Why is he all wet?' She looked at Bruce but asked the question of Ari, as if the responsibility must be his.

'Since arriving in this area,' said Ari patiently, 'this boy has rescued a woman from the sea. Am I speaking the truth, son?'

Bruce nodded modestly but Mrs Nissenbaum remained unimpressed. 'There's too many women here,' she said. 'Better to leave her. Conserve the men, okay. Let the ocean have the women, I say.' There was a brief pause, then she said, 'Thirty dollars a week for the room.'

Bruce glanced gratefully at Ari who winked in return. 'That's very nice of you,' he said to Mrs Nissenbaum. He had time to study her now. She was a wooden woman with jowls and heavily reddened lips. Her hair was accidentally tinted several colours and her eyelashes laden with mascara. Detachable lashes projected like teeth.

'Maybe if you feel at home I could give you a better deal still,' she said brazenly. She cocked her eye and the right eyelash broke partially free and curled upwards giving her the fierce questioning aspect of a war god in a Chinese opera. Bruce involuntarily shivered. 'I think thirty dollars is real generous, Mrs Nissenbaum,' he said.

She knew the eyelash was adrift but it did not worry her. She reached up and pulled it back into position on her lid. 'In advance,' she said firmly, holding out her hand. 'I got to take a week in advance.'

'Sure,' said Bruce, reaching for his pocket. His seventy dollars came out like a wet wedge of tobacco. He looked at it doubtfully. 'I guess it needs drying out,' he suggested.

'That'll teach you to run after women, even them that's drowning,' sniffed Mrs Nissenbaum. 'Okay, I'll take the thirty when it's aired. Ari will show you the room. No members of the opposite sex, that means women, allowed in the room after nine o'clock, no dogs and cats, no parties, noise, drunkenness or drugs. What I says, that goes. Okay?'

'Okay,' nodded Bruce. 'I don't figure on getting a dog or a cat anyway.'

'And there ain't no women around after nine o'clock anyway,' added Ari.

Mrs Nissenbaum loosed off an enormous smile that completely wrecked her face. Her false teeth appeared to be floating in the cavern of her mouth. 'Welcome to Sunny Gables then,' she said. A hand like a spade came out and folded over his. Bruce winced. 'I'm sure we'll be friends,' she continued. 'This is a great little place to live. You just swing with us. Ari will tell you, won't you Ari?'

Ari's nose bowed meekly. 'A great little place, Mrs Nissenbaum,' he agreed. 'Just a great place.'

'Some of the beds are new,' she continued. 'And the water's clean. And in the evening we have a guy comes and plays the banjo.'

In the early evening, as promised, the man who played the banjo arrived at Sunny Gables and set up a little dais upon which he sat to play to the guests. Loose Bruce walked into the lobby after the performance had begun and stood at the rear behind the rows of chairs, looking over the heads of the old folk as if they were children.

The banjoist was dressed, for some reason, in a kind of old-fashioned military uniform with which went a sombrero. Bruce wondered if he might have been in the Mexican army at some time. His voice, however, was mid-American. Once, long before, he had been able to sing as well as play the banjo, but although he tried gallantly now, the higher notes took off into silence with only a smile in the eyes and a moving of the mouth to show that they were being attempted. When he had real trouble with a few notes, or he slipped up on remembering the words, which he also did at times, the audience sportingly joined in to push him up the hill. With some it seemed that their voices were the strongest part of their bodies and they entered the spirit with almost raucous abandon.

A great favourite seemed to be, *They Tried To Tell Us We're Too Young* – 'as sung by my own personal friend, the late, great, Nat King Cole.' Everybody joined in and Bruce stood awkwardly outside the company, too embarrassed to join it. He knew the words, however, and after being pushed and prodded by several eager old people in the back row of the seats, he began to mouth them silently. When the song had finished a long delicate hand reached up and took his encouraging him to take a chair. He sat down awkwardly.

'I'm K-K-K-Katy,' said a beautiful, grey-haired lady. 'I'm not trying to st-st-steal you, young man. I already have somebody who loves me.'

'That's nice,' was all Bruce could think of under the circumstances. 'That's very nice indeed.'

'He is an ex-theatrical st-strong man,' she recited, keeping her voice well modulated, below the sound of the banjo man's tune. 'He was known as Lou the Barbender. He's J-J-Jewish, you know.'

Bruce had never met anyone like this before. 'Jewish?' he echoed, as though she had said he was Gibraltese. 'That's very interesting.'

Katy bent closer. She had a fine perfume about her hair. He wondered why girls did not smell like that now. 'He lives next door,' she whispered, 'in the other Niss-Niss-Nissenbaum place. Enemy territory. We have to meet in secret.'

That for the moment seemed to exhaust the information she was inclined to give about herself and her lover. The banjoist, with a unique blend of the slang of three generations, exclaimed: 'Bounce me, brother, we're going to rock, because this is where it all is!'

An appreciative snort came from the audience and they began to sway about while he lurched himself into some barely recognizable tunes of the fifties. A lady came around with a tray of drinks and, impecunious though he was, Bruce felt like he ought to ask if Katy would like one. She seemed overwhelmed with pleasure.

'Th-th-that's real kind of you, young fellow,' she told him. 'I'd like a Kosher Cola.'

Bruce, trying to look as if he bought Kosher Colas every day, took the drink and paid his thirty cents. A pale, slim man in a faded but still shapely suit came in, his hair carefully combed, a boot-lace tie at his neck and a pair of fawn spats topping his polished black boots. He sat down with the casualness of a dude and turned on the television that stood in the corner. He took no notice of the banjo-player but turned the volume of the cowboy series he had selected until it was to his satisfaction. Then he sat back easily to watch.

'That's Joe D-Danziger. They call him Sidewalk Joe,' whispered Katy seeing Bruce watching the man. 'He used to be a g-g-gangster, you know. In New York. Nobody crosses him.'

'He looks dangerous,' agreed Bruce, looking at the man's frail hands against his cheek.

'I don't really think he is,' confided Katy. 'I guess he re-retired from that life a long time ago.' She looked around. 'Like all of us.'

Bruce looked towards the other side of the room. 'Who's that?' he nodded. 'The lady tearing the pages out of the book?'

'That's Molly Manders. Everybody calls her Molly Mandy. She looks for treasure on the South Beach. Her granddaughter's got a motor cycle. I've seen it.'

Bruce was becoming accustomed to the inconsequential sentences. 'Why would she be doing that? Tearing pages from her book?' he inquired.

'Once she's read a page she r-r-rips it out,' shrugged Katy as if it were perfectly natural. 'No point in c-c-carrying around pages you've read, now is there? When you get older you learn to conserve your energy.'

With a sudden rattle of his banjo, the player indicated that his evening's performance was almost through. Immediately everyone got to their feet and attempted to stand stiffly. Bruce was the last one up. 'It's the National Anthem of our country,' said Katy as if he had recently arrived from Mars. 'Do you know it?'

'Yes ... sure,' mumbled Bruce. He tried to remember how long ago he had last sung the words.

'It's a lovely song,' said Katy, skipping a couple of bars. 'We ought to be real pleased and proud to be Americans.'

two

Mornings begin early on South Miami Beach. As the first sun pushes through the streets, so the people emerge from the shabby little hotels and hurry along Washington Avenue to the fruit and bread shops. At the fruit store they know there will be bruised and damaged produce being sold at half price and at the bakery the same bargains in day-old bread and cakes.

Ari the Greek scorned such scavenging, as he called it. 'I got my pride still,' he said to Loose Bruce as they trotted along the beach in the warming morning. 'Sure I pick up my social security with the rest of the people, but me, I spend it in style. I buy *fresh* fruit and *new* goddamn bread. Maybe I give the apples a little push so they fall on the floor and then I get a discount on them being damaged, but that ain't the same as lining up at dawn for the left-overs. There's no style in that, son. No style.'

Bruce found himself puffing a little as they trotted the long beach. The early waves fell nonchalantly on the sand almost at their feet.

In the distance behind them the cruise liners from the Caribbean were lined along the quays in the port, ahead the tall buildings of contemporary Miami Beach stood like topless palms along the shore. At that distance the sand diminished into early mist. Pelicans flew cheek to cheek and the municipal trash cart bearing its label 'Rubbish Gobbler' cruised Ocean Drive. There were a lot of cats and dogs mooching the streets and along the shore, because the old people liked pets. Mostly they were not allowed to keep animals in their rooms, but they adopted strays and fed them regularly in appointed places with scraps saved from their own tables.

'See that,' said Ari pointing to four people feeding dogs and cats in a yard between two blocks. 'It don't matter what happens to humans as long as the animals get fed.'

'Seems to me,' puffed Bruce, 'that all these people about here need *something* to *do*.'

'Sure, sure,' agreed Ari. Bruce watched his clockwork legs with admiration. There was brown perspiration like rusty water on his face and his large nose wobbled as he ran, as though it were on a hinge, but he spoke without panting. 'They *got* things to do,' he added, nodding his nose towards a man sitting facing but not seeing the ocean, a transistor radio clamped to his ear. In the other ear was a deaf aid. 'But they ain't the *right* things. Feeding the birds and the cats, dancing, playing cards and dominoes, arguing, all that sort of stuff. But it ain't real, son. There ain't no ambition around these parts.'

They came within shouting distance of the lifeguard's watchtower. Bruce had done enough running. 'Ari,' he said, 'I guess I'll have a word with my buddy up there.'

'You're bushed,' grinned Ari. 'You ain't used to it.'

'No, I'm in good shape. Just thought I'd see him. Keep running.'

'While I'm running I'm living.' Ari's slogan floated back over the sand as he trotted on. The sun eased itself higher. The ocean was unoccupied except for a cargo ship moving indolently towards Port Everglades. Bruce climbed the ladder to the lifeguard platform.

'Busy?' he asked.

'Nope. But you never know in these parts,' drawled Ossie. His matted grey hair hung over his brown forehead. There was a hole in his antique hat. 'Could be an out-of-season hurricane. Could be an invasion from Cuba. Or Mrs Blum could make another run for eternity. You just never can tell, man.'

They stood on the platform and turned from the shore to the grass and the sea-grape trees. The multi-coloured costumes of the old folk of South Miami Beach were coming from many directions, from the lateral streets and the steps of the cramped hotels, many of them carrying flimsy fold-up chairs. Groups were already forming on the grass. Greetings were called, newly arrived letters were waved ('I got word from my son, the sailor'), musical instruments were tuned, cards were shuffled. On the small enclosed terraces and balconies of the hotels others sat looking wistfully at the activity on the ocean front. They did not move very much. They just sat and watched and if anyone could think of something to say they said it and the others were grateful. A discussion of whether a walk was possible that day might occupy half an hour.

'Something new every day,' shrugged Ossie, looking out over the people. 'Non-stop excitement, man. Ever seen anything like this?'

'Not till now,' admitted Bruce shaking his head. 'What the hell are *you* doing here, anyway?'

'Now that's what I was going to ask you,' said Ossie.

'I heard the sun was out down here,' replied Bruce. 'I just didn't realize what it was shining on. Is there anybody under sixty for miles?'

'Pompano, Fort Lauderdale,' said Ossie nodding his head along the shore towards the vague, warm distance. 'Daytona Beach, that's the place. Plenty of chicks up there, so I hear. The kids drive around in cars on the beach. Or Key West.' He revolved and nodded in the other direction towards the unseen Florida islands. 'They got all the hippy people down there. That's where all the flowers have gone. You can smell the grass burning.'

'Maybe I'll head that way. Down the Keys.'

'It's nice, so they say. A guy told me there's a lot of hot, wild screwing goes on and people have iguanas and frogs as pets. And they all sit on the quay and watch the sun set, and they clap when it goes down. It's different, I guess.'

'What the hell *are* you doing here?' repeated Bruce.

'Well, it's kinda peaceful. The one thing that old folks are – they're kinda peaceful.'

'Mrs Blum didn't seem so peaceful. I still got the bruises.'

'Right. But she's the exception. The rest keep good and quiet. I was in Vietnam and when I got back I didn't enjoy getting the blame for it, you know? Sometimes I got blamed for losing and sometimes I got blamed for not losing sooner, and sometimes I got blamed for not losing, and sometimes I got blamed for being there at all. Christ, I didn't know what the hell it was all about. I just went and I came back and every bastard's throwing shit at me. So I figured that down here it would be peaceful and it sure is.'

'Sure. But there don't seem a lot of future to me. Where d'you live?'

'I got an apartment. It's okay. I was sharing with a girl from Omaha who kinda wandered in this direction, just like you. But she's gone. She went off with one of the old guys. One with a lot of dough. I guess she saw more future in that.'

'So what d'you do?'

'I just sit here and then I go home. There's a diner next to the place I live so I eat there. I get drunk pretty regular and last week I went to the burlesque. They got big boobs those chicks there.'

'It's the food, the nourishment,' said Bruce knowingly.

'Could be. There's a broad does things with a snake. It's real neat. But it ain't like doing the genuine thing. Going there, I mean. There's no future in that either.'

'How old are you?' said Bruce.

'Just about thirty-five,' said Ossie.

'You look older, pal. It's this place growing on you.'

They stood looking out over the grass. The people now numbered more than a thousand. 'We ought to think of something they could do,' decided Bruce. 'Maybe organize a revolution.'

'Right,' nodded Ossie. 'Lead them on Washington. All the

old biddies and the old guys, burning and raping and pillaging on the way.'

'There ought to be something,' said Bruce thoughtfully.

As they watched, a heavy red motor cycle eased down as it cruised throatily into Ocean Drive. It came to a stop outside Sunny Gables and Bruce and Ossie stopped speaking and stood on the watchtower admiring its bright powerful form. 'Gee, it's not too often you see a sight like that down these parts,' said Ossie. 'Beautiful.'

The rider, slight in black jacket and jeans, pulled away a vivid orange helmet and visor. At a shake of the head a sunlit cascade of fair hair rolled down. Bruce grabbed Ossie's binoculars. 'A Yamaha Mama,' he breathed as he looked. 'And beautiful, so beautiful.'

Ossie forced the return of the glasses and turned them on the girl. He felt the breeze of Bruce going past him. 'I'll tell you what she's like later,' the younger man called as he stumbled hurriedly down the ladder. Ossie was quickly after him, sliding expertly on the wooden rail. They landed in a heap on the sand and then ran towards the street, dodging through the assemblies of old people, and braking a few yards short of the girl who was looking towards the entrance to Sunny Gables. She heard their breathing and turned and saw them.

'Nice little runabout you got there,' said Bruce, looking patronizingly at the broad red back and silver shoulders of the machine. It glistened like a sweating horse in the sunshine.

'It gets me from A to B,' she answered evenly. 'And I take my grandma on it. I'm waiting for her now.'

'Molly,' said Bruce, pleased he had remembered. 'Molly Mandy.'

'Mrs Manders, that's right,' said the girl. 'You know her?'

'Well, in a way. We're fellow guests.' He nodded at Nissenbaum's hotel.

'There? You?'

'I like old folks.' He smiled winningly at her. 'And younger folks. I just have no firm preferences. Look at my friend here. He's old.'

'I'm Ossie,' said Ossie stepping forward modestly. 'Old Ossie.'

'And me, I'm young Bruce. Loose Bruce they call me,' Bruce grinned with boyish assurance.

'You should get somebody to tighten you up with a wrench,' said the girl.

'I'd sure like to ride that bike,' said Bruce easily.

Surprisingly she nodded. 'Okay. Get on the back. I'll drive.'

Bruce's eyebrows went up with pleasure. 'You wait and keep grandma glad,' he said to Ossie. 'We'll be back next week.'

'Five minutes,' forecast the girl. She eased her tight backside across the saddle and Bruce climbed on behind. He rubbed his hands with brief chivalry on his jeans and placed them with careful enjoyment around her waist. 'Not too tight, Loose Bruce,' she called over her shoulder. 'I'm not going to leave you, sonny.'

She kicked the starter and the motor cycle growled like an animal. It strained to be off and she did not contain the urge for long. They roared south on Ocean Drive and were gone in a moment into the Miami dust. Ossie sat down on the grass and waited.

Molly Mandy appeared on the steps of Sunny Gables wearing a purple motor cycle outfit and a green crash helmet. Ossie introduced himself and told her what had happened.

'And this young guy's gone off with Gabby, has he?' she said, looking concerned. 'Poor fellow.'

She and Ossie exchanged comments on the heat of the Florida day. Although they had never met before he had seen her with her metal detector on the beach and she had seen him sitting above in his watchtower and they had exchanged waves. 'Glad you came down to earth,' she said with a smile. 'You looked like some kind of angel sitting up there.'

Within five minutes Gabby was back, curving in dust along Eighth Street and guiding the thick wheels along the sidewalk. Loose Bruce, pale down to his shoulders, dismounted unsteadily. The girl pushed back her visor, kissed her grandmother, and glanced back at her passenger.

'I guess you really enjoyed that, didn't you, Bruce?' she inquired. 'I certainly did.'

'Yes,' muttered Bruce uneasily. 'Very different. I'm glad we missed the ocean liner on the quay. I don't go for collisions with ocean liners.'

Gabby smiled fully at Ossie. 'Maybe you'd like a little ride someday?' she suggested.

'Thanks,' replied Ossie with great care. 'When I dice, I like to dice with dice.'

'Okay,' she said easily. 'Get aboard grandma.'

Molly laughed with delight and got into her helmet. The old lady clutched the young waist and the machine eased forward picking up speed as it drove once more south of Ocean Drive.

'Some experience, I guess?' suggested Ossie.

'Great,' breathed Bruce. 'Just getting your legs around something as special as that is just great.'

Ossie shrugged. 'You didn't seem to appreciate it too much.'

'I wasn't talking about the motor bike,' said Bruce.

K-K-K-Katy was preparing to go to the weekly twenty-five cent dance at the South Miami Beach Community Centre. It was always an event to which she looked forward and she sang short snatches of old stage songs, the words adorned by her attractive speech impediment. On occasions, years ago, she had used it to devastating effect. Allied to a baby face and flawless blue eyes, the stutter had made men tremble.

She had been a chorus girl in the wanton days of the thirties in Buffalo, and she still had the long legs and the urchin grin. She was proud of both and decided gratefully that they were now with her for good. All the charms you were going to lose, she calculated, you lost by the time you were sixty and she had just seen that birthday off.

The weekly dances had recently taken on a new significance for now she was escorted by her one-time strong man, Lou the Barbender. He had toured every state and had even astonished the populace in Cuba and Mexico. Their paths, they decided, must have touched at times in their respective heydays because they remembered many of the same names. They had fallen into conversation one morning beneath the sea-grape trees and now they were in love. It was strange, K-K-K-Katy reflected, how love reverted in these late days to the childish extremes of holding hands and stealing kisses. Lou still had immensely strong hands, and he could still bend thin iron bars and tear two thirds of a telephone directory down the middle, and she still had the lips that had been desired by so many in the past years. Occasionally she wondered where all those suitors had gone.

The room was small and overburdened with Katy's worldly goods. There were trunks and suitcases, hundreds of smiling dead photographs, faded paper flowers, press cuttings, knick-knacks she had accumulated over the years and two dozen dresses hanging from the picture rail around the walls. These included the wedding dress that she had never worn. She had been ready and eager to marry a nice Jewish financier in Chicago in 1941 when he was called, not to the war which had opened only a week before, but to gaol for frauds that kept him there for the next twenty years. When he came out he said he had thought about it and changed his mind about marriage and so the dress remained unused. She wondered if, perhaps, after all, it was not too late for the dress. Lou would look remarkably fine in a tail coat (she knew he had one because he had mentioned he had kept such a garment from the days of his act). And she knew for sure that the dress would still fit her because every year, on her birthday, she tried it on.

She had bathed in the one bathroom on that floor of the Sunny Gables Hotel where she had lived for the past five years, and had been delayed because, as occasionally happened, one of the other guests, a fat man, had become wedged in the narrow bathtub and needed to be levered out by some of the stronger male residents.

Now she selected a fine lavender dress that swept down her long legs and put a saucy flower in her ear. She could still do a shoulder high kick and she performed several of these, standing facing down the narrow room with the window wide open in case of miscalculations. She sang a few bars of a song, worked up a movement, and then flung the leg spectacularly towards the ceiling one, two, three times. She smiled with satisfaction and then waited for the banging downstairs. It came on schedule, one, two, three, four ill-tempered thumps on their ceiling with a rubber-ended walking stick. They always did that when she kicked. In her youth, when she could really kick high, people used to complain from the room above.

Cheerfully she went downstairs and on to the confined balcony in front of the hotel. Several of the inmates were sitting out there staring in the direction of the setting sun as though wondering why and where it was going. She said a bright word to them and two nodded kindly but the others did not take much notice. She was still considered a flapper.

She timed her exit excellently, for as she went out with the paling daylight, Lou the Barbender, uncomfortably resplendent in his tailed suit, appeared on the porch of the Waving Palms Hotel only a few feet away. She smiled and he grinned shyly but they did not speak, and would not do so until they were two blocks away. The rival Nissenbaums appeared a minute later, both having suspicions of the alliance, and confronted each other truculently over the wooden fence that divided their dominions.

'Fraud,' said the Sunny Gables Nissenbaum.

'Skinflint,' replied her sister-in-law.

That was all. They sniffed the South Beach air and, their salvos fired, turned and retreated into their doors. They did it every evening.

Two safe blocks away, Katy held on to Lou's great hand. She sniffed at the warm evening, smiled at the calm palms, and felt that there were possibilities abounding. She allowed her dancing shoes to sound loudly on the sidewalk and did a short, complicated triple step between some ornamental trees. Lou smiled his admiration. She felt very good; like a young girl going to a college ball. She had a strong intuition that something was going to happen to her soon. She could not have realized just how much.

Loose Bruce had wanted to go to the burlesque show, but Ossie had dissuaded him, saying that at the weekly dance in the Community Centre there was always complimentary food and plenty of it and some of the old guys carried whisky flasks in their pockets.

They lined up at the door without attracting a great amount

of interest. Old folk have generally seen everything and one more surprise is not surprising. Bruce towered over the line for the pay booth and Ossie was only just shorter. Behind them among the elderly chatter they heard the girl's voice talking to her grandmother. They turned simultaneously, their heads almost colliding as they twisted inwards. She looked up and regarded the two hopeful faces coolly.

'Wow,' the girl said to the old lady. 'Old folk get younger all the time.'

'Never did see *two* of them fellows here before,' said the grandmother.

'Maybe they're a cabaret act,' the girl whispered loudly. 'They look kinda strange, like that.'

Bruce and Ossie paid their twenty-five cents each and hung about inside the door.

'Why don't you go to the washroom?' suggested Bruce watching for the girl to enter.

'I never do,' replied Ossie coolly. 'The old guys ask you to zip them up.'

They loitered beside a dusty indoor palm until the girl and the old lady came in.

'Hi,' said Bruce with what he believed was a long smile.

'Hi,' said Ossie touching his forehead with what he imagined was a sign of good manners.

'Good evening,' said the girl soberly. She looked superb in a cool blue dress. Her face was lovely but her eyes without encouragement. 'Come on grandma, let's find you a chair,' she said briskly.

Bruce and Ossie followed behind as they walked. They watched the graceful loop of the girl's backside alongside the little plodding bumps of the old lady. 'Man,' said Bruce thoughtfully, 'I sure don't care for your date.'

'How much does that job of yours pay?' asked Bruce. 'Being a beach guard?'

Ossie picked his teeth carefully. 'About enough,' he drawled. 'And expenses.'

'Expenses! Jesus, how can you get expenses? You can't *spend* anything. You just sit there on your ass all day looking at the goddamn ocean. Christ, you don't move unless Mrs Blum makes a run for it.'

'And bonuses,' continued Ossie. They were sitting on the Community Centre chairs watching the old folk dancing in a large revolving oval, moving as if they were some substance in a slow mixer.

'Now I've heard it all! What kind of bonuses?'

'Ten dollars for a rescue. That's the rate.'

'Ten bucks. Did Mrs Blum rate ten bucks?'

'Sure.'

'Well, what about my fifty per cent? I rescued half of Mrs Blum. The heavy half.'

'Twenty per cent,' offered Ossie easily. 'It's my pitch remember. When I get paid, you get paid. Okay? Two bucks.'

'Cheapskate,' said Loose Bruce. But his face brightened. 'Say, you're real slow man. Why not get a few of the old women to make like they're drowning. *Give* them a dollar a time. You'd be *nine bucks* in profit every time! Ten rescues a day would be worth it. Ninety bucks, seven days a week, that makes . . .'

'They get suspicious,' Ossie pointed out solemnly. 'The authorities. The guy I took the job from tried that. Got his own folks to be like they were drowning. Come to remember it, his ma really *did* drown. While he was pulling out his sister, his ma drowned. So it don't work.' .

'You've got a negative outlook,' complained Bruce. 'According to you *nothing* works. Something's got to.'

He looked about him. Again it came to him that he was in an unreal world. The old folks performing their polkas and other odd ancient dances as if some time machine had projected him to a past age. Ossie, who had seen it before, sat munching free sandwiches and drinking sarsparilla, his grey head nodding to the music as if he at least partly understood it. The women heavily outnumbered the men and many ladies danced together, some clutched to each other as if they were in danger of sinking. At that time of life, however, they had abandoned any feminine shyness and soon two plump and beaming sisters advanced upon Bruce and Ossie and demanded that they get to their feet and dance.

Neither knew what foot went first but excuses were loudly

elbowed aside and they found themselves in the revolving crowd bouncing up and down and in and out to some Slovak dance from years back.

They saw that the girl was dancing, however, and the jig conveniently gave way to another, a progressive dance where the people stood in lines, stayed with a partner for a few steps and turns and then moved on to someone else. Bruce adeptly inserted himself three places from the girl and soon they came face to face. They clapped hands together as the dance required.

'This is beautiful,' said Bruce. 'Gee, I love this dance. What's your name?'

She sighed. 'Okay. My name's Gwendolina but everyone calls me Gabby.'

'I don't wonder,' said Bruce.

She grimaced, then laughed. 'I'm from St Pete's, Florida, and the lady you are about to hold in your arms is my grandmother. You'll like her. Goodbye.'

Bruce found himself pushed along the line by the eager Ossie, who grinned happily at the girl he now turned in his hold. 'I'm in steady employment,' he said, 'and my name's Ossie. I'm a lifesaver.'

'I'm not drowning,' she said, disentangling his arms. 'Yet.'

Bruce quickly broke out of sequence and slipped into the line again on the left side of Ossie, so that when the dancers moved up again he was facing the girl. 'It's me again,' he smiled winningly. 'I'm Bruce.'

'I'm Bruce, fly me,' said the girl wryly.

'Loose Bruce,' called Ossie sideways down the danceline. 'Ask him why he's called Loose Bruce. Go on, ask him.'

'I'm six feet almost one inch, fair hair, brown eyes, friendly nature and alone.'

'Alone? I wonder why that could be?' said Gabby.

Ossie made a quick break from the line and pushed in before some old five foot fellow who was patiently looking forward to dancing with Gabby.

'You're spoiling the dance,' he said sharply to Ossie.

'Sorry. I'm not sure how to do this one. I'm just all confused,' said Ossie moving in on Gabby. He smiled his mature smile at her. 'I save people from the ocean,' he said. 'All day.'

'He gets ten dollars a time,' Bruce called up the line. 'He wants you to put your grandmother in the sea and he'll split it with you. He's all heart.'

The dance stopped and everyone clapped, Bruce and Ossie louder than anyone. 'They spoiled it,' said the five foot man who had been looking forward to dancing with Gabby. 'They shouldn't be allowed in here.'

Ossie smiled overwhelmingly at him and then at the puffy lady at his side. She blushed pink and, nagging, pulled the small man away. Gabby and her grandmother sat down and Ossie and Bruce sat on either side of them, Ossie triumphantly next to the girl. 'Why don't you join us,' suggested Gabby caustically.

'Gabby,' said the old lady. 'Are these two trying to pick us up?'

'I'm afraid so, grandma.'

'Well I don't want to be picked up. I'm fancy free. My heart's my own.'

A man with red bursting cheeks pranced to the centre of the floor and threw his arms wide. 'Ladies and gentlemen, nice people,' he beamed. 'Now we come to the time of the cabaret. You all like the cabaret, don't you?' There was a chorus of approval. 'Yes of course. Well tonight we have your old favourite, Lou the Barbender, the strongest man on Miami Beach. Also a lady who's just come down from Pittsburgh who can sing, and a gentleman who's real hot playing the zither.'

The two young men watched almost mesmerized as a big woman in a blood-red dress rushed immediately on to the stage, pushed the compère violently to one side and flung herself into a hideous song with enormous and tuneless gusto. All around the people groaned and buried their heads in their hands, some shouted rudely at her to quit. But she appeared not to hear, went right through three verses and the terrible chorus, eyes closed, mouth wide, not caring for anyone or anything. She left the stage to a fusillade of catcalls and boos. The compère returned shakily. 'Thanks people, I just knew you would enjoy that,' he smiled.

'Mother Courage,' said Ossie. 'That's who she is. Mother Courage.'

'They've all got guts,' put in Gabby turning to him. 'You need guts to survive down here.'

'I figure they ought to *do* something,' said Bruce, anxious to talk with her. 'Not dancing or singing. Not *made up* things. Get me? Something they'd be a hundred per cent occupied with. You know?'

'I don't know. But I see what you mean,' she said. 'Like building a dam or riding pony express.'

'Something like that,' agreed Ossie.

'My grandma searches for treasure with a metal detector,' said Gabby quite proudly.

'I've seen her,' said Ossie. 'When she finds it I'm going to help her carry it home.'

Lou the Barbender had now taken the centre of the floor. He lifted a ten pound weight with his little finger, a feat which brought excited gasps from the encircling ladies. He was red-faced in his tailed suit and every one of his shirt buttons had burst, but he looked formidable in an old-fashioned way.

Bruce looked beyond the strong man to where the man they called Sidewalk Joe, the old New York gangster, sat like a well preserved dandy at the edge of the floor. Bruce turned and caught Ossie's eye. He briefly jerked his head sideways and the two young men stood up carefully and, with an excusing nod to Gabby and her grandmother, sidled their way through the audience to the deserted sandwich table. They both picked up leftover segments of bread and put them in their mouths.

'I've got it,' said Bruce. 'It's beautiful.'

'Okay,' said Ossie sceptically. 'What is it?'

'Crime,' said Bruce seriously, biting into the rye bread. 'Organized crime.'

three

Captain of Detectives Albert Salvatore drove over the Julia Tuttle Causeway from Miami Beach towards the City of Miami at eight o'clock on a shining Florida morning. His head told him that his police college reunion he had attended the previous night at a hotel on the beach had been a raucous experience. He had been obliged to telephone his wife Betty at midnight to report that he was in no condition to negotiate his passage home and had slept on an uncomfortable floor in a room in the hotel.

The splendid but everyday crystal air and water of the region was all about him, with sail boats and power boats on the lagoons and the habitual Goodyear silver blimp in the sky. And had he been a reflective sort of man, which he was not, he might have given thought to Julia Tuttle after whom the concrete causeway on which he drove was named. Mrs Tuttle, an adventurous widow, had literally discovered Miami less than a century before when it was swamp and jungle and inhabited only by Seminoles. She had sailed down the Miami River with her family, a piano and a pair of Jersey cows and found herself in a region of such warm lushness that she sent a sprig of orange blossom to Henry Flagler the railroad builder in New York. By this he could see, on that cold January day in 1895, that Miami was without frost. So he built a railroad to the south and opened up the great vacation city.

From the Julia Tuttle Causeway, Salvatore could look over silvery lagoons to both north and south, joining the long peninsular of Miami Beach and the island of Key Biscayne to the city of Miami. Further north the lagoons thinned to become the amazing and little known Intra-Coastal Waterway, a canal running almost the whole length of the eastern seaboard of the United States. In winter, using lakes and rivers and the canal itself, small boats from as far north as Canada could voyage to Florida and into the Caribbean without once having to risk the open sea. From the point where the wide lagoons bottlenecked into the slim canal the banks were joined by a series of cantilever bridges, opening at their centre to allow the passage of larger craft. There were ten of those mechanical bridges between Hollywood Beach at the northern extreme of Miami Beach proper to West Palm Beach several miles further up the coast. They crossed the Intra-Coastal Waterway at Hollywood, where there were two bridges, Fort Lauderdale, Pompano Beach, Boca Raton, Delray Beach, Lake Worth, Palm Beach and West Palm Beach. Each bridge carried above it a highway connecting Route A95 and the Florida Turnpike with the beach resorts. That morning Captain Albert Salvatore had, perhaps fortunately, no inkling of the drama and frustration these cantilever bridges were to cause him in his pursuit of the most unusual gang of criminals Florida, probably even the entire United States, had ever known.

He was not, and this he admitted even to himself, the most spectacular of police officers, nor did he look it. He was slightly undersized, but slim enough, with a worried face that continued its habitual frown right up to the summit of his head via a channel naked of hair. He found this embarrassing and his wife Betty blamed it on his scratching his head when puzzled or frustrated, which was frequently. On special occasions he tried to conceal this channel by combing the hair from its sides over the exposed skin. His children had been heard to refer to him as 'Old River Head' and this had frightened and annoyed him. He was running out of people whom he could love and who loved him in return.

Crime in greater Miami contained a high element of misdemeanours which the police officially referred to as 'self-adjusting'. This included various feuds within the Miami branch of the Mafia or between the Mafia and other organizations whose members appeared in the area on spring vacations as regularly as the big league baseball teams who came there to tune up for the new season. These crimes, while they had to be investigated, could generally be relied upon to look after themselves, vengeance and sometimes even justice being delivered within the framework of the secret society itself. The same went for political crimes, a bomb explosion or a shooting, among the many Cubans who had settled in Florida following the coming to power of Fidel Castro in Havana. The various factions within the tempestuous Cuban community occasionally took primitive revenge on each other. But the Cuban eye for the Cuban eye was the same as the Mafia tooth for the Mafia tooth. All that remained for the police to do was to take photographs and police notes.

There was a third area of self-righting crime, the hot-weather misdemeanour of passion, usually domestic, which required no great effort either to solve or to bring to justice. These three types of activity took up a fair part of Salvatore's professional life and he could handle them. Handle them with such ease, in fact, that the recent intrusion of a man called George Zaharran, a retired policeman, into his working hours, a minor thing in itself, had become a major intrusion and irritant.

He guessed that Zaharran would turn up somewhere that morning because it was Monday and he had become a habit on Monday. Salvatore owed him professional favours from the distant past but he found it difficult to find the opportunity, or the inclination, to repay them now. Zaharran was elderly, fat and almost immovable. He had set himself up as a private investigator, or a criminalistic inquirer and investigator, as he preferred to be known, had, over two or three years, achieved a series of almost spectacular failures and was now begging for work.

Zaharran, in fact, did not appear until after eleven that morning – thus lulling Salvatore into false complacency – and then it was in the coffee shop where the police detective went for a twenty minute break from his office.

It was all but impossible for Zaharran to conceal himself anywhere, this added to an enormous slowness of movement being one of his prime failure factors, and even though he contrived to sit shadowed by a large and dusty indoor plant in the coffee shop, Salvatore immediately spotted him. But it was too late to escape. Zaharran emerged.

He was like a brown elephant, wearing fawn shirt and trousers, lumbering forward, small-eyed, large-limbed, fat-bodied, with a look of pleasured astonishment on his worn face. 'But Captain Salvatore ... what a break ... I just didn't know you numbered among the clientele of this place! May I buy you a cup of coffee?'

Salvatore sighed. 'Jesus Harry Christ,' he said. 'You *know* I come in here, Zaharran. Every goddamn day I come in here. And now you're in here also. You bother me at my office and you bother me now when I'm taking a private cup of coffee. Why not come to my home maybe?'

'My cover's blown,' sighed Zaharran sitting heavily on the stool next to the policeman.

'Like it always was,' returned Salvatore unkindly.

'In the early days I was good,' said Zaharran, more in reminiscence than protest. 'You got to give me that. I helped you a lot then. Remember the case at Key Biscayne – the big house robbery? And the kidnapped kid at Pompano ...?'

'Okay, okay. But that's gone. You're retired, Zaharran. Why don't you be like other retired guys and retire?'

'If I gave up the work of detection I would just go to pieces,' said Zaharran illogically. Salvatore stared at the human wreck beside him. He melted sufficiently to order a second cup of coffee which he passed to Zaharran.

'Coffee,' beamed Zaharran, his face a movement of creases. 'Now you buy me coffee. You're seeing things my way.'

'I don't,' said Salvatore bluntly. 'You're retired and that's retired. If you want to go on investigating then get your own cases.' He tried logic. 'Listen, we got trained cops, plenty of trained cops. How can I pass on even a crumb to you? How can I? How can I justify the cost?'

Zaharran felt about his fawn pockets and produced a bent business card. It said: 'George Zaharran, Criminalistic Inquirer and Investigator. Formerly of the Police.' 'Here,' he said as if making a donation. 'Take this with you, captain.'

'Jesus Lionel Christ,' sighed Salvatore. 'I have plenty of these already. I got a whole drawer full of them.' He held the battered card between two fingers. 'And they don't get any cleaner either. I guess the Sanitation Department might have a case against you Zaharran, handing out dirty cards like this.'

'Let them try,' shrugged Zaharran. 'I'd sue them for violation of civil rights. Violation of the rights of the elderly, the poor and the needy.' He looked thoughtful. 'Maybe I could sue you for that, Salvatore, or the police department. Violation of the rights of the elderly, the poor and the needy.'

'We do it all the time,' said Salvatore unimpressed. 'It's no good violating the rights of the big people is it? You can't win.'

He finished his coffee and rose. 'Got to go,' he said. 'Lots to be done.'

'Wish I could help,' said Zaharran sadly. 'I miss it like hell, you know. Maybe some small routine cases. Missing children, stray dogs ...'

'We have all the personnel we need. You should concentrate on divorce, Zaharran, like most private investigators do. That pays.'

Zaharran made a worse face than he had. 'No dice,' he said. 'I always fall out of trees and I'm too big to get under a bed. I know, I've tried.' He leaned forward with last minute urgency and fumbled again in his gaping pocket. He produced a small sheaf of business cards encircled with an elastic band. He separated them hurriedly and handed them one by one to the reluctant Salvatore.

'Zaharran Real Estate,' said the first card. 'Zaharran Paper Novelties' said another. 'Zaharran Mailed Astrology' said a third. And as an additional reminder, 'George Zaharran, Criminalistic Inquirer and Investigator. Formerly of the Police' said the fourth.

Salvatore sighed and took the cards. 'If you should ever feel yourself in requirement of any of those services,' prompted Zaharran, 'do not hesitate to call me. I can recommend the mailed astrology personally.'

Nothing was going to stop Salvatore leaving now. He reached the sunshine of the door. Zaharran called after him: 'The businesses are for sale too ... Five thousand ... a thousand dollars the lot ...'

But the policeman had gone. Zaharran gathered himself together, asked the man behind the counter if he wanted any paper novelties. He did not. So Zaharran himself lumbered out into the sad eternal sunshine.

*

The potent aroma of lokshen pudding hung over South Miami Beach. It drifted from the kitchens of the compressed hotels and out on to the dry sidewalks of Ocean Drive, Washington Avenue and the short streets between them. In Flamingo Park it loitered about the trees in the late sunshine, it wafted to the windows of The Four Seasons Nursing Home, it triumphed even in competition with the Latin smells that issued from the Cuban eating places. It was a balm and a reassurance to the thousands of Jewish people in the twilight streets. While there was lokshen pudding there was hope.

'Jeez, that Jerusalem smell gets everywhere,' protested Ari the Greek sitting under the Tree of Knowledge in Flamingo Park. He did not know why it was called the Tree of Knowledge, it was just that it had a notice to that effect and Ari, in general, believed what notices said. Also, it seemed appropriate to him that an outnumbered Greek should sit beneath its boughs.

'It's bad enough being a fit kinda guy down here,' he confided to Bruce who sat one side of him. Ossie sat on the other considering him quizzically. 'I mean the ladies, they outnumber the guys by plenty to one. So they bother you. "Can I do anything for you Ari?" "Gee Ari, you sure look young and healthy." "Don't you get lonely Ari?" The shit that's circulated in these parts, you would not believe. When a guy's on his feet and breathing down here, he's in trouble, just believe Ari. And get the smell of that pudding.'

'We thought up an idea,' said Bruce getting in while Ari took a breath.

'Yeah, an idea for business,' said Ossie. Ossie had been fired that day as a beach guard. They said he wasn't working hard enough. There were not enough rescues on the books. He had an idea they were looking for an excuse to get rid of him.

'Business!' exclaimed Ari. 'Business! Listen kid, let me tell *you* about business. Don't tell me. And especially business in these parts and this locality.'

'We had an idea ...' restarted Bruce hopefully.

'Teeth,' said Ari with conviction. 'Now teeth are good business. Have you just seen the teeth they sell around here? Jeez, but an alligator couldn't accommodate some of the teeth they sell in these parts. Just you see how many folks are about South Miami with their faces all screwed up. That's the teeth they've got. Get good teeth and you've got good business. And taking blood pressure. Now *there's* a good business. You don't need no stock, no capital. All you have is a Band Aid and a pump and you charge a buck a time to tell people they're still alive. A buck to find you're still alive! And walking sticks! Now there's another racket. What you got to pay for a walking stick is robbery . . .'

'Robbery,' put in Bruce quickly but quietly. 'That's what we had in mind. Robbery.'

Ari's nose was trembling all over his face. 'And just to get a pair of reading glasses! So you can see the bad news in the newspaper. They charge you . . .' He braked. 'What did you mention, son? Robbery, you said?'

'Sure, robbery, that's what I said,' nodded Bruce. 'I said robbery.'

'Robbery,' confirmed Ossie from the other side.

'And kidnapping.'

'Hold-ups.'

'Burglaries.'

'Frauds.'

'Extortion.'

For once Ari was silent. His mouth opened and shut a few times.

'Ari,' said Bruce patiently. 'We're thinking of forming a select group of the people around here.'

'Like a gang?' nodded Ari with unusual accuracy.

'Okay, a gang. There'll be Ossie and me and maybe half a dozen of your generation. Four guys and two old ladies, or three and three. We'll work on the details. We use hoods and gloves. We pick off selected targets in the South Florida region. A break-in here, a hold-up there. You know the sort of things.'

'But no violence. We'll avoid violence.'

'Yeah, you need to avoid violence if you figure on getting your gang from these parts,' said Ari practically. 'Half the poor bastards can't stand up.'

'We've got to pick carefully,' put in Bruce. 'Hand selected.

They've got to be fit.' He waited, then added pointedly, 'Like you, Ari.'

The nose turned towards him like the bow of a ship turning to port. The Mediterranean eyes were sharp. 'You want me, *me*, to get myself mixed up in this?' he said accusingly. 'Me? Say I got caught and put in prison. I can't afford that kind of time, son. Jeez, even probation would be a life sentence to somebody my age.'

'There's money in crime,' encouraged Ossie.

'There is,' agreed Ari. 'I'm going in for blackmail. Twenty bucks or I tell the cops.'

'And it gives you something to *do*,' emphasized Ossie. 'You can't just go on running all your life.'

'But I just run on the beach and down the street,' Ari pointed out innocently. 'I ain't got no highway patrol up my ass. Mine's legal running.' He glared at them, but with a touch of uncertainty. 'The whole thing's crazy,' he muttered.

'Listen Ari,' said Ossie. 'You're a guy of *action*. You can *do* things. You may be sixty but you can *do* things. But what do you *do*? Tell me that, what do you *do* down here on South Miami Beach?'

'I run,' said Ari predictably. 'And son, while I'm running I'm living.'

'Sure. But you ain't running nowhere. And you ain't living nohow. Don't you feel like a little excitement now and then? Don't you kinda feel that you'd like to *use* yourself . . . ?'

'Sure, sure,' agreed Ari gently. 'But there's business and there's business. Why don't you give the teeth a whirl. There's not many folks satisfied with their teeth. There's real good money in . . .'

'Robbery,' said Bruce again. 'Nothing violent or unpleasant. Just now and then a neat little robbery and get out quick, back here to Ocean Drive. And that's the beauty of it. The cops will never guess that the operators come from down here. Like you say, most of the people have trouble standing up. It's a perfect cover.'

'And what will you guys do? Wait for the old folks at home?'

'Aw, Ari, would we?' Ossie was pained. 'We'll be right there with you. We'll plan it all and we'll be there. You've got people down here with plenty of cool, and they're fit even if they're old, and they've got experience in a million things.'

'Not many in robbing,' pointed out Ari. 'Anyway, what experience do you guys have? What crime experience?'

The young men looked shamefaced. Neither replied for a moment, then Loose Bruce looked up and said: 'Not much. We'll come clean about that. Not a big deal.'

'I once slugged a guy straight through a bar window,' admitted Ossie.

'And I used to steal my mother's clothes and sell them,' muttered Bruce.

'For Chrissake,' said Ari in mock admiration. 'That's sure powerful stuff.'

'What about you?' asked Bruce shrewdly.

Ari looked reminiscent. 'Well I naturally ain't told anybody about it, but I used to steal horseshoes in Chicago. When I was a boy. Steal them and sell them.'

'Not exactly Dillinger's scene,' said Bruce.

'You asked me what I'd done. And a little bootlegging down here in these parts in the Prohibition days.' He smiled fondly at the memory. 'They was good times. I made some dough too. Everybody knew Ari the Greek then.'

'If you could have some more good times,' suggested Ossie, 'you could be Ari the Greek again.'

Ari's wide mouth spread in a grin beneath the parapet of his nose. 'Well, I guess it might be interesting. And I ain't busy just now. And if they catch me and give me twenty years I'll cheat by dying. Okay, you got a deal.'

Delighted, Bruce and Ossie shook the old Greek's hand. 'Right,' whispered Bruce. 'Now we need you to recruit the others. You know the fittest and the people who might be interested around these parts. Just draw up a list and we'll take a look at each one, then you can move in. Then when we've got the gang we've got to get the guns.'

Ari's face contracted against his nose. 'Guns? You said no violence.'

'Okay. Right, no violence. But you got to have guns, Ari. You got to be fierce, otherwise there's no point. Who ever heard of a gang without guns?'

Sidewalk Joe was sitting in his usual place in the shade of the giant calendar. He was dealing the cards but like the other old men around the table he could not resist a sidelong glance at the concrete reminder that while he played poker his days were numbered. The big square said it was 17 January, the time was 10.46 a.m. and the temperature was seventy-six and climbing. It was going to be the usual day on South Miami Beach.

'Morry,' said Joe, looking at a piece of paper at his elbow. 'As of this moment you owe eighty-six.' He was wearing his light brown suit, a homburg and spats over his black boots.

Morry nodded agreement over his cards. Joe ran a strong finger down the paper. 'And Charlie. You're down seventy-one. Benny you owe just thirty.' He added the totals carefully with some satisfaction. 'That's one hundred and eighty-seven cents altogether, which according to my calculations is one dollar, eighty-seven cents.'

'This game could hit the roof,' muttered Benny. 'All that dough.' He whistled softly and shook his head.

Joe said: 'Okay, let's play.'

The sun travelled across the populated lawns, snaking between the sea-grape trees. Someone began to pluck on a Jew's harp. He played it well and some of the old people smiled in memory and rocked their heads gently to the faraway tune. The grass area was filling up as the folks converged on it from the hotels, all carrying their square canvas chairs. Some pigeons and a clutch of seagulls waited patiently in two groups for well-wishers who they knew would soon come to feed them on scraps rescued from early morning trash cans. A family of Florida sparrows sat separately but also expectantly. Lonely people often befriended birds.

Mrs Blum, ready to make her first suicide bid of the week, was sharply disappointed to see that the familiar grey-haired and handsome young beachguard had been replaced in the watchtower by a large plain woman. She vowed to complain to the authorities. It would be no fun being rescued any more.

Ari the Greek sat carefully in the shade watching Sidewalk Joe and the others crouched over their poker game. Mrs Blum plodded by him bulging from her many coloured swimsuit and muttering disconsolately. On the beach he could see the solitary searcher Molly Mandy stepping slowly, her metal detector held out before her oddly like a reverse dog on a lead.

They had made out a list, Ari, Bruce and Ossie, a dozen names of which they had eliminated seven for various reasons such as arthritis, bad eyesight and liability to panic under fire. The names remaining were Ari himself, Sidewalk Joe, Lou the Barbender, K-K-K-Katy and Molly Mandy.

Ari knew better than to break up Sidewalk Joe's poker school, as he sat peacefully in his raft of shade while it changed course with the sun's journey through the bright sky. After an hour Joe rose from his collapsible chair and carrying it with him (everybody carried their small chair when they moved even if it were only a few yards) he approached Ari. As he had been sitting with his back to Ari this impressed the Greek a good deal.

'How d'yer know I was looking for you, Joe?' asked Ari moving up to make a piece of shade available.

Joe opened his little chair and occupied the shade. 'I got the scent of you, Ari,' said Joe. 'I just felt you was in this area.'

They sat, like the two elderly men they were, looking out at the people and the ocean. Joe nodded towards the seabirds sitting watching the people, taking turns to curve off for a noisy white flight in the blue. 'Baygulls,' said Joe. 'Jewish seagulls.'

'So I hear,' replied Ari amiably.

'I hear things too,' said Joe. 'I heard things and I see things.'

Ari looked at him with a mixture of alarm and admiration. 'You do, Joe? That's smart. Very smart. And what about do you do this seeing and hearing?'

'Who's the two young guys?' asked Joe. 'Like I see them at the dance. Like I see them in earnest session with you in Flamingo Park. Like they look like guys do when they're working something out, when they're looking for action. I seen it all before. What they planning? Robbing the Social Security? I don't mind. The Social Security been robbing me for years.'

Ari nodded admiringly. 'I knew you couldn't lose the nose.'

Joe glanced at him. Beneath the homburg peered deep blue eyes. His age sat quietly on him. 'You couldn't lose your nose either Ari. Christ, that's some nose you got.'

'From a Jew that's a compliment,' nodded Ari. 'But I was not speaking of the physical organ of the nose. I was talking about the way you smell things out. Like situations.'

'What's the deal? I was getting bored playing poker for pennies.'

'I figured that. We wondered if you'd be interested in joining a little business hustle. Just a quiet heist or two. No violence.'

'These two guys. They want somebody to do their dirty work,' guessed Joe. 'Innocent old men.'

'They'll be right there,' promised Ari. 'And it's splits. Not the Federal Bank. Just pee-wee league stuff. It'll be great, Joe. Just like the old days for you.'

'In New York City,' murmured Joe, his bright eyes clouding sentimentally. 'They was good times, Ari. Forty years ago now. Good times. I worked with three gangs who got wiped out, all except me. Real good times.' He returned to the present. 'But not now, old friend. I couldn't do that now. I ain't stole nothing in years. Only the usual things, fruit, bread and that sort of material.'

Ari moved closer in the shade. The gulls were disturbed by a dog and whirled around the heads of the people, screaming abuse. Before Ari could speak Joe became engrossed with the birds. 'Barbecued gull,' he said. 'Now that could be a great idea. Catch 'em and cook 'em.'

'Oily,' said Ari. 'Kosher maybe, but oily.'

'I was just dreaming,' said Joe. 'So you want me to join the operation? Who else is on the payroll?'

'I got to keep that a secret until the gang is all got together. You understand that now, don't you? I have a feeling you're interested, Joe.'

'Sure I'm interested. I get weary taking cents off these millionaires. But I don't want to shoot anybody. Got that. I'm too old to kill people. That's for the birds.'

'No shooting,' said Ari sincerely. 'That's already in the rules and regulations. But we got to have guns because it won't look like we mean business without guns. You can't hold-up a mail truck with a wooden leg can you?'

'Right. No. That figures. Okay, I'm in.' He stood and folded his chair. Ari shook Joe's hand warmly. Joe looked around cautiously. 'Take it easy, Greek,' he said. 'Cut out the warm friendship stuff. When people see a Jew and a Greek shaking hands they know something suspicious is likely.'

Ari swallowed and then grinned and said loudly, 'Thank you, thank you sir, for your generous contribution to the Orthodox Church.'

'Great,' muttered Joe sourly. 'I can see I'm going to enjoy working with you.' Joe returned to the poker school and Ari walked through the people towards the ocean, deep green and blue embroidered with a double cuff of surf. An old compatriot tried to waylay him to tell of his boyhood in the Peloponnese, but Ari had heard it eight times already and had excused himself, leaving the old man looking thoughtfully around for someone else to tell.

Down on the sand, a patient figure in the sun, Molly Mandy dowsed for treasure. The metal detector swung easily, regularly, in front of her, her ears enveloped and engrossed in the earphones. Ari eased himself over the parapet wall and walked towards her. She did not detect him until he was a few yards away. Then she heard the metal lace-holes of his shoes. 'You ain't running, Ari,' she said surprised. 'You tired of living?'

'Today I made it early, real early,' said Ari. 'Because I got business.'

She took the earphones away from her head and handed them generously to him. 'Just listen in to that,' she invited. 'I guess you can fit your ears in. It's a good thing you don't listen through that nose.'

Good-humouredly Ari acknowledged the remark and put the earphones to his head. Molly Mandy moved the detector to and fro on the beach. Ari launched a slow, big smile. 'I like it,' he said. 'It's beautiful. Just beautiful.'

'Like the music of the stars,' she said sweetly. 'And folks ask me what pleasure I get from this? Sure I find things – but also it makes lovely music.'

Ari returned the earphones to her. He hesitated, dug his toes in the sand and said: 'Molly, I got something to ask you. A couple of years ago, I hear, you found some guns buried down here on the beach.'

'Right,' she replied readily. 'Lots of guns. I still have them in my room. Would you like to see them?'

'I would, Molly,' said Ari gratefully. 'I sure would.'

four

Lou the Barbender was worried. He walked, bowed, along Washington Avenue, a large man among the smaller old folk on the sidewalk. He wondered whether he ought to spend a dollar on a blood pressure check but he dismissed the notion. He liked to be lifting a weight or bending some iron at the time they took the pressure but that always drew a crowd and today he did not feel like a crowd.

Some days he met K-K-K-Katy in a steamy coffee shop along the avenue, a favourite with many of the South Miami folk because although the air conditioning was not efficient, it had daily bargains in food. He was heading that way now. He wondered how Katy would take to the idea of becoming a criminal so late in life.

The bargain of the day was unexciting. The owner had painted across the window 'SPAVLOV'S DO IT AGAIN! Today's great Special: Rice, Noodles and Chicken. NOW WITH FREE BREAD!'

Katy had ordered the special. The waiter came back with the plate and recited. 'Rice, Noodles and Chicken. Now with free bread.' He put the plates down.

'I know, I know,' sighed Lou. 'Spavlov's have done it again. Free bread for God's sake. What d'you want? That my eyes should sparkle?'

'S-S-Something's happened,' said Katy when the man had

grumbled at people who bit the hand that fed them and gone off. 'I can tell, Lou, b-baby. What's gone on? Maybe a bar you couldn't bend?'

'It's serious,' Lou told her. 'Very and most serious. I have to put a straight proposition to you, Katy.'

'T-T-This is i-i-it,' said Katy to herself. Curiously she often stuttered when talking to herself. 'M-m-marriage.'

'What could that b-b-b-be, honey?' she inquired, leaning over her rice. The free bread fell from the plate but she deftly caught it before it hit the floor.

'It could change your life, and mine,' said Lou. His face was large with emotion. 'For ever and ever.'

'It often does,' she said girlishly. 'But we won't mind.' She wondered if she ought to do a few high kicks. She felt like it. Old people are just young people with nothing to lose. They often feel free to be eccentric. Katy got up and did three high kicks in the coffee shop. Lou and most of the other customers watched her passively then, when she had sat down again, he leaned towards her.

'Can I interest you in joining a gang?' he said bluntly.

'A g-g-g-gang?' She was as astounded as she was disappointed. 'I thought you were asking me to marry you, Lou.'

'I will, I will,' he said as if the matter had been settled long before. 'But this is a different question. We've been invited to join a gang. You and me.'

'A gang?' she almost shouted and he put a heavy hand on her mouth. Her eyes revolved and he released her.

'Like Al Capone. That kind. But older folks.'

'And what's it for?' she whispered.

'What gangs are for. Robbing, kidnapping and such activities.'

'Gee, it sounds exciting. But who's asked? Somebody crazy? I don't want to join if the man is crazy.'

'Ari,' said Lou. 'You know him, the Greek. The guy who runs in those little pants.'

'He's got a gang? He don't look like he's got a gang.'

'He's collecting one. Well, he's the front man see. There's two young guys behind it. They figure it will give some of the more active people around here something to do.'

'It sure sounds nice,' said Katy seriously. 'But I wouldn't like to break the law.'

'Gangs *have* to break the law,' said Lou patiently. 'That's why they're gangs.'

'I see. Yes, that's logical I guess. But I don't enjoy the sight of blood. If it was a different colour it wouldn't be so bad. Like pale blue. So I couldn't guarantee to shoot anybody, Lou. I just couldn't see myself doing it. Not unless I really didn't sympathize with them.'

'There's no violence planned,' said Lou. 'None *planned*, I said. But in the gang business it could develop. It just could. That's why they asked me. I'm strong.'

'But why me? I'm just a little old lady.'

'You're a girl,' he said suddenly softly. Their eyes met and she blushed and laid her shapely hand on his.

'So we get married as well, do we?' she whispered. 'I mean you did mention it in passing just now.'

'Yes, sure, sure. But we'd better not have any kids, Katy. The gang business being risky.'

Her eyes shone happily towards him. 'It was sure a funny proposal,' she said. 'But I accept. I've loved you ever since I saw you bite through that pack of cards.'

'There was no aces and no kings,' he said modestly. 'But it was my own teeth. So we join the gang then?'

'Oh sure, it sounds fine. But . . . but what do they calculate to steal? I mean things are guarded. You couldn't even walk out of here with a piece of their free bread without the alarm going off.'

Lou nodded his heavy head. 'Okay, okay. You're right Katy. But it's going to be all scheduled see. Every detail. And these guys figure that nobody is going to suspect a gang of old folks to be operating the crimes. You get it?'

'What if the cops get us?' said Katy. 'They'll put me in a women's prison and you in a men's prison. It's no use being married if we're in different prisons, now is it? What's the sense of that?'

'We *don't* get caught, that's all,' said Lou decisively. 'If we do we say we thought it was for charity.' Thought lay thickly on his brow. 'For myself, Katy, I'd like to do it. I been missing the excitement these past few years. After what I've done. You know I've been in theatres in every state and in Mexico and Cuba. I was the strong man of Havana before Fidel Castro had any chance of growing a beard. I guess I'd like to take a final fling.'

She laid her hand on his again and looked at him intensely. 'Right, let's do it. Let's join,' she said. 'Who knows, maybe we can steal a few things for our new home.'

'Guns,' said Molly as she led Ari up the winding stairs of Sunny Gables Hotel. 'Sure I got guns. When I dug them up on the beach I thought maybe I ought to tell the police, but then I thought, maybe not. I figured they might come in useful some-day, like if Fidel Castro invaded the United States. So I stored them.'

She opened the door of her room and felt a small blush in the gloom of the passage. 'No man has ever been in this room, Ari. Not since Melford died.'

'I'll respect that, Molly,' said the Greek. 'I only want to view the guns.'

'So you shall.' She worked the lock with some difficulty and then let the door creak open. Ari looked in. Right opposite on a sideboard against the wall was a Russian one-man rocket firer.

Dumbstruck, Ari stepped cautiously in the room. 'I keep that one there for decoration,' said Molly blithely. 'I think it's just cute. The others are in the bathroom.'

Modestly she led Ari through the tight living room, pausing to indicate a dim photograph. 'That was Melford with the Elks,' she whispered. 'There, that's him, smiling. He was a great Elk, Melford, and he enjoyed smiling. But even Elks die.'

'It's a common happening,' agreed Ari. 'Myself I try to avoid the matter. I think maybe I'll get overlooked and I'll be around for ever. But I guess that won't happen.'

'You don't get luck like that,' agreed Molly seriously. 'Not on South Miami Beach. Somebody goes every day. Here's the guns.'

She opened the bathroom door and Ari's eyes bulged. Ranged around the walls was a complete armoury, pistols, short rifles, grenades, sub-machine guns and a flame thrower displayed over the toilet cistern. 'Jeez,' muttered Ari. 'Jeez.'

'Melford mounted them. Before he died of course. He was with me when I found them buried on the South Beach. Melford thought they must be something to do with all the Cubans we have down here. They're into guns, the Cubans you know, I found them with my detector. Gee, it was like the Fifth Symphony when I got this lot on the earphones. They were only just under the sand in a kind of box. Melford said it had Soviet writing on the side.'

'And you ... you and Melford,' said Ari still staring, 'just dug them up and brought them here?'

'Just like that,' she said proudly. 'We had a car then and we loaded them in and unloaded after dark.'

Ari gingerly touched the butt of one of the pistols. 'Ammunition,' he muttered. 'How about ammunition?'

'There's no ammunition,' she shrugged. 'We didn't find any. Except one little itsy-bitsy bullet and that's right over here. Above the washbasin. I hide it among my lipsticks. Don't you think that's clever, Ari?'

'A stroke of genius,' nodded Ari, still looking disbelievingly at all the guns, 'hiding the bullet. But no ammunition?'

'Well we figured, Melford and me, that if there was ever any complications concerning our guns we could always say there was no ammunition so there was no danger, was there?'

'They're Russian guns, and Russian ammunition is hard to come by,' admitted Ari. 'You don't see a lot of it around.' He reached up and brought down the pistol he had touched. It felt ugly in his hand, heavy and menacing. 'Not a pretty baby,' he said. 'But just what we need.'

'Who's we?' inquired Molly without suspicion. She was another who could not easily be surprised. 'Why do you want the guns, Ari?'

Ari knew he might as well tell her. He had thought of making some excuse about a hunting trip but since there was no ammunition he could hardly expect Molly to believe that. 'We've got a gang,' he said looking straight at her.

'Gee, how nice!' she said warmly, her hands clasping. 'Are you going to rob people?'

'That's the general idea,' he nodded. 'But we don't want nobody getting hurt, and especially the members of the gang. It's just a kind of hobby. Something to amuse a few folks around here.'

'Well,' she said decisively, 'if you have *my* guns, *I* want to be a member of the gang. I'm getting bored with treasure hunting anyway.' She put out her hand and took the pistol from him. Suddenly she whirled on him, thrust her legs apart, and, crouching, jabbed the muzzle at him. 'Okay buster,' she said, trying for a harsh deep voice. 'Hand over the goodies.'

Ari swallowed uneasily. The aperture of the weapon was pointing at his nose. 'Not the nose please, Molly,' he said, 'that's an easy target.' Cautiously he took the gun from her. 'I mean, you're sure it's not loaded?'

'No, sir,' she assured him. 'My Melford checked every single one. But he said the grenades work okay. You just have to pull the pin out. See, like ...'

Ari just beat her to the pin. 'No, leave it where it is, Molly. You should just *not* do anything like that.'

Prudently he led the old lady from the bathroom. He still had the gun. He sat down, staring at it thoughtfully. 'And you want to join?' he asked, his old eyes rising.

'I've *got* to join,' she said triumphantly. 'I insist. No Molly, no hardware.'

'I need to make a call,' said Ari. 'You don't have a phone, do you?'

To his surprise she did, housed beneath a knitted tea cosy on the sideboard. He pushed the Russian rocket firer gently away and dialled the number. 'Boss,' he said, when Loose Bruce had answered, 'she's got the guns. Enough for an army. All clean. Yes, just great ain't it. There's two other items of news. The first is she wants to join. If she don't we don't get the munitions. Sure ... sure ... she's fit. She walks miles on the beach every day and she's watched *Kojak* because she does the cop's crouch with a pistol. So I guess she'll be fine.'

'Sure ... sure. Okay, I'll tell her. What's that? Oh yeah, the other items of news. We've got everything here, everything but a ballistic missile, it seems to me. But there's a difficulty. It's all Ruskie stuff meant for Castro. It was buried in the beach some-

.where. Everything. But the only ammo is *one* bullet. Yeah, that's right. You got it. One. I guess we'll have to conserve our ammunition.'

Loose Bruce looked carefully along the row of lined, expectant faces. They sat on the chairs and on the bed in Ari's room at Sunny Gables Hotel, Ari himself squatting on his light canvas chair. Ossie arranged himself awkwardly on the table behind Bruce. Because he had no job and little cash Ossie had now moved into a small room at the hotel, he and Bruce having shone twin smiles at Mrs Nissenbaum who melted and agreed to take the rent at the end of the month.

Outside it was a sullen day. Clouds lay heavily on the sea and the air was warm as soup. The ancient air conditioning box fitted to Ari's window heaved and grunted as if it were containing some captive animal.

Bruce looked along the eager faces. Ossie's eyes followed his track. What they saw was not encouraging and yet, ironically, just what they wanted. This collection of has-beens with their bright eyes and old limbs looked like anything but a gang intent on criminal pursuits.

Ari the Greek sat on his beach chair trying to look strong, his prow of a nose pushed out, his eyes steady, his muscles below his sweatshirt flexed, ready for action. Next to him sat Molly Mandy who, for effect, had brought with her the detector with which she scoured the beach. She held the upright lightly with one hand, like a soldier leaning on a rifle. Sidewalk Joe fingered his bootlace tie and narrowed his New York eyes.

Lou the Barbender was next, the large face spread like a map, intent on every word which had been said. He kept inserting short encouraging remarks into the discussion. 'My strength is still my own.' 'I can break in anywhere.' 'I can handle three cops at once.'

Next to him, her delicate hand in his heavy paw, sat K-K-K-Katy, her fine legs crossed, so excellent that both Bruce and Ossie found their eyes continually drawn that way. If ever I get to go dating a sixty-year-old woman, Bruce thought, that's the one I'm going to date.

'It's important,' Bruce heard himself saying, 'that everyone here realizes what all this is about. We don't want any backers-out later who'll say they didn't get the idea straight. The group will carry out criminal activities. Is that clear? Robbery, hold-up, kidnapping. Criminal activities. Okay?'

All the heads nodded. Only Ari spoke his agreement.

'This could put us all behind bars. Is that understood?' said Bruce. Again the heads nodded. Ari's this time as well.

'And, although we will avoid it if we can, there could be some violence.'

'There could be some violence,' repeated Molly Mandy as if she were looking forward to it. The rest nodded.

'Now, this is the last call. Anybody want to quit? I'm asking you to speak up now.'

Nobody wanted to quit. Their heads shook all along the line.

'Okay, that's settled. Now I'm going to hand you over to Ossie, who's the tactical guy. He was in Vietnam. He's going to tell you what to do next.'

'What about the profits?' asked Sidewalk Joe. 'How about the split?'

Bruce said : 'Equal shares, after the deduction of expenses.'

Sidewalk looked back steadily, then nodded. Nobody else said anything. Bruce felt uneasy. 'Right,' he swallowed. 'Now Ossie is going to go over our plans. Questions and suggestions afterwards. We're going to run this gang on democratic lines.'

'You can't,' interrupted Joe again. 'You can't run a gang like that, son. I know. There's got to be a big guy, the boss, and there's got to be a not-so-big guy and he's the second boss.'

Ossie looked at him. 'Bruce and me thought we kinda fitted those roles,' he said. 'If that's okay with you, Sidewalk?'

'Sure it's okay. It's just important to know, that's all. The bosses always get the longest stretch in the penitentiary. We got to know who they are.'

'Okay, we'll take that responsibility,' swallowed Bruce. 'Now, can we get down to business? Okay Ossie, let them hear it.'

Ossie leaned forward but doubt was still touching his face as he looked at them. 'We have a plan,' he said. 'For the first assignment. We've gotten a real nice lot of Russian guns, mostly pistols, but I might as well tell you the bad news. There's only one bullet.'

He heard Sidewalk Joe say 'Christ', but he went on talking. 'Maybe this is not such a bad thing. If there's no ammunition, nobody here is going to the penitentiary for murder.'

'It's not the penitentiary I'm worried about,' said Katy thoughtfully. 'It's going up to God with a murder on my conscience. Now that I wouldn't care for.'

'Right,' agreed Ossie. 'So if there's no bullets nobody gets hurt.'

'What do we have to do, yell "bang"?' asked Sidewalk.

Ossie sighed. 'We use the guns as threats.'

'And what if we find we got guns against us?' said Sidewalk. 'Like fuzz guns.'

'We run,' shrugged Ossie. 'Or we surrender.'

'Good thinking,' said Sidewalk.

'Got any better ideas? The way we figure it we ain't going to have call to use any guns anyway. They're just kinda props. It's just for effect, Mr Sidewalk.'

'Which guy has the bullet?' asked Lou.

'Me,' put in Bruce decisively. 'I may have to blow my brains out.'

'Right,' Ossie began again. 'Any more questions about the guns?'

'Excuse me,' said Katy shyly. 'But I can't use a gun. Up to now I've never had a reason.'

'That's okay, Katy,' said Ossie. 'Tomorrow, if we can fix transportation, we are going on a little trip.'

'Goody,' he heard Molly Mandy whisper. 'Oh, goody.' He shuddered.

'I know a place,' he went on, 'that's pretty quiet. It's off one of the Everglades tracks and we can take a couple of hours for instruction without anyone seeing us.'

'There's alligators in the Everglades,' pointed out Molly nervously. 'I don't care for alligators.'

'And snakes,' added Katy. 'Fl-fl-flying snakes.'

Ossie sighed. 'I'm afraid, ladies,' he said, 'that we have to take some risks. The whole operation is a risk. Now there's still time to back out. Anyone want to back out?'

Nobody did. Katy lowered her eyes. Ossie went on. 'We're

going to have some weapons training. I'll handle that with maybe some assistance from Sidewalk, okay?'

'Maybe we ought to take some water pistols and bows and arrows,' suggested Sidewalk sourly.

'I can shoot a bow and arrow,' said Mandy.

'For Chrissakes,' put in Bruce angrily. 'Can we just get this matter straight without making a musical out of it? Okay. We go to the Everglades tomorrow. And I want you to keep your eyes open in that vicinity because that's where we're planning to run our first hold-up.'

'Are we going to rob the Seminoles?' said Lou blinking ponderously. 'Ain't no good robbing the Seminoles. They're poor Indians. They ain't got a bean.'

Ossie sighed. 'No, it's not that. But we think we have an idea how to make some good pickings in that area. First, we got to get this training done. We got to look right. We got to *scare* people. Okay?'

'Okay,' they all agreed.

'Right. We meet here at ten tomorrow morning. Got that? Ten. Anyone you know can fix transportation?'

'I know a guy with a little bus,' said Sidewalk unexpectedly. 'I can get that.'

'Great. What about the dough?'

'Nothing,' said Sidewalk. 'I just have to lean on him a little.'

'That's the sort of talk I want to hear,' put in Bruce encouragingly. 'Let's be like that. Let's lean on people.'

They went out singly, at intervals of two minutes, in case of observation. Molly Mandy was the last to go. She turned at the door and said to Bruce and Ossie, 'Well, off I go to practise looking *fierce*.' She ground her teeth as she went out.

Bruce and Ossie sat down and looked at each other disconsolately. 'Jesus,' said Bruce. 'What are we going to do with this goddamn bunch? I ask you?'

'Make them into a gang,' replied Ossie. 'You wait. It'll work.'

'I've got a name for them,' said Bruce sombrely. 'The Ocean Drive Delinquent Society – the ODDS.'

'It sure fits,' nodded Ossie.

five

South Florida's Everglades Parkway, otherwise known and marked on maps as Alligator Alley, cuts directly, east to west, across the foot of the state from Naples on the Gulf of Mexico to Miami on the Atlantic, a distance of about a hundred miles. After Naples there are no settlements of any size, apart from Seminole Indian Reservations, until Andytown is reached just short of Miami – Fort Lauderdale.

The Seminoles, once the proud water-Indians of the region, are now reduced to an area of rough country to the north of the highway, with one large compound to the south. The rest of the area is swamp, saw-grass and entwined trees, the home of the alligator, snake, swimming bear, panther, bald eagle and flamingo. It is accessible only by air-boat, a light craft powered by a large fan on its stern, and tenuous man-made walkways linking occasional firm islands in the four hundred square miles of watery jungle.

There are, in addition, a few dirt roads turning off the main highway and pushing for a mile or so into the Everglades, generally to places of interest to tourists.

At one of these attractions, a bogus Seminole encampment, a busload of tourists from the Miami–Fort Lauderdale area were watching an Indian wrestle with an alligator. The air was humid and there was no great enthusiasm from the audience, their guide from Smileytime Tours, the Seminole called Blue Squirrel, or the alligator itself now lying somnolently on its back. Molly Mandy watched with only half-attention, her mind on other things. The tourist guide was a red-cheeked young man with a croaky voice. 'Now folks,' he called. 'Just watch that critter's tail when Blue Squirrel turns him on his front again. He don't like what's been going on and Blue Squirrel sure needs to watch that sneaky tail.'

Blue Squirrel reached carefully and turned the five foot alligator on to its feet again. Its tail struck at him spitefully and he jumped. A minor buzz of interest came from the tourists.

The Smileytime guide called out: 'And that ladies and gentlemen is the end of the performance today. I guess you want to show your appreciation to Blue Squirrel in the usual way.'

The people applauded and Molly Mandy in a brightly flowered straw hat slipped away towards a wigwam which bore the sign 'Telephone'. The audience drifted, leaving the Indian looking annoyed. 'Mean bastards,' he said to the alligator. 'Every time that guy says "show your appreciation", they think it's enough to *clap*. Never a goddamn dime.' The alligator opened its jaws as if laughing at the joke. Blue Squirrel closed them again with a firm push of his foot.

Molly Mandy was in the wigwam. 'Everglades one,' she whispered into the phone. 'Everglades one calling Everglades two.'

'E-E-Everglades two,' said the excited K-K-K-Katy in a call box three miles away on the highway.

'We're just leaving. Okay?'

'Okay. We're ready. G-G-Good luck, M-Molly.'

Molly left the wigwam. The rest of the party was already aboard the bus. The stripe-shirted guide, sweat running down his chin, was stretched on his toes counting his charges.

'Wait for me!' shouted Molly running towards them holding her pretty flowered hat in place.

'Ah!' exclaimed the guide, 'I thought maybe the Seminoles had got you.'

'Wish they would,' said Molly brightly as she boarded the bus. 'We women don't have fun like that these days.'

Some of the passengers laughed but she got a few frowns and turned-away faces as she went down the aisle. She reached her place next to a stiff-looking woman who had said she was from Boston. Molly settled herself. 'You *know* what the Indians do to white women,' she mentioned mischievously. The Boston lady shuddered.

It had been very hot and the majority of the tourists were from Canada and the Northern United States. The doors closed and the bus started along the track towards the main highway. The people sat gratefully in the air conditioning and discussed the afternoon's diversions.

'I got to tell you, Marge, to me that alligator looked just like it was made of rubber.'

'Doped,' said Marge decisively. 'Doped snout to tail. That

Indian didn't have a scratch or a mark on him. Doped.'

The driver sighed idly into the mirror. Every day he heard the same comments, the same complaints. They did not believe those parrots at the Parrot Jungle really rode bicycles and roller skates. It was all a trick, rubber parrots worked by electricity, wasn't this sun hot, and the whole of Florida was below water level and one good tidal wave would drown the whole state, and the hotel charged too much for drinks, and, gee, wasn't it hot, those guys had to be cruel to make those dolphins do those tricks, anyway they were rubber dolphins, worked by electricity, same as the alligators and the parrots. Never mind, they just had two feet of snow in New York State. God, this dirt road is sure bumpy. The Mafia ran everything in Miami, even a dum-dum knew that. The horse racing and the Jai-alai games and the dog tracks. You couldn't win anywhere. Florida was out to rob you. Gee this road. And what's that, Al, some guy off his motor cycle? Lying in the dirt road ...

Katy felt very hot and uncomfortable in the motor cycle gear, and the crash helmet hung like a ton on her head. She lay face down in the red dust, a centipede walking determinedly towards her left eye. She watched it nervously. To her relief it did a smart left turn when it realized that her eyelash was not another centipede. It marched past her view like a platoon of soldiers.

The motor cycle was spreadeagled in the dirt a dozen yards away, a long convincing scar cut into the track by its handlebars. She had offered to attempt to ride the machine, but Ossie had said it would be just as realistic if it were a set-up. He rode the bike along the track to make the tyre impressions and skidded it at the decided point.

She heard the bus come around the bend and hoped that the driver wasn't too tired or preoccupied to see her. It would be a shame to miss the very first operation. She smiled at the dust under her nose as she heard the engine check and then come to a halt.

In the saw-grass a few yards from the bus Ari and Lou crouched, the useless Russian pistols in their hands. On the other side of the track Sidewalk Joe waited, similarly misarmed. Bruce and Ossie watched through binoculars two hundred yards up the track. All wore hoods which reached to their waists.

'Right,' whispered Bruce. 'It's stopped. Any second now.'

The door of the bus slid open and the guide and the driver appeared on the step. At the windows the faces of the tourists pressed to get a better view. From the undergrowth on either side the three masked figures stepped out simultaneously. Everybody in the bus screamed.

'Okay,' said Sidewalk Joe, moving in first, according to plan. 'This is what they used to call a stick-up.' He pushed the large Russian gun into the tourist guide's projecting middle. 'What's your name, son?'

The young man, his face crimson with alarm, swallowed. It seemed like he would never make it. 'Larry,' he said painfully. 'Larry K. Burlestone.'

'Right,' said Sidewalk Joe beneath his mask. 'Larry K. Burlestone. You're going to be the late Larry K. Burlestone if these good people don't contribute to my benevolent fund.' He shouted the words up the bus. The passengers were sitting stiff with apprehension. 'Okay, my buddies will be coming along the bus for contributions. We'll accept anything and everything. Any trouble and lovely Larry here will be ready for the mortician. And the same goes for anybody else who tries to pull anything.'

Lou and Ari moved into the bus. Each had a canvas bag for the loot. Molly watched them as they advanced. She clutched her purse realistically.

'Rape! Rape!' cried a plump woman, halfway along the centre aisle.

'We don't do requests, lady,' muttered Ari standing along the centre aisle. He leaned forward and took off her necklace, opened her pocketbook and helped himself to a billfold. All around the other passengers were surrendering their valuables, some fearfully, some sullenly, some with brave curses. Lou took Molly's handbag.

'I've counted it,' warned Molly from the edge of her mouth. 'Every last cent.'

Lou was quietly collecting the belongings of three New England gentlemen. They handed them over haughtily. Lou smiled below his hood. 'This is where you say "you'll never get away with this",' he reminded them. None of them spoke.

Ari opened the wallet of a large scornful-looking man and was confronted by the man's photograph and an FBI identification card. Ari's breath stopped for a moment. He handed the wallet back. 'Nice to have you aboard, sir,' he said from beneath the hood.

Lou was patiently making his way along his section of the bus. 'Contributions please,' he recited. 'All gratefully received.'

A quarrelsome woman refused to be parted from a diamond and emerald ring. 'Never,' she said bluntly to Ari. 'Just for a start, mister, it won't come off that finger. It never has come off.'

'Gee, I'm sorry,' said Ari. He called towards the front of the bus. 'Charley, get a hacksaw.'

'It came off!' exclaimed the woman at once. 'That's the first time it's come off in twenty years!'

Ari examined it. 'Nice stuff, lady,' he said. 'You should look after rocks like this. Hope it's insured.' He dropped it into his bag. He looked around. The others were finished and making their way towards the door at the front.

'Ladies and gentlemen, on behalf of the poor of South Florida, we would like to thank you for your response to our appeal,' said Sidewalk Joe. 'You been real generous. We've got to be on our way, but we will always remember you and hope you will remember us. We are going to take your guide Larry K. along with us for a while. That's just to make sure you stay good and quiet. If you all stay in your seats and button up for ten minutes you'll find that Larry will come back to you – all his pieces joined on to his other pieces. If you don't, then we may have to separate him.' A shudder, beginning with Larry himself, echoed down the bus.

'I'd like to say something,' said Larry bravely. 'Is that possible, sir?'

'Just don't shout "Help",' replied Sidewalk. 'Okay, go ahead.'

'Ladies and gentlemen,' said Larry turning his sweat-soaked face to his customers. 'Smileytime Tours apologize for this interruption. We hope that you will still remember us next time you are planning a tour in Florida.' His smile was yellow. 'Smileytime, anytime – that's our slogan.'

There was a predictably mixed chorus of cheers and groans and outright boos from the robbed passengers. Lawsuits were already being planned. Larry was taken from the bus by the gang. The driver was warned once again not to move a yard. The gang and their hostage stepped out into the heavy sun. Katy had gone off on a prearranged route, leaving the motor cycle, which they had stolen, lying in the dust in the path of the bus.

From their concealment two hundred yards away Bruce and Ossie watched. 'They're on their way,' said Bruce. 'All to plan. Let's blow.'

They climbed through the undergrowth and pushed their way to a clearing in the swamp. A Volkswagen mini-bus was parked there. Ossie climbed into the driving seat and started the engine. Bruce opened the rear doors. A moment later the three hooded members of the gang and the prisoner came through the saw-grass. Larry K. was hoisted into the back of the Volkswagen and the others sat around him, still in their hoods.

'This will ruin Smileytime Tours,' said Larry loyally.

'Shit,' said Sidewalk Joe. 'Great publicity, all the newspapers, TV, radio. Everybody will want to tour with Smileytime.'

Larry brightened. 'You sure?' he asked. 'You really think that could happen?'

'Sure,' put in Ari. 'You'll get more loot from this than we did. Just wait and see.'

After five minutes they dropped Larry K. by the side of the dirt road at a place where he had a long walk to a phone and a longer walk to the Everglades Parkway. He sat down resignedly at the side of the swamp waiting for his bus to pick him up.

The gang were joined by Katy, who appeared from the vegetation, and they set off for the main highway in soaring spirits.

They took their hoods away, each one revealing a sweating face smirking with triumph. 'Great! It was great!' hooted Ari. 'It worked! We did it!'

Lou embraced him so heavily he winced and Sidewalk grinned his New York grin. Katy giggled and Bruce and Ossie shouted their relief.

'We got some nice trinkets,' said Ari looking down into his canvas bag. 'Some real pretty things.'

'Put it away,' said Sidewalk sharply. 'Jeez! Never look at the takings until the door is locked.'

Ari looked up shamefacedly but the warning was timely because now they had reached the Everglades Parkway and Ossie had turned the vehicle east towards Andytown. Occasional cars passed in either direction and a worried silence fell on them. Then at the traffic lights at the termination of the parkway a highway patrol car drew easily alongside.

'Sing,' hissed Bruce. 'Everybody sing.'

It was Katy who began. In her old piping voice she opened up. She sang *'That old gang who sang heart-of-my-heart,'* and the others joined in robustly.

The highway patrol men grinned and one leaned from the car and called to Ossie: 'All had a good day?'

'Oh a great day, thank you officer,' he grinned back. 'Everybody.'

The policeman waved cheerfully as the lights changed. 'One thing I like to see,' he said to his driver, 'is old folks having a good time.'

The headquarters of Dade County Police is on Biscayne Boulevard, Miami. It was here that the victims of the Everglades bus hold-up were taken. Three hours had elapsed since the robbery, the Florida sun had sunk without a trace, and the tourists were becoming irritated and hungry. They sat on benches around the large, untidy but boring room, waiting their turn to step to one of the tables where policemen sat and wrote laborious lists of valuables stolen by the gang.

Molly Mandy was conscious of a small blush of apprehension as she was beckoned forward to one of the tables. But the officer who was listing took it as natural nervousness of the police – a sound deduction – and he smiled professionally at her as he nodded towards the seat on the other side of the table.

'Now, ma'am, this won't take too long. First your name and address.'

'Molly Belle Mandifield,' she lied primly, touching her gentle finger tops together. 'I'm not going to tell you my age, I'll tell you where I live. I live at 1017, Pine Street, Longville, South

Carolina.' That was a lie also, but she had wisely decided to keep the law away from South Miami Beach.

'And you're on vacation in Florida?'

'Yes. And I've had a real good time, till now.'

'Local address?'

She decided to bluff it out. 'Sunshine Apartments, Pompano Beach,' she said, naming a hotel where she had once spent three days on her first arrival in South Florida. She had doubts about the untruth. 'But I'm leaving tomorrow,' she added firmly. 'Going home. And I'm glad, just take it from me, I'm glad.'

'Okay, I see. Well, we'll get in touch if we find out who did this to you.'

'What do you mean "if"?' she inquired, leaning forward as though she were the interrogator. 'Is there any *doubt* that you're going to catch them? I hope not.'

The policeman looked pained as if he were personally disappointed in her. 'We hope not too, lady, but we got a few million people in this corner of the US and maybe they could hide. We've not heard of this gang before. This is the first time they've tried anything.'

'I hope you're watching the ports and airports and the state boundaries,' sniffed Molly. 'I hope you remember that.'

'Night and day,' sighed the policeman. 'We've got them trapped in sixty thousand square miles. Now can we get down the list of your missing property?'

'Okay,' she replied sweetly. 'Eight dollars, thirty-five cents, my ruby ring and good luck travel charm.'

'Like a medallion on a chain?'

'Right,' affirmed Molly. 'It's supposed to take care of me when I travel.'

'It quit on the job. Anything else?'

'No.' Molly dabbed at her eyes. 'I'm just a poor robbed woman.'

The policeman looked up with a suspicion of sympathy. 'Sure, sure,' he muttered. 'I'm sorry lady. We'll get them, don't worry.'

'I'll pray for you,' said Molly turning away. As she did so she raised her eyes towards the ceiling.

*

Captain Salvatore sat disconsolately on the edge of his desk in the police station office. He was thinking, his sparsely covered head bent, his eyes dull, his top lip hanging over the bottom.

He spread a sheaf of statements in his hairy hand like an ape playing cards. 'Hooded hoods!' he snorted. 'Guns, scared old ladies. For Chrissake, what is this, I ask you?'

Detective Stewart, a blinking young man, shrugged: 'It's armed robbery, chief.'

Salvatore regarded him painfully and then revolved thoughtfully to the other policeman in the room, Detective Cook.

'I'll tell you something, Cookie,' he said, nodding towards Stewart. 'Our boy here has sure improved since he went on his refresher course at police school. It's armed robbery, he says. Jesus Harold Christ! I *know* it's armed robbery. I already made that deduction, Stewart. What I meant was, for Godsake, this is Florida! Sunshine, citrus, palm trees, safe swimming in the ocean. Nice people getting a suntan. It ain't Harlem.' Salvatore sighed, the effort shaking his frame. 'Tourists, the state's most valuable commodity. Robbed, in broad daylight. In Florida sunshine!' He seemed to take it as a personal hurt. His unkempt face sagged.

'We don't know any gang in this state who operates like that,' ventured Cook. 'Hooded, guns ...'

Stewart tried. 'Maybe it's the Purvisco Mob,' he said. 'Down for a vacation.'

Salvatore stared at him desperately. 'The Purvisco Mob? You get more beautiful by the hour, Stewart. The last operation the Purvisco gang pushed got them a million bucks from the State Deposit Bank in Chicago.' Dull-eyed he looked down at the list in his hand. 'Two pearl earrings, imitation,' he read. 'A pair of sunglasses, eight dollars, a diamond ring, a ruby ring, imitation. Three candy bars, genuine.' He paused and looked up sourly at Stewart. 'Does that sound like the Purvisco Mob?'

Stewart looked aggrieved. 'It was only an idea,' he said.

'And a lousy one,' said Salvatore. 'I can't see me telling it to the chief. Who was the FBI man on the bus?'

'Guy called Brown, I expect that's an alias,' shrugged Stewart. 'Nobody in the FBI is called Brown.'

His captain's odd eyebrows went up in the direction of Cook.

'What was he doing?' repeated Salvatore. 'Have we checked him?'

'He was on vacation,' said Cook. 'He likes seeing Indians fight alligators. He's okay. I've checked him. And his name's Brown.'

The Ocean Drive Delinquent Society returned quickly to South Miami Beach, scattered with hardly a flutter and merged with the hundreds of inhabitants of God's Waiting Room. In turn they deposited the bags of loot taken from the bus in the bathroom of Molly's narrow apartment, among the armoury of Russian weapons.

At nine that evening they rendezvoused in the apartment, K-K-K-Katy bringing with her a bottle of genuine New York French Champagne. 'I was saving it for something to celebrate,' she said before looking in Lou the Barbender's direction and pouring a measure in each glass held by the gang. 'But maybe we've got something.'

'Beautiful,' murmured Loose Bruce, sipping at his glass. 'Just beautiful.'

'It sure seemed like it,' said Ossie cautiously. 'But ladies and gentlemen, we're waiting for Molly to get back. She's been held up with the police for quite a time.'

'I l-l-l-liked it,' said Katy decisively. 'Gee, it was so exciting! And that gun felt so comforting.'

'Like old times,' nodded Sidewalk Joe contentedly. 'Took me right back to the thirties. Maybe it wanted a little more drama, like there was no shooting, no ketchup, and nobody turned stool pigeon or double crossed, but it was close enough.'

Ari said: 'Jeez, did you see those folks' faces? People sure don't like being robbed.'

'How much did we get? That's what I want to know,' said Sidewalk quietly. 'I just know it ain't much.'

'Right,' said Ossie. 'You're right. But it was the first pitch. That's what matters. We did it.'

'Maybe we should have waited until some millionaires went to see the Indian wrestle the alligator,' suggested Lou solidly. 'Maybe it would have been big time then.'

'And maybe not,' put in Katy. 'All the m-m-millionaires I've ever known never had a cent on them. It's all in banks and safe deposits and stock. They don't go around loaded.'

There came three soft knocks on the door, followed by two others. 'Molly,' said Bruce. He rose from the table and opened it. Molly slid in like a spy.

'Was it okay?' said Bruce right away.

'Oh, just wonderful,' she smiled. 'There's a poor cop called Captain Salvatore going bananas at police headquarters. They just got no idea. No idea. Gee, is that champagne? Oh, you kept some. That's real sweet. I like the bubbles in my eyes.'

'What happened then?' asked Ossie when she had taken a long drink from the glass. 'Did you get through with the questioning okay? You handled it?'

'Easy,' she said blandly. 'Like falling in love. Gave them a list of what was stolen from me. By the way, can I have my pocket book back?' She looked accusingly at the Greek. 'It was you, Ari, I could tell even with the hood. The way you keep doing that cute little run. It must be a nervous twitch, Ari. You did it in the bus.'

'Watch that, Ari,' warned Bruce. 'It's a clue. We don't want to hand out no clues. No jogging when we're robbing.'

'We're going to do some more soon are we? Say we are,' said Molly. 'I want to be under a hood next time.'

Ossie studied the line of waiting, anticipatory faces. 'It's something we've got to discuss,' he said. 'First, I guess we all want to see what we made on the operation.' He reached for the first canvas bag and carefully slid the contents on to the table. It made a pile of wallets, jewellery, cigarette cases, lighters and cash. The robbers leaned over. Ossie began to sort it, pushing the money to one side. Bruce began to count that. Katy put a jeweller's eyeglass to her eye and examined the trinkets critically. Every bag was emptied, each set of contents sorted and counted. Eventually Ossie turned to them.

'Four hundred and ninety-three dollars, thirty-seven cents,' he said. 'Assorted jewellery, such as you can see. It's not dynamite. There's a couple of nice cigarette cases, but they've got initials on them and those would have to be removed before we sell them.'

A small pout of unhappiness blew from Molly's face. 'Sell

them?' she repeated. 'Sell them? Somehow that seems so dishonest.'

The heads of the gang turned to her in slow astonishment. Bruce and Ossie matched eyebrows. Ossie said gently, 'So is armed robbery dishonest, Molly. In fact, it would be pretty well impossible to run a gang like this without some element of dishonesty.'

'I know, I know,' sighed Molly. 'You think I'm crazy. It's just that doing the robbery's exciting and there's a risk. But, well, how can I explain it? Selling the stuff seems . . . well . . . mean.'

'I know a fence,' said Sidewalk practically. 'He'll take everything, but his rate ain't so good.'

'Maybe we would show a better profit by each taking a few things to the pawnbrokers and secondhand shops,' said Katy. 'A little at a time.'

'We need a fence,' said Ossie decisively. 'I vote we give Sidewalk the assignment of getting this arranged.'

'You're supposed to fix a fence before you do the job, son,' warned Sidewalk. 'That's why you don't have the stuff hanging around where people can smell it out.'

'I know, I know,' sighed Ossie. 'But we're beginners, remember. Next time we'll have things arranged a little more on the line. And that's another thing. Next time. Now do we vote that we're going on to do something else? Now we know we can handle a crime are we going to try and improve on it, or does anyone want to quit now?'

Nobody wanted to quit, although Molly insisted quietly: 'I'd be a whole heap happier if we didn't have to *sell* it.' No one took any notice of her.

Katy got up and putting the loot in two of the bags she carried it to the bathroom. The money she left on the table and Bruce divided it up equally between them. He put the bills in his pocket. 'Now at least I can eat,' he said.

From below them came the sound of somebody playing an evening piano. They played sadly and badly and the fractured notes floated like memories.

'You'll be hearing soon,' said Bruce as one by one they sidled out into the warm corridor. 'Just be ready.'

He and Bruce went out of the elderly hotel and walked along

Ocean Drive and across Washington Avenue. They went to a
bar next to the burlesque show. It was half-dark in there, a blue
rinse light coming from the television set hoisted up near the
ceiling at the far end. Three or four male customers gazed up
as if the machine was bringing them some celestial message.
Ossie and Bruce went to the far end of the counter and turned
their backs on the screen.

'So what do you think?' said Bruce.

'Well it worked. I mean it *worked*, didn't it? These old guys
seem to slide right into it. And apart from Molly not wanting to
sell the stuff, the old ladies seem right there, with it.'

'Less than five hundred bucks in cash, phoney rings and some
dented cigarette cases ain't exactly the great train robbery,'
pointed out Bruce. 'We might as well get jobs.'

'Right, okay. I agree,' said Ossie. 'But now we know they can
do it. Next time we'll strike something rich.'

'Like what's rich?' said Bruce. 'You got any ideas?'

'A house,' said Ossie quietly. 'Jesus, this area's full of loaded
houses.'

'A burglary,' said Bruce.

'You're quick, real quick. What I think we should do is to
smell around for a while. Keep your eyes on the newspapers
maybe. Then when we come up with something considerable,
go to work on it.'

'It'll be quieter than a stick-up,' agreed Bruce finishing his
beer. They went out and got some hot pastrami sandwiches
from a takeaway, and cans of beer from a package store. Ocean
Drive was quiet except for the insistent pushing sound of the
waves.

'My dad always thought I'd make a good preacher,' said
Ossie biting into the sandwich as he walked along.

'Shows how wrong fathers can be,' mumbled Bruce with his
mouth full.

'Maybe I'll still be, one day,' said Ossie. 'I got a feeling for it.
I just see all these old folk sitting along here in the day and,
man, you know, I just feel like getting up there on a box or
something and giving them the Jesus call.'

'They're Jewish,' Bruce pointed out through the bread.
'Ninety per cent Jewish. They'd say "Jesus, who needs it?" '

'So it would be hard. I don't give a shit. I tell you sometimes up there on the beach tower I've been tempted, you know seriously tempted, to start throwing my arms about and start shouting things.'

'You want to be loved,' Bruce told him.

'I guess that's it.'

They reached the Sunny Gables Hotel, looking sick in the orange floodlight which was thrown across its front. 'Maybe if we make a few more bucks,' said Bruce, 'I'll get me a better room. That one I got is so small I can turn the air conditioning on just by breaking wind.'

'You don't say.'

'Sure. It's enough to work the thermostat. Just breaking wind.'

'You got some nice habits,' said Ossie.

They walked into the front of the hotel. Gabby was standing in the shadows. They saw she was pointing a gun at them. They stopped and regarded her with alarm.

'Okay, you two,' she said quietly. 'I want to know what you're doing with my grandma.'

She looked very businesslike behind the small hole of the gun. She jabbed it towards them and ushered them towards the stairs.

'Put your hands over your heads,' she said firmly. 'And don't put them down.'

'You're enjoying this,' murmured Bruce. 'Domination over men.' He caught Ossie's grinning eye. They both raised their hands and allowed themselves to be prodded up the stairs. Gabby was three stairs behind them.

'Don't try to pull anything,' she warned sombrely. 'I promise I'll shoot.'

'We ain't pulled anything in weeks,' answered Bruce easily. He could tell by the back of Ossie's neck that he was smiling. Ossie's got the bullet, he thought. The stairs were narrow and turning and they could hear hesitant footsteps scraping down. They were on the first landing and the elevator clanked open almost at Ossie's elbow.

'In there,' said Gabby. 'Go on. Get in.' She pushed the snout of the gun into Bruce's middle. 'You get it if anybody tries anything.' Obediently they got into the elevator. It was old and trembling. Most of the residents of Sunny Gables were afraid to use it, the elderly having a profound distrust of the elderly.

'Which floor is your room?' she said to Bruce. 'I want to go there. Right now.'

'Gee, I thought you'd never ask,' he answered. He pressed the button for the eighth floor which was the top. The jerk caught the girl off balance and they both hurriedly caught her and steadied her. She regarded them with deep dislike.

'I want to know what you guys have been doing,' she muttered. She rattled the gun in Bruce's ribs.

At the next floor a thin, weak eyed man was waiting and he stepped into the cage, somehow blindly inserting himself between Gabby and Bruce. Gabby found herself with the gun pointing at the old man. She manoeuvered it behind his thin back until it was covering Bruce again. He grinned sympathetically. The thin old man focussed his eyes carefully on the elevator door and when it stopped at the next floor staggered out with tiny steps. He had not spoken to them.

'That guy,' said Ossie conversationally to Bruce. 'Have you noticed? All day he goes up and down in the elevator. Every time I get in this elevator he's either aboard or he gets aboard.'

'I noticed,' said Bruce. 'Maybe he doesn't know where he lives.'

'Maybe he lives in this elevator,' said Ossie. 'Right here.'

They were completely ignoring Gabby. Her expression hardened. 'You two think you know all the answers don't you? Oh yes, you're real smarties. I might have known you were up to something. Using an old lady's guns. Jesus, how low can some people get?'

They had reached the eighth. Bruce and Ossie with exaggerated politeness stood back to allow Gabby to exit, but she pushed them both out with a nudge of the gun. 'Okay, where?' she said.

'Right here,' said Bruce reaching the door. 'I hope it's not too untidy, lady.'

'There may be blood on the floor before too long,' she replied. She was keeping up the hardness, but they knew she was unsure because of their lack of concern at the gun. They walked into the room. Bruce quietly let off wind and the air condition-ing obligingly whirred. Ossie nodded at the feat. 'I'm impressed,' he said.

'What's it all about?' insisted Gabby at once.

'Grandma didn't tell you?'

'She wouldn't say.'

'Great. Good for Molly.'

The familiarity of the name immediately angered the girl. 'Jesus, you are such shit!' she burst out. 'She's seventy. Come on you bastards, what was it all for?'

'For armed robbery,' shrugged Bruce. Ossie nodded. 'You *need* a gun for armed robbery,' he added solicitously.

Gabby's large eyes opened larger. The muzzle of the revolver dropped and so did her attractive mouth. Loose Bruce and Ossie grinned together. 'Robbery ...?' she said at last. 'Rob-bery? My grandma ...?'

Bruce said : 'Well on this raid she didn't have the gun because she was the plant, you get me? We need somebody among the er ... victims ... and that was Molly. She had a good time, believe me.'

'I ought to shoot you, both of you,' she muttered.

'It ain't no good,' said Bruce easily. 'That weapon ain't loaded. We got the guns but there's only one bullet. And he's got that.' He nodded backwards at Ossie. Ossie looked puzzled. 'No man, you've got it,' he said.

Bruce went serious and pale. 'But you ...'

'You had it,' said Ossie quietly.

'I've got it,' said the girl firmly. 'It's in the gun.'

They whitened together. 'Jesus, Gabby, baby, watch what you're doing!' pleaded Bruce. 'Point it at *him*.'

'I was brought up with guns,' said Gabby. 'My old man was a game ranger. What's in this could go right through both of you. And maybe it will.'

'Look,' said Ossie hurriedly. 'Let's have a little sense in this. We wouldn't have let your grandma have a loaded gun.'

'No,' said Bruce fervently. 'Not for anything, Gabby. We thought there was only one bullet and we thought one of *us* had it.'

73

'One of you may get it,' she said. 'My grandma stole it from you. Great gang leaders you are. Letting a little old lady steal your ammunition.' She was very sure of herself now.

Expertly she flicked open the chamber of the gun as if to make sure the bullet had not got out. Both men jumped on her in the instant. Bruce caught the gun and Ossie caught the girl. She could fight and the room was narrow. Ossie fell over Bruce and Bruce got Ossie's boot in the chest. The girl rolled beneath them. The table fell over and one of its legs collapsed. Bruce managed to sit astride her. Ossie pushed him aside and muttered, 'I'll hold her, I'm stronger.'

'It's rape now, is it?' spat Gabby. 'You horny bastards.'

'Nobody's getting raped unless it's me,' Ossie assured her. 'We just wanted the gun and the bullet on our side. Now are you going to be a good girl?'

She nodded sullenly. Gently he got from above her. Her lovely breasts heaved under her sweater. The man and the girl regarded each other. Bruce, seeing the expressions, moved in quickly and helped her into the chair again. All three sat down panting. Bruce had the gun. Ossie took it from him and dropped the bullet from the chamber. 'Next time,' he said to Bruce, 'I'll make you sign for it.'

One hour and fifteen cans of beer later they thought they had convinced her. She kept pace, argument by argument, and can by can, with them, but in the end she shrugged. 'Okay,' she said. 'I'll go and talk to her again. I want to make quite sure she knows what she's doing.'

'Like I say, it's only occupational therapy,' said Ossie persuasively. His strong eyes regarded her seriously and she had to look away after holding on to the gaze for a moment. 'These old people down here,' he went on, 'just need something ... a little excitement. We aim to provide it.'

Gabby hung her head thoughtfully. 'I want to go and talk to her again,' she repeated. 'I want to hear it from her. Okay?'

Bruce looked doubtful. But Ossie said: 'Okay. But don't try anything, sweetheart.'

'I know,' she said. 'She's in it too. I won't tell any tales. Don't worry your junior heads.'

She went out. Bruce and Ossie drank another can of beer each silently. Then Bruce said: 'You're too old, man. She's my generation.'

'That's right,' agreed Ossie. 'That's why I've got a lap start. Just see, sonny, she'll come to daddy.'

'Listen, we *can't*,' said Bruce. 'We could screw up everything if we both start making pitches for her.'

'Maybe she'll have a say,' pointed out Ossie logically. 'Women have a curious idea they can make up their own minds. Anyway, don't let it bug you – or me. And have a little sympathy, man. Jesus, you're so young you'll have them by the hundred before you're too old and tired. Me, I'm nearly through, it could be my last chance.'

'You poor old bastard,' commented Bruce looking at the cheerful brown face and the chopped grey hair. 'My heart bleeds. It bleeds.'

They had another two cans of beer before the girl came back. She came quietly into the room. Bruce farted silently and set the air conditioning going. 'At least the air conditioning works in here,' she said. 'My grandma's only goes when it thinks it will.'

'Maybe I'll fix it for her,' offered Bruce.

Ossie smiled. 'What did she say, the old lady?' he asked.

Gabby sat, surrendered, on the chair. 'I've got to tell you that grandma told me she loved every minute,' she sighed. 'She's not crazy about spending the loot, but she liked doing the job. I've never seen her so frisky. To tell you the truth I only came back from St Petersburg because I was worried so much about her. She used to be such fun, like a young girl, but this place, this graveyard, is getting to her. And when I get back today she's hopping about like a buck rabbit.'

'Maybe she'll make enough to get away from South Miami Beach altogether,' said Ossie cagily. 'Go some place where she can be old and content and not have to live in a crummy hotel like this. What do *you* do for her, anyway?'

It was a shrewd inquiry. She hesitated. 'Not enough,' she admitted. 'But I worry. That's why I came back. Just now I'm not in a very strong situation myself. I had some trouble. I got mixed up with a guy who has a wife and it hit the fan just a few weeks ago. And he's got a vice-presidency and kids. I don't have a job or even a proper home of my own right now. God, I just had to sell my motor cycle, and that was hard, really hard.'

Bruce did not like the way the conversation seemed to have been carried on without him, almost as if nobody expected he was mature enough to understand. 'She got any other family, your grandma?' he said solidly. 'Don't anybody else take an interest?'

Gabby looked carefully towards him. Ossie smiled to himself. 'Well, no, not really,' said Gabby. 'They don't give a damn. They sent her off down here before I was old enough to stop them. Go and have a good time on Miami Beach, they said. The sun always shines down there. Jesus, the sun! What the hell's the sun? If somebody cut their throat down here they'd put them out in the sun to get better.'

'Right,' said Bruce gravely. 'That's absolutely one hundred per cent right.'

'What are you going to do next?' inquired Gabby expectantly.

'The gang?' said Ossie. 'Oh well, we were just getting around to thinking about that. It's still in the planning sequence you understand.'

'We can't reveal anything at this stage,' said Bruce importantly.

'Are you interested?' said Ossie, more to the point. He leaned towards her. Bruce looked annoyed that he had not said it. Gabby's face came up to meet Ossie's and nodded. She shrugged. 'I'm right out on a limb myself. People keep throwing dirt at me anyway. Maybe I could deserve some of it. Sure, why not?'

The young man and the older man regarded her passively, their beer cans held negligently. She appeared to have forgotten them, to have gone down into some cellar of her own. Her brown neck was arched forward and her beautiful profile became thoughtful, the lids and lashes dropped low over the large eyes. The air conditioning stopped and Bruce, silently lifting his leg, started it again. The girl said, 'That's the neatest way I ever saw of starting it.' It was an aside. Bruce looked shocked and ashamed. Ossie nodded approvingly towards Gabby.

'Okay, what did the stick-up make?' she asked eventually.

Bruce and Ossie turned to each other, their separate embarrassments meeting halfway. 'Well,' Ossie hesitated, 'it didn't show much of a profit. Not that much.'

'It was a kind of try-out,' apologized Bruce. 'Just to see if it could be done.'

'How much?' she insisted.

'Oh, roughly about five hundred dollars,' said Ossie.

'Approximately that,' confirmed Bruce as though trying to share the blame.

'Big time eh? You could have sold the guns for more than that.'

'Right. Okay. But we'll need the guns again. And next time we'll be after bigger fry,' said Ossie.

'What's it to be next time? Busting into a juke box?'

'Listen,' said Ossie leaning forward and touching her arm with his can of beer, 'you just joined.'

'Sure, he's right,' said Bruce. 'We were only waiting for *you* before going into the big-time.'

'Just as well I got here,' she said, ignoring the sarcasm. 'Seems like it wasn't a minute too soon.'

Ossie looked at her squarely with such concentration that she had to lift her head and return the look. 'One thing, baby,' he said slowly. 'One thing you're not going to do and that's take over.'

She converted her calm stare into a shrugging laugh. 'Okay. Okay,' she agreed. 'I'm not going to spoil your party. You Tarzan, me Jane.'

'What about me?' said Bruce.

'There's only Boy left,' said Gabby.

Gabby and Ossie both laughed at Bruce's lost face. Ossie tapped him on the head with his beer can. 'Don't take it too hard, son. It's *our* gang. She's just been coopted.'

'*Our Gang* is right,' commented Gabby. Before they could reply she had lapsed into her thoughts again.

Bruce opened three more beers. The last three. 'What are

we supposed to be thinking about?' he asked the other two.

'The next target,' said Ossie patiently. 'Where the ODDS strike next.'

'What's the ODDS?' asked Gabby almost absently. 'What's it stand for?'

'Ocean Drive Delinquent Society,' replied Bruce smugly. 'Don't you think that's a smart name?'

'It is, it is,' agreed Gabby, forestalling any further argument. 'The Lostra Nostra.'

Ossie opened his mouth but she got there first again. 'There's a three million dollar house at Palm Beach,' she said thoughtfully. 'It's called something Spanish, Casa Velentia, that kind of place. I saw it in the Miami newspaper. They're having some sort of gala night there for charity. Why don't we just look into the possibilities. If we can get in during the extravaganza ...'

'What's an extravaganza?' asked Bruce.

'The night,' Ossie said. 'It means the charity night, see?'

'Why didn't she just say?' sulked Bruce.

'If we get in,' she went on, ignoring the exchange, 'while all the guests are there, we might find there's some pickings. Maybe from the people themselves – they're bound to be loaded at that sort of party. Or maybe we can hook on to a few treasures from the house itself. It will be a matter of finding out what the possibilities are.'

'Casing the joint,' said Bruce smugly. 'Reconnoitring.'

'Just so,' agreed Gabby easily.

'When's the charity night?' asked Ossie grinning at them. 'How long do we have for planning?'

'In a couple of weeks, I seem to remember,' said Gabby. 'I'll check with the newspaper. How does it sound?'

'Sounds okay,' said Bruce like a military tactician. 'Worth taking a look I'd say.'

'What's the charity?' asked Ossie. He leaned back for some more beer but realized it had all gone. 'How many beers have you drunk?' he asked Gabby.

'Jesus, I don't know,' she said. 'You hand me them, I drink them. The charity is the Senior Citizens' Goodwill Fund.'

'What better?' said Ossie. 'We qualify right away.'

six

The members of the Ocean Drive Delinquent Society gathered in Molly Mandy's room. It was their third meeting that week, and they arrived, their excitement and expectancy scarcely contained in their expressions. Carefully they moved the Russian flame thrower from the sideboard and all stood around while Ossie opened a drawn plan. Gabby and Bruce stood slightly behind him.

'It would seem, ladies and gentlemen, that if we're lucky, this operation at Palm Beach is tailor-made for us.' He looked around like the chairman at a board meeting. 'We have given you time to familiarize yourselves with the surroundings of the house, Casa Velentia, and here we have an architect's drawing of the place, which Katy managed to extract from the municipality at Palm Beach without the municipality being aware of it. Good work Katy.'

Katy blushed and, half standing, gave a little old-fashioned bow. 'Th-Th-Thank you,' she said. 'I just went in there and said I was an interior designer and I needed the plan, and they gave it to me. They were real nice.'

Ossie and Bruce both smiled fondly at her, causing her blush to surface again. 'In this operation – which Gabby will explain in detail in a moment – we need three inside helpers and the rest will have their own responsibilities in carrying out the raid.'

Molly Mandy shyly raised her hand. 'Ossie,' she said quietly. 'Could I please be one of the ones who wears a hood this time?'

'Everybody will get a chance to wear a hood in time,' said Ossie.

He paused, circled the faces. Molly smiled her motherly smile, Sidewalk adjusted the bright buckle on his spats, Katy crossed her legs, Ari's eyes looked a long way behind his nose and Lou worked the strength of one set of fingers against the others, bending them one way and another, like a man wrestling with himself. Katy glanced at his hands affectionately before going back to the strategy unfolded on the plan.

'We've discussed this matter in great detail,' said Ossie. 'We want it to go right and we want to make sure we come out with a profit. So if you'd give your attention to Gabby, she will run through the plan for the operation.'

Gabby stepped forward and there was an endearing little round of applause for her, originating from her grandmother but being taken up generously all around. 'The girl's got brains,' confided Molly Mandy in a loud whisper to Sidewalk Joe. 'That's what this outfit needs – brains.' Bruce and Ossie looked at each other and winced.

Gabby performed a short bow. Ossie observed her closely. So did Bruce. The tight shirt over the excellent breasts, the brown arms and brown arched neck, the face beautiful and sure.

'Ladies and gentlemen,' she said, 'I want to tell you the general outline for our plan for the robbery of Casa Velentia . . .'

'Can I wear the hood this time?' put in her grandmother at once. 'Please?'

'You just have *got* to wait, grandma,' said Gabby. 'Everybody will have an important part to play.'

'I'd still like to wear the hood,' muttered Molly. 'After all, I made them.'

'I made the gloves,' nodded Katy. 'Crochetwork – it's a lost art.'

Gabby sighed and ignored them. 'There's going to be a lot of good things going for us in this operation,' she said. 'A lot. For a start, the charity gala is in aid of the Senior Citizens' Goodwill Fund of Palm Beach. The house belongs to Mr and Mrs Peter Van der Vatt and they plan to have a few tame old folks present to give it some atmosphere. Like exhibits. We have arranged that two of our members will be among the tame old folk. That will be pretty useful when it comes to creating a diversion.' She looked along the faces, each watching her pointedly. 'We'll require two people with strong acting ability for that part,' she said.

'I was an actress, you know,' put in Katy with modest enthusiasm. She glanced around. 'Well, a chorus girl anyway.'

'I still want to wear the hood,' muttered Molly doggedly.

'Grandma,' threatened Gabby, 'button up or I'll put the hood on now.'

Molly looked chastened and fixed her upper lip deliberately across the lower as though charging it with the responsibility of silence. Her eyes remained firmly and fondly upon Gabby.

Gabby continued. 'We've carried out a little research on Casa Velentia,' she said. She picked up the architect's plan. 'It's a real nice place. The main reception will be in the salon which opens out on to the garden, the swimming pool and the beach. The room we are most interested in is the room directly above this salon.' She brushed a slim fawn finger like a feather across the map. Bruce and Ossie watched the beautiful finger intently. Gabby glanced up, saw their expressions and pursed her lips as if cautioning them to pay attention to the map.

'In the room above the salon,' she said, returning to the drawing, 'there is a safe. There are a lot of goodies in the house itself but the real sweet things are in that safe.'

'What kind of safe?' asked Sidewalk Joe. 'There's all kinds.'

'Yeah, what kind? How strong?' confirmed Lou professionally.

'That's where we've stalled,' admitted Gabby. 'We don't know as yet. All we *do* know is it's concealed. It's in the wall or maybe the floor.'

'It's a long time since I busted a safe,' said Sidewalk. 'Safes have changed.'

'On the other hand,' said Gabby, 'our information is that no new safe has been fitted in the house for at least fifteen years.'

'If it needs strength, I've got strength,' said Lou. He looked at his fingers as though counting them. Kate glanced at him and then at his powerful hands with soft admiration. Lou caught her eye and blushed through his elderly tan. 'Sure I have,' he repeated.

'Concealed safes,' said Sidewalk, 'are pretty much the same. They ain't got enough room to be too fancy. If we can't open it by hand we can always blow it open.'

'That will be very noisy,' said Molly thoughtfully, 'blowing it open.'

Sidewalk nodded patiently. 'It will be,' he conceded. 'Real noisy.'

Bruce looked across at him. 'You can get some explosive?' he said.

'I guess so,' nodded Sidewalk. 'Me, I can always get explosive.'

Ari the Greek looked at him with long-standing admiration. 'He always could get things,' he said half to himself. 'Sidewalk Joe. Always could.'

'We'll fill in more details before Wednesday,' nodded Gabby. 'Just now I think maybe we ought to fix who is going to do what.'

The gang leaned forward in anticipation. 'Katy and Ari ought to be our plants,' said Gabby decisively. 'We thought this out and – in the event of us needing a diversion – one of them has got to throw a good, realistic heart attack. Okay?'

'That's Katy,' said Ari firmly. 'I don't like pretending those things. Not heart attacks. Like it's tempting Providence.'

'Sure,' agreed Katy. 'I'd like to do that. Can't say I ever had much scope for tragedy. Not as a chorus girl.'

'You don't,' agreed Lou sagely. 'Not in the chorus. Not as a general rule.'

They waited for him to finish. He looked around, embarrassed, muttered, 'Well you don't,' and shut his mouth firmly.

'Okay, that's agreed,' said Gabby. 'And we need a waiter. I have a thought for a waiter – Bruce.'

'Me?' exclaimed Bruce, backing away. 'A waiter? But I drop things.'

'Sure,' said Gabby sarcastically. 'That's going to be a great help. But we need you, Bruce, to keep things coordinated on the lower floor, in the salon and to help Katy and Ari get clear if we blow the job. It won't be difficult to get you in there as a waiter. Just try not to start dropping trays until it's time, that's all.'

Bruce nodded. 'I'll practise,' he promised.

'We need a look-out,' continued Gabby. 'Someone to keep watch for trouble outside, while we're working in the house. That will be you, grandma.'

'But my hood. What about my hood?' insisted Molly plaintively. 'You promised.'

'We need you as a look-out,' said Gabby firmly. 'Because you can *whistle* real loud. And we need a look-out who can whistle if there's trouble coming.'

Molly smiled. 'Sure can,' she said. She put her fingers into her mouth and let go an ear-wrenching whistle.

They all fell away from her, consternation on their faces. 'Sounds like some crazy bird,' said Sidewalk staring at her.

'I can whistle too,' put in K-K-K-Katy quietly. She put her fingers to her lips and after a hesitation not unlike her habitual stutter let go an even louder shriek. It was like Molly's, only longer. The gang held back, amazement, admiration and protest on their faces. Katy smiled sweetly. 'At one time,' she said confidingly to Gabby, 'all American girls could whistle.'

'It's a lost art,' agreed Molly.

'Let's not search for it,' suggested Gabby. 'Okay. Check. We've got the look-outs and we've got the plants, we've got the waiter. The others – there's Lou, Sidewalk, Ossie and me – we'll do the job on the safe.'

'Maybe I could ask a question,' said Ari.

'Sure, questions are welcome.'

'Why do we have to rob the safe with so many people in the house? Maybe it would be easier just to get in there when there was only the family at home.'

Sidewalk Joe looked at him impatiently. 'All the best house robberies used to be done when the place was full of folks,' he said. 'Nobody notices a few more faces around and a little noise nobody notices. And a lot of folks is like a smokescreen when it comes to getting away too. Get it?'

Ari looked abashed and said: 'Yes, I see, Sidewalk. I was only a no-good bootlegger. I was never in the big time. But I see the point. Believe me, I see the point.'

'Anything else?' put in Ossie.

Bruce said: 'One thing we ought to get right is the raid party. The guys who are going to get into the upstairs room will all be dressed like they're going to the gala.'

'In fact they *will* be going to the gala,' added Gabby. 'Tuxedos, everything. We'll have some tickets specially stolen. They won't know. It's going to be easier getting into that room from inside than out. But we'll need to get away through the window, so somebody will have to be outside with a rope ladder to throw it to the window. That should be the look-out.' She regarded her grandmother doubtfully. 'Could you throw a rope up to the window, grandma?'

Molly looked scornful. 'Sure I can. I can throw a rope like I can whistle.' They backed away quickly in case she whistled again but she did not. She just smiled and said, 'I'll throw the rope.'

Gabby nodded. Lou said: 'I got my own tuxedo. It's smart, real smart. I'd like to wear that.'

'Right, that's okay,' agreed Bruce. 'There's nothing like a well dressed gang. But everybody, the waiter, that's me, the tame old folks, Katy and Ari, the look-out and the safe gang will all have their hoods with them, okay? If it all hits the fan and you can get your hood on, then get it on smart. Then run like hell.'

Charity begins in everybody's home in Palm Beach, Florida. There are few weeks in the season when there are no benefits or galas in aid of some worthy cause. These are invariably well patronized and always by the same people. Some are not especially generous in either heart or pocket, but it is socially required to attend such functions, to note who is missing and who is present, how much they give, and then to host a richer and more ostentatious charity ball or benefit at a later time.

Mr and Mrs Peter Van der Vatt, an elegant, wealthy couple in their thirties, had planned for half a year, organizing the details of their gala night for the Senior Citizens' Goodwill Fund. Casa Velentia, their expensive and expansive home, was ideal for such an event. Its neo-colonial arches and verandas looked out serenely over inch-clipped lawns to a swimming pool like a bevelled turquoise and then down the gentle slope to the ocean, a limb of it captured in a stone boat dock where their several boats were tethered. At night amber lights and lanterns oozed from the house, there were diffuse illuminations among the flowered shrubs and burning brands along the ocean shore. All around the elegant Florida palms bowed in the night breeze as though approving every touch and detail.

Two hundred guests were expected, at a hundred dollars a plate, and as they strolled about the grounds an hour before the scheduled start of the event, watching the musicians setting up their music, checking that the chefs were abreast of time, and that the barbecue was glowing, that the glasses were shining, the Van der Vatts experienced only one regret. It was a pity, they agreed, that their own household servants were insufficient to fulfil the needs of so many guests.

It had been necessary to import outside help and some of the temporary staff looked anything but the correct thing in such surroundings. There was, Mrs Van der Vatt noted particularly, one young, tall, fair man – obviously uncomfortable in his waiter's suit, who had already knocked a salver of glassware sideways and now, even as they walked from their measured lawns towards the wide terrace doors of the house, was scraping a trembling pile of vanilla ice cream from the seat of a chair. He looked up as they approached and had the grace to blush.

'It kinda slipped,' he said apologetically. 'Ice cream does.'

Mrs Van der Vatt winced as he picked up a great gob in his hand and dropped it back into the dish. She rolled her eyes at her distinguished husband but said nothing. Taking his sympathetic arm she went with him into the house.

The sight of the main room reassured them. It was a salon with fine proportions, copied from one of the most famous colonial houses in Virginia, dominated by an exquisite chandelier especially made for the Van der Vatts by Claudio Picci in Florence. Below this, sitting like a stalagmite under a stalactite, was an ornate cake of great girth. It was iced and curled and embossed. At its summit were two miniature old people, the man in a frock coat, the lady in an old-fashioned dress, each supported by a walking stick, the other hands coyly touching. Around the third layer of the cake was inscribed 'Palm Beach Senior Citizens' Goodwill Fund'. It was an impressive work of charity. It was intended to be.

There were some tasteful paintings riveted to the walls and some good drawings tucked away into modest niches. A portrait of Mr Van der Vatt's father (for it was he, Cornelius Van der Vatt, who had bought Casa Velentia for them as a wedding present ten years before, sat regally above the carved fireplace.

It was in this room, penned in a small minstrels' gallery, that the musicians would play, with an additional Cuban guitarist strumming down by the shore for the enrichment of any romantic moments that the guests might enjoy there. He was also keeping an eye on the boats. At the last party some high spirits had taken one of the more sumptuous craft and rammed the dock wall with it, causing it to sink immediately. The Van der Vatts did not want that sort of expensive unpleasantness again.

'Honey,' said Peter Van der Vatt, 'I want to tell you, I think it's just perfect. I don't see how it could be improved.'

'I think so too,' she said with elegant modesty. Then her voice changed. 'Even so, we're bound to get some bitchy remarks from some people, the Costellos for sure. Have you ever seen a woman take a bite out of anything – but anything – making the face she makes? You'd think the whole goddamn world was out to poison her. That look of suspicion.'

'Maybe the world is,' he sniffed. He looked around thoughtfully. 'Baby,' he said, 'these old folks we've invited. They're going to be okay are they? I mean ... okay?'

'Sure, sure,' she said, understanding at once what he meant. 'I told the welfare authorities that we wanted them clean and civilized – and quiet. We don't want them making a fuss or drinking too much. But at the same time it's no good having them too well turned out. They've got to have just a suspicion of poverty, darling, otherwise, you know what people are, they'll just wonder why they're giving money to people who are okay anyway.'

'And that's no way to get the biggest subscription for any charity in Palm Beach,' he smiled fondly. 'No way at all.'

'It's fixed,' she said confidentially. 'I told them to send half a dozen senior citizens who look a bit sad and just a little threadbare. They know what I mean.'

'Right,' he nodded. 'It's no good having the merchandise looking better than the people who are paying for it.'

They did not consider there was any lack of charity in their observations. To them they were practical, basic economics, the sort of considered thinking that had made both families rich and powerful and the givers of the best benefits in South Florida. Charity was proverbially cold. It was no good being sentimental about it.

When the tame old folks arrived an hour later Teresa Van der

Vatt had planned it so that there would be a sufficient number of guests present to give them heartfelt applause as they trooped through the house and on to the lawns, but not so many that the demonstration would put a brake on the more pleasurable events of the evening.

The six dowdy old people had been carefully selected by the welfare office, who were particularly pleased with the pair who had come forward (not many old folks wanted to volunteer) and who seemed to have all the steadfast humility that was required by the occasion. This pair had also been recommended by that nice young lady from St Petersburg who spent so much time helping the elderly of South Miami Beach pass the time of day.

Ari the Greek and K-K-K-Katy were almost bursting with the excitement of their mission. As they walked with the other selected tame old people, two men and two modest women, through the ranks of the guests at Casa Velentia, Katy performed a short stagey shuffle, which brought a patronizing burst of extra applause from the watchers.

'Now wasn't that just cute, Wilbur? Did you see? She did a dear little dance.'

Ari, not to be left out, suddenly broke into his running-and-sparring routine which delighted the audience further. 'Wow, that old guy's fitter than me, Audrey. Just look how he moves. What a mover. Real great!'

A group of the guests waylaid Katy and asked her name, squeals of delight coming from them as she told them what it was with an embroidered version of her celebrated stutter. 'They d-d-didn't call me after the song,' she added to their enchantment. 'They c-c-c-called the song K-K-K-Katy after *me*. I'm that a-a-ancient!'

Just then Ari caught the eye of Loose Bruce the bogus waiter, balancing a difficult tray and trying to send out warning signals about becoming too conspicuous by their antics. Ari got the message and moved closer to Katy. 'Cool it Katy,' he whispered. 'We don't want to get too much attention. We don't want them to remember us after tonight. Not to remember us too well.'

Katy simmered down and walked more sedately. Ari was about to begin shadow boxing again, something he did without thinking, when Bruce's gaze found him once more across the heads of the guests and he dropped his fists and slowed his feet.

A worrying photographer and a bleak lady journalist materialized through the crowd, and the tame old people were halted while photographs were taken of Mr and Mrs Van der Vatt posing smiling with their guests and then with the old people themselves. The columnist agitated her pencil, whirling it around like an épée, jabbing at each of the elderly folk in turn to demand their names.

Then the short procession corralled into the house for photographs with the giant iced cake surmounted by the two miniature figures. There was no doubt about it that this was the centrepiece of Mrs Van der Vatt's dreams of making her evening as spectacular as possible. It was a cake like a castle, four tiers, carved, embossed, finished with great art. It was so tall that its summit was only two feet below the centre crystal of the fine and famous chandelier.

The musicians in their pen began playing their spidery waltz and down by the shore the Cuban guitarist sang calypsos from the West Indies, where he had never been. The lights eased through the flowers and trees, the palms slyly nudged each other: the sound of conversation, polite laughter, touching greetings and touching glasses mingled with the insinuating music. The night was airy and warm. There was a strong possibility of a moon.

Loose Bruce looked at his watch as he attempted to serve drinks without drenching everyone. The movement of turning his wrist emptied a glass of champagne wastefully on to the ground and he grinned with wry embarrassment at the astonished lady who was holding out her hand in readiness to receive it.

Ari and Katy were holding court by the swimming pool. Ari, who told a good tale when given the opportunity, had the men gravefaced and the women reaching for their handkerchiefs as he related some touching but completely fictitious episode of his younger life. Katy, her face suitably subdued, listened too and realistically reached out and held his gnarled hand. The society ladies blinked, the men swallowed visibly.

Three hundred yards away, in a concealed grove, the other members of the Ocean Drive Delinquent Society quietly left two cars. Everyone knew where to go and what to do when they got there. Ossie, Lou the Barbender and Sidewalk wore tuxedos and smiles. Gabby was in a long and rippling evening dress below which she wore a set of overalls. Molly appeared modest and becoming in her gown. Her hood was in her handbag.

Molly, with Sidewalk as her escort, went first, strolling surely through the front gates of Casa Velentia, producing stolen tickets for the persual of the security guard. 'Gee, honey,' Molly said loudly, unable to resist embroidering the occasion, 'I feel like tonight we're doing something in a real good cause.'

'For folks not as fortunate as ourselves,' echoed Sidewalk. It was a far cry from the old New York hoodlum days.

Gabby, on Ossie's arm, followed two minutes later. Lou strolled alongside them like a large keeper. They produced the tickets and Gabby smiled brilliantly at the gateman. He blushed under his lamps and smiled back. 'It looks like Mrs Van der Vatt's done it again,' mentioned Gabby to Ossie, squeezing his arm.

'There's nobody throws a benefit like the Van der Vatts,' agreed Ossie.

Gabby turned to Lou. 'Come on Daddy, we're going to miss all the fun.'

Lou's face became crammed with surprise because he was not the most facile of men. Then he grinned and said: 'Okay, daughter, I don't want to miss it neither.' The gateman's pleased smile took in all of them and he waved them on.

Loose Bruce saw them right away. He turned his face to where Ari and Katy were holding court and latched on to Ari's eye. They both nodded.

Gabby eased herself through the crowd. Inside the house there were people sitting on the fine staircase and others moving up and down between them. Gabby saw the grand iced cake with its symbolic figures and winced. Ossie took a glass from the tray offered by Bruce. He handed it to Gabby who looked coolly around before sipping it. 'The rooms upstairs are all open,' said Bruce quietly. 'Room "A" as we had it on the plan is the place to change. It has a door directly into room "B" and the door is unlocked, but I still don't know where the safe is.'

'It's in room "B". We'll have to find it,' said Ossie quietly over the rim of his champagne. His voice made furrows on the surface.

'Okay Gabby, let's move.'

Lou took a glass from Bruce's tray and emptied it quickly. He caught the younger man's warning look, took another and lifted it more sedately to his large lips. 'Room "A",' muttered Bruce. 'Pass it on to Sidewalk.'

'I got it,' said Lou with more confidence than either he or Bruce felt. 'Everything's going to be fine.' He moved away, to where Sidewalk, his back to the room, was admiring an obtuse drawing. 'Room "A",' he said from the corner of his mouth, standing behind the old New Yorker and looking in the other direction. 'The door's open. In one minute.'

'Okay pal,' said Sidewalk. He was apparently absorbed in the picture. Within himself he felt the warmth of danger, the twist of excitement in his gut that he had been missing all these years. This was true therapy; better than poker any day.

At the side of the grounds Molly stationed herself among the guests, patrolling a path that gave her a view both of the front and rear entrance of Casa Velentia.

She was observing the gate near the beach, ostensibly standing and admiring the profile of the Cuban guitarist against the creamy sky. His proverbial song floated through the trees. She smiled, suddenly pleased to realize the words.

Some folks buy and some folks pay.
Some folks come and steal it away.
Whatever you got, you won't have long.
This is the story of this song.

She put her hand in her handbag and felt the hood and the shape of the pistol.

It was ten o'clock. The Van der Vatts' exquisite Boule wall clock chimed its exquisite chimes, attracting as many glances as if it had produced a cuckoo. For the members of the Ocean Drive Delinquent Society it was Zero Hour.

Gabby slipped into the small ante-chamber they had designated room 'A' in their plans. There was a cool excitement about her, a sensation trapped burning in her stomach and showing nowhere in her outward calm. At least she too was *doing* something. The room was furnished as a dressing room with two subdued lights and an illuminated mirror. She undid her long dress, forcing herself not to hurry, and folded it carefully before putting it into a plastic bag. She was not going to leave that behind. Now she was wearing the dark overalls that her clever grandmother had made. She turned to the mirror, approved of the fit around her bottom and tidied her hair. The door opened carefully behind her and Ossie came in. He grinned when he saw her at the mirror. Lou and Sidewalk Joe were just behind him. Sidewalk locked the door.

'Nice party,' said Ossie finishing a glass of champagne. He put it unhurriedly on the dressing table. There was no need of conversation. Each took out his hood and put it on. Lou found himself sweating and made two attempts before he could locate his head. Sidewalk took a piece of gum from his mouth and casually parked it on the side of the dressing table before easing on his hood. It is difficult to chew gum under a hood.

Each had a gun. Gabby had the one with the bullet. She had insisted on that and they had not argued. The girl glanced around her through the eye-holes of her hood. Her large eyes filled the spaces. She nodded at Ossie. He had a strange feeling that she had taken command.

Bruce had said the communicating door was open. Now, the others watching, Ossie turned the handle anxiously. It opened soundlessly and they crept like thieves into the gloom of a generous library. Sidewalk and Ossie had the torches. Lou checked the window. Below in the shrubbery he could see the upturned face of Molly. He waved without hurry as though he were on the street. Molly acknowledged the signal then swung the lightly weighted rope and threw it like a sailor. Lou grabbed for it wildly. He was a strong man but with no finesse. He caught it awkwardly and pulled it in, hand over hand. The other end was attached to a nylon handle. Lou secured it clumsily but safely to the pipe of an air conditioning duct. He waved confirmation to Molly who sank into the shrubbery like a lady sinking into a lake. Then Lou turned into the room. They were searching for the safe. Gabby looked towards him and he patted

the knot that held the ladder. She lifted her hand in acknowledgement and waved him to help find the safe. It was Lou who
saw the bump in the floor below the table.

'I got it I think,' he said close to Ossie's ear. He pointed.
Below the table there was a smooth, regular bump under the
carpet.

Ossie crouched and went below the table. Sidewalk dropped
down too. He ran his hand over the carpet like a man stroking
a cat. 'Could be,' he nodded at Ossie.

Lou lifted the heavy table by himself and placed it gently
aside. Ossie knelt close to the carpet and felt the swelling again.
He glanced sideways and Sidewalk wordlessly handed him a
knife. He pushed it into the carpet and made a slit. The gleam
of brass came through as he eased the carpet aside. 'Looks like
it is,' he whispered tensely, running the knife crossways. He
pulled the segmented carpet clear. Beneath it, now revealed, was
a round brass plate like a small hill. He glanced up at Lou. The
strong man bent and felt the plate. He nodded. Ossie looked
towards Sidewalk. He nodded too.

The mound was about the size of a large dinner plate but
Lou's outsized hands spanned it without difficulty. He placed
his powerful fingers against the metal and pressed before turning the pressure to the right. Nothing happened. He turned the
force left and then right again. The plate moved.

The others eased back to give him room. Beneath the hoods
they were all set-faced and sweating. Gabby glanced towards
the door. The sounds of the party drifted through to them. She
looked back at Lou.

The Jewish Barbender was carefully turning the plate and it
was obediently rising from its setting. 'It's just the cover,' muttered Sidewalk. 'The safe's underneath. Watch it ain't wired,
buddy.'

Lou nodded. He reached up and took Gabby's slim hand.
She knelt beside him. He took her fingers and guided them
towards the edge of the plate, now raised a quarter of an inch
from its fitting. Gabby glanced at him. 'Wires,' he whispered.
'Feel for wires.'

She fingered carefully around the edge of the brass and

eventually had made the full circle. 'Nothing,' she said. 'Can't feel any wires.'

Lou nodded and went back to his task. Then someone tried the door and they stiffened as the handle turned and turned again. Gabby unhurriedly drew her gun. The others saw her and stared through the eye-holes of their hoods. Ossie's eyes met hers. She lowered the weapon. Someone laughed outside the door and then went away.

They breathed and crouched again. It was very tight and hot under the hoods. Lou lifted his off his face. He was layered with sweat. His big hands went back to the plate. He turned again. Easier now. He turned it twice and felt it disengage from its thread. With extreme caution, like a man de-fusing a mine, he laid the brass disc aside. Beneath it was another brass plate, concave with a large nut of the same metal hugging a bolt. Lou looked quizzically at Sidewalk. Sidewalk scratched his chin through his hood. 'It's another goddamn cover,' he said quietly. 'Try it.'

Lou began turning the nut, about the size of a coffee cup. The brass slid beautifully around on its thread. Gabby had a passing thought that it was an elegant safe, if inconvenient. The nut came away easily. Lou had it in his hand.

At that instant they knew they had done something wrong. There was an eerie creaking below them and the floor trembled as if in an earthquake. Alarm jumped to the faces below the masks.

Then, suddenly, convulsively, the projecting bolt from which the nut had been taken shuddered and disappeared before their eyes. There was a terrible crash below and many cries.

In the room beneath them, the great chandelier, made specially by Claudio Picci in Florence, descended from the ceiling and crashed through the giant ice cake with the little elderly figures on its summit. The miniature candy man shot from the top like a high diver. The thousand crystals and their curved ironwork decimated the cake and thundered into a cascade across the table, scattering delicacies and drinks over every edge.

The people all around reeled back in horror, the men shouting and cursing, the women howling hysterically. Peter Van der Vatt and his wife stood immobilized. K-K-K-Katy, remembering her instruction to have a heart attack at the first sign of any emergency, threw herself backwards with an awe-inspiring cry. Ari caught her and shouted for assistance. Nobody answered.

'That ceiling's coming down next!' shouted the society columnist, filling her pad gleefully. 'Everybody scram!'

There followed a disgracefully mad scramble towards the safety of the open air. Several heavy men actually stood on poor prostrate Katy, pushing Ari aside in his efforts to protect her.

Ari got her to her feet. 'B-B-Bastards!' she cried. 'Kick an old lady when she's down!'

'I don't think the heart attack routine is going to work,' suggested Ari in a whisper. 'They've screwed it. We'd better get going.'

Above them the would-be robbers looked down through the massive hole in the floor like people peering down a well. 'Jesus,' breathed Ossie. 'We've fucked it up. Let's blow.' They blew.

At both gates there was a rush of people to get away from Casa Velentia. Many believed the whole house would explode any second. Others in disorder cried: 'Terrorists! Cuban terrorists!'

At her watching post Molly Mandy witnessed the panic. She knew what had happened. 'They blew it,' muttered Molly to herself. She joined the running crowd.

In five minutes the house and grounds were almost deserted. The police and fire brigade arrived to find Mr and Mrs Van der Vatt standing amid the wreckage of their extravagant cake and their expensive chandelier. Down by the ocean the Cuban calypso singer, who had witnessed much in his life and remained unimpressed, and anyway was paid by the hour, leaned back against an equally imperturbable palm tree and sang:

People they come, and people they pay.
There come a big bang – people go away.

It seemed to Detective Salvatore that the chief looked like God in a bad mood. Hubert Morriston sat, heavy and hunched, behind the extensive desk at Miami Police Headquarters, his eyebrows brooding, his mouth a tight line, his chin a deep police blue. From hand to knuckled hand he tossed a viciously honed dagger which had once been an exhibit in one of Florida's most carnal crimes and which he now used as a paper knife.

'I knocked,' apologized Salvatore as he went tentatively into the office. 'I just didn't hear whether you called me in, chief.'

'I heard you, Salvatore,' grunted Morriston. 'I heard you fine. I was just trying to make up my mind whether I wanted to see you this morning or whether maybe I could put off the evil day.'

'I'm sorry, chief, but I don't *plan* the crime in this district, I just try and find out who's committed it.'

For a moment the detective thought that his superior was about to throw a knife in an attempt to part his already sparse hair. But the chief grasped it instead, tightly with both hands as if forcing himself not to give in to the temptation. 'I *know* what you do, Albert,' he said with exaggerated patience. 'At least I know what you're *supposed* to do. But for Chrissake, there's crime and there's crime. Okay, a few dead Cubans after a shoot-out is one thing, but this terrible business at the lovely home of Mr and Mrs Peter Van der Vatt is something else, and something else I don't like.'

'Can I sit down, chief?' asked Salvatore. 'I don't feel so good today.'

The chief looked as though he might refuse the request, instead he grunted. 'Take a seat but don't get too comfortable because this is not a comfortable situation. Hooded mobsters in one of the fanciest homes in Florida. And in the middle of a goddamn benefit.'

'Chief,' said Salvatore painfully, 'please remember, they didn't get away with anything. Not a dime. There was no larceny.'

Morriston stared at him, an elongated stare, like a shaft, as if he could not believe what he was hearing. 'Detective Salvatore,' he said eventually, 'they brought the whole fucking ceiling down. A chandelier worth fifty thousand dollars and a cake of great sentimental value.' Salvatore thought his chief was going to begin an explosion of shouting and he minutely edged his chair away, but Morriston seemed to find at the very moment of ignition a small reserve of unsuspected inner calm.

'You and me, Salvatore, we're just men. Everyday Joes. We got nice houses and nice kids and nice wives. Okay?'

'I got a nice house,' agreed Salvatore. 'I ain't so keen on the wife and kids.'

'Okay, okay. But what I'm trying to put to you is that we don't have no chandeliers worth fifty thousand dollars and made by some brilliant bastard in Italy. We don't have that kind of ornament in our homes, now do we?'

Salvatore, reassured by the new quiet in his chief, nodded. 'Maybe we could help to fix it. To piece it together,' he joked. 'It sure seems a lot of dough for a light fitting.'

'Light fitting!' Morriston had used up the inner calm. His face blew up before Salvatore's eyes. 'Light fucking fitting! Jesus Christ, Salvatore, how did you ever get to be a cop? This is fifty thousand bucks worth of broken, beautiful glass. And guess what, Salvatore – the insurers don't want to pay up because it was in the course of a robbery. The Van der Vatts are insured for damage and they're insured for robbery ...'

'But they're not insured for damage during a robbery,' sighed Salvatore knowingly. 'Which means?'

'Which means we're in big shit. Lots of it.' Morriston quietened as though the realization that they were in it together turned down his anger. 'What do we have to go on? Anything? Anything at all? Speak to me, Salvatore.'

Salvatore backed down from repeating the obvious. He grappled for words.

'Speak to me, Salvatore,' repeated Morriston. It was a mutter, half a threat, half a plea. 'Just tell me *something* I can tell the commissioner because Mr and Mrs Van der Vatt have already told the commissioner what they think and I got to tell him something different. Anything different.'

'Hooded gang,' shrugged Salvatore. 'Same as the bus robbery. Fingerprints on a champagne glass and a wad of parked gum in the room next to the library. We're having them checked but it takes time, chief. And the FBI go fishing on Thursday. You try calling them.'

'How did the guy *get* a glass of champagne?' asked Morriston quickly. 'I mean did he go down to the party in his hood and take a glass of champagne and walk about drinking it like the goddamn invisible man?'

Salvatore frowned. 'No, chief. I guess he must have been one of the guests. On the other hand, there's no proof that the glass was anything to do with the robbery. Maybe the gang didn't ever go in that room. Maybe somebody else put it down there while he was having a quick screw. We just don't know.'

'People,' sighed Morriston, 'don't have quick screws at Mrs Van der Vatt's parties. Or even slow screws. They're not that kind of party. Maybe we ought to make a list of things we don't know. There's so many I keep forgetting.'

'We could pull some suspects in,' said Salvatore hopefully. 'You know, the same guys we always pull in. At least it gives you something to tell the commissioner.' He looked at Morriston carefully, then said decisively: 'I'll get them pulled in.'

Morriston began staring again. Salvatore did not enjoy it when he stared. 'Why don't we call Rent-a-Suspect?' Morriston said. 'Ten custom-made suspicious characters at a hundred bucks a time. You ought to consider that, Salvatore. Seriously consider it. You won't solve any crimes, but at least you'll *look* like you're busy.'

'What else can I do, chief? I've got five men on the case. What else?'

'Get your ass off that chair and walk around in circles in your office until you've thought of something! That's what! I'll tell the commissioner to tell the Van der Vatts that you're seriously considering the matter. Boy, that'll satisfy them! They'll go home smiling all over their million dollar faces.'

Salvatore rose, shrugging as he did so. 'I'll try,' he said. 'I'll really try, chief.' He made for the door. 'This job is okay when you've just got the Mafia and the Cubans to deal with. At least with them you know where to look.'

'I think maybe you ought to apply to join the Mafia, Salvatore,' said Morriston. 'You'll be safer there. I'll get you an application form.'

Salvatore habitually opened one eye and then the other as though he expected each day to attack him as soon as he awoke. This day was Sunday, he told himself as soon as he had examined the horizon revealed by the first eye. That was good because he was, unless the circumstances were exceptional, relieved of the hassle of the office. But it was also bad because it meant he could anticipate the hassle from his family. Sometimes it was easier to handle the office hassle because, at least up to a certain level, there he was boss. At home he was the last of a long line.

His normally morose spirits took a dive to an even lower level when he remembered that all the neighbours he did not like were coming to his house for a lunchtime barbecue. He hated the people and he hated barbecues because he was the one who had to do the cooking and the dry fumes of the charcoal always got into his head. His only consolation was in imagining that the grilling meat he turned on the spits was the bodies of those guests who surrounded him with their hideous Sunday neighbourliness.

'Albert!' Betty's voice came wearily up the stairs to him. He pretended to be still asleep. If he did that she sometimes went away. This time she didn't.

'Albert!' she called again flatly. 'The children say there's a dead man on the lawn.'

'Tell him to go away,' Salvatore called back. She must know their children were congenital liars.

'He's dead, I tell you. How can I tell him to go away if he's dead?'

'Problems, problems,' grumbled Salvatore. 'Why can't anybody solve their problems without consulting me.'

'You're supposed to be a cop,' she shouted back.

'It's Sunday, for God's sake,' he said. He rolled reluctantly from the bed. He did not believe there was a dead man on his lawn, so he took a cautious look at himself in the mirror.

He never looked any better. Even he had to admit that. His hair was fleeing altogether, his eyes were holding up sullen bags. Daringly he poked out his tongue. 'Oh God,' he said. 'A dead man.'

To see the lawn it was necessary to go into the next room. He did not hurry. He put on his robe and stretched his arms before grumblingly going out into the passage and into the room of his son. He looked from the window and saw them standing almost religiously around the stretched-out body of a large, living, fat man.

'Zaharran!' he bellowed angrily. 'Get off my lawn! Get out of here you bum!'

'He's dead,' called the eldest son, Franco. 'How can he answer?'

'He's not dead,' Salvatore howled back. 'You quarter-wit!'

Betty called up the stairs. 'Albert, go and see. We've got people coming, remember. If there's a body on the lawn, get rid of it. Somebody's done it to get revenge on you, I expect.'

Dispiritedly he went to the head of the stairs. 'People get revenge on me all the time,' he pointed out loudly. 'Revenge is all I get from people. But that man ain't dead, Betty. That man ain't capable of doing a decent living thing like dying. He has come here to bother me, to attract attention to himself.'

'To get revenge?' she suggested from the bottom of the stairs.

'Revenge. Sure revenge. That's what he wants also. Everybody wants it.'

'Well go and see what it's all about,' she sighed. 'It's too much for me all this. If he is dead then get him moved. Then get the barbecue going. You can find out who killed him tomorrow.'

'Okay, okay, okay,' he recited the words as he descended the stairs. He wrapped the robe tighter around him, although the morning was growing hot. His scowl increased as he strode down the lawn.

His four children for once acknowledged his superior presence and backed away. Zaharran was lying like a dumped pile of sand. His battered face was as composed as it would ever be, his hands were clasped religiously across his great stomach.

'He's dead as dead,' said Francesca, the youngest girl. 'I'm going to get him some flowers.'

'He's not dead!' The children jumped as their father shouted.

Betty was leaning out of the kitchen window. 'Is he dead?' she called in the same voice she used to ask if the Sunday newspapers had arrived. 'Or isn't he?'

'He's not dead!' cried Salvatore again, turning round and directing the verdict to her. He pushed his slippered foot forward and touched Zaharran. 'In the first place,' he said in his detective's voice, 'note how the hands are clasped across his gut.'

'That's how dead people are,' said Clara, the second daughter. 'I've seen it in hospital films on TV.'

'Idiot,' Salvatore told her. She poked out her tongue at him. 'They put the hands across the body *after* death. Nobody *dies* in that position.'

The children, who hated disappointments, wanted the man to be dead. Franco said: 'Maybe somebody killed him and then put his hands across there, like as a mark of respect.'

'How do you kill somebody then respect them?' asked Salvatore. He was now enjoying his superiority. 'Idiot. Anyway, you may like to notice that the dead body is breathing. See, it's rising up and down. That's called breathing.'

'Death convulsions,' said Clara. 'There's things called death convulsions. I know. It's on TV.'

'Zaharran,' said Salvatore to the body. 'Get up. You're frightening the children.'

'No he's not,' protested little Francesca. 'Can we bury him? I want to bury him.'

'Zaharran,' repeated Salvatore, 'get up or I get the garden hose on you.'

The heavily folded eyes reluctantly opened like those of a tortoise. The children gasped and backed away before coming forward again to view the miracle. A fissure appeared in the prostrate man's face. It was his smile. 'Captain Salvatore?' he breathed. 'What ... what am I doing here?'

'Playing dead,' answered Salvatore. 'And if you don't beat it, and quick, you won't just be *playing* dead.'

'But I collapsed,' pleaded Zaharran, his eyes widening with what he faintly hoped might look like innocence. 'Collapsed, blacked out. And I wake up right here in your yard. What a coincidence.'

'It's my *lawn*,' Salvatore pointed out. 'These houses don't have yards, they have lawns. The grass you are bruising with your body, Zaharran, is my lawn.'

'Could ... could I ask for a drink?' inquired the big man pitifully.

'I'll get you one,' said Clara eagerly. She moved towards the house.

'Water,' her father called after her. 'Just water.'

'With maybe a little Scotch,' Zaharran called too.

'I will. I will,' the girl called back.

Salvatore continued to glower down at the human hulk. 'We got people coming for a barbecue,' he said. 'We're going to be using the lawn.'

'Okay, okay,' acknowledged Zaharran. He put up a hand as big as a sail. The children stared at it. 'I maybe wondered if you needed a few leads on the masked gang, that's all.'

'Zaharran /.. George,' said Salvatore moving urgently forward. His children stared at the change in his attitude. Their father knelt by the prostrate man and helped him into a sitting position. 'Scotch!' he bellowed over his shoulder. 'Plenty of Scotch. Not too much water.'

He almost fell on his knees beside Zaharran. 'You've got something?' he pressed. 'You know something? I don't have to warn you about withholding evidence, do I? What is it, George? What have you found out?'

'Nothing,' said Zaharran simply. 'Not a thing.'

'Jesus Harry Christ!' bawled Salvatore. 'What's all this about then?'

'I got some ideas, that's all.'

'Ideas? Is that all?'

'That's what I said. Ideas. But they're good ideas. I just want to know if you'll retain me on the case. So I can follow them up.'

Clara appeared with the Scotch and water. 'Take that Scotch back,' shouted her father. 'Get back with it.'

'But you ... but you ...' pleaded the girl.

'I don't care. Take it back.' He leaned threateningly over Zaharran. 'Don't bother me any more, Zaharran,' he said. 'Or I have you arrested. Vagrancy. I could get you for vagrancy. I know I could.'

Zaharran considered it, then shook his bison head. 'No way,' he said. 'I have a home.'

'Wandering abroad then. Or trespass. Yes, I could get you for trespass.' He glared at the big man. 'Anyway, why am I discussing this with you? Get your ass off my grass and beat it.'

Zaharran rose slowly. The children backed away and looked

at him respectfully, something they had never afforded their father. The older man began to shuffle towards the gate. 'There's a reward?' he said.

'Reward? For God's sake, you know there's a reward. You read the newspapers.'

'I'll work for that,' said Zaharran as if making the decision right there. 'I'll operate on my own.'

'Do that,' growled Salvatore. 'But keep out of my hair.'

Zaharran stared at the policeman's famished hair but said nothing. He lounged towards the gate. Francesca hurried forward and opened it for him. He raised his unkempt hat. She smiled. 'I sure wish you were my daddy,' she said.

The members of the Ocean Drive Delinquent Society, hung with gloom and disappointment, sat beneath the Tree of Knowledge in Flamingo Park, South Miami Beach. It was a day of fresh wind which seemed to spring on impulse from the ocean, thrilling the gulls and cormorants and the planing pelicans, but keeping most of the human denizens of the district away from the shore. The old gang with Ossie and Bruce sat in the way of a class receiving instruction, with Gabby facing them. Indeed there were often to be seen small groups like this sitting in small semi-moons along the lawns of Ocean Drive, studying Hebrew history and destiny, Mexican embroidery, book binding, philately, the art of the jazz drummer and such subjects, so the meeting beneath the tree attracted little attention.

'Anybody can make a mistake,' pleaded Lou the Barbender, the shame of the crashing chandelier still pressing his strong shoulders. 'I didn't know it wasn't a safe. I'm just strong, not brainy.'

Gabby shrugged. 'There's no blame. It was a joint responsibility,' she said. 'If anything, the fault lies with the leadership. We just made a mess of it.'

'The chandelier made a mess of the cake,' reminisced Ari. 'I saw it. It's a sight you don't generally see, a chandelier go crash through a cake. Not something you can experience every day. Very rare ...'

They were not inclined to let him finish. 'Okay, okay,' said Ossie firmly. 'The post-mortem's over. We screwed it up.'

'More like unscrewed it,' said Bruce making a turning motion with his hand. Nobody even smiled. He shrugged and returned to disappointed silence.

'Now we come to the crunch question,' continued Ossie as though no one had spoken. 'Do we quit or do we have another try? On the law of averages we've just got to get something right soon. On the other hand we've taken a lot of risks for not much in return. I think we need a vote on it. And as he put the proposition to them a cop left a police car along Ocean Drive and walked idly to take a look at the rough seascape. He was screened from the group by the foliage of the Tree of Knowledge and nobody saw him until a moment after Ossie had put the question. 'Do we try another crime or do we declare this society closed?'

'Try another crime,' they all answered loudly, not one of them feeling that it was sufficient merely to raise a hand. Elderly persons, like children, like to assert themselves vocally. The words 'Try another crime' came out strongly just as the strolling policeman rounded the tree. He could hardly have failed to have heard it. Gabby paled as she looked across the heads of the gang and saw the blue uniform appear. Ossie was swift.

'Okay,' he said with extra loudness. 'We'll try another time.'

The cop smiled a fatherly smile when he saw the small class. He was a well-nourished policeman, amiable and ambling, with a smile dropping easily into well-used creases on his warm face. 'What's the lesson today, teacher?' he said to Gabby, approving in his look that one so young was aiding the old.

'Aspects of presidential responsibility,' Gabby replied at once. 'The class are trying to learn some of the Articles of the Constitution.'

'That's interesting,' said the cop, expanding his face into an even bigger smile. 'What they going to do with it when they know?' He did not wait or require an answer. 'Maybe,' he suggested, 'I could come by with my buddy one day and give you a lecture on police work. I been a cop twenty years. Seen things you'd never believe.'

'Oh, we'd like that, wouldn't we now class?' enthused Gabby.

'Oh sure, great.' 'Yes please, sir.' 'Oh boy, I can't wait,' echoed the gang, all nodding and returning the policeman's smile. 'Can we see how your gun works?' asked Molly, always the one to ask the additional question. 'I'd like to see that.'

'I promise,' said the decent cop. 'I won't promise to shoot anybody but I promise to show you. Maybe next week. I'm on this patrol next week as well.'

'Tuesday,' said Ossie decisively. He wanted to get rid of the man.

'Right, Tuesday then,' beamed the officer. 'Same time, same place. Gee, I'll enjoy that too. Look after yourselves.'

He waved and sauntered on towards the crashing green ocean. The gang remained silent, watching him go. He suddenly turned and saw their expressions. 'Just carry on,' he called back. 'Don't let me disturb the lesson. I'm just a cop.'

'Everybody wave,' ordered Ossie quietly. The gang all waved towards the friendly cop and he waved back before continuing his walk to the beach.

seven

Gabby and Ossie were walking by the sea at night. The wind and the day had gone, drifting in close company across the flat land towards the Gulf of Mexico, leaving the Miami night in its customary condition, warm and blue, with the firm promise of a later moon.

The girl and the man walked a yard apart over the sand. Neither was wearing shoes. They had hardly spoken for five minutes. They progressed thoughtfully as if each were alone.

'Listen,' he said eventually but without looking towards her. 'If you want to quit and go back to St Pete's I'm certain everyone will understand. I would.'

'You trying to ditch me?' She stared down as if she had lost something in the shingle.

'No, not at all, Gabby. It's just been such a bomb.'

'We'll think of something. Next time it will work. I know it.'

He glanced at her and the beginnings of a grin touched his face. She continued walking, ploughing her feet into the sand, her face and her breasts pushed forward like an intrepid explorer in an unknown place. She did not return his look. They were walking towards an horizon of waiting stars. Across the sky, among the stars, a plane moved like a small spark.

'Do you think I'm beautiful?' Gabby suddenly asked. She still did not look at him and they continued their walking.

'Yes,' he said simply. 'Excessively.'

'I think you're beautiful too,' she said. 'I go for men with untidy grey hair.'

'Maybe when we do a successful robbery I'll get it cut,' he said.

They returned to their silent journey. For several minutes neither acknowledged that the other was even there. It was Gabby who spoke again. 'Where are we headed?' she asked, looking behind her and suddenly realizing how far they had travelled along the beach. The sand faded far behind them and the white stripes of the sea showed clearly for a great distance.

'Don't ask me,' he said. 'We just started walking.'

They stopped, Ossie turning back and looking into the distance. The lights of Miami Beach were heavily along the shore. She extended her hand to him. He had been waiting for it. Their faces turned and their eyes met frankly for the first time.

'The boy's not going to like this,' said Ossie. 'Bruce is crazy about you.'

'I was never very enthusiastic about youth,' Gabby replied. 'Not even my own. I can't wait to be thirty. But maybe we won't tell him. Okay?'

'Okay,' he agreed. 'We won't tell.' For a moment neither seemed to know what was expected of them next. There was no awkwardness about it; they simply stood there, facing each other, a gap still between his rough blue shirt and her breasts, their hands still held. He grinned. 'What happens now?' he said.

'You're not so old you can't remember,' she said. 'How old are you anyway?'

'Going on,' he said. 'Beyond that I'm not prepared to comment.'

'You're beautiful,' she repeated softly. 'I don't know why I didn't see it before.'

'You've been too busy being a gang leader,' he smiled. He had been a tired man for a long time. Suddenly he felt a freshness come from her and pass into him.

She said: 'I love your tired face. I love the weary blue eyes and the lines on your forehead and the ...'

'Maybe I can get a word in,' he said. 'You are the most stunning girl in America, well in Florida ... okay, let's settle for Ocean Drive.'

'Thanks. Do you feel like kissing me?'

'I'd forgotten,' he said. 'I thought that was old fashioned.'

They leaned towards each other curiously, like experimenting children, and they kissed without fuss. Then he moved a pace across the sand and put his hard arms quietly about her waist and eased her body to him. The breasts pushed softly against his shirt, as though begging attention. Gabby's arms travelled up around his dark neck and she pressed her face to his. He felt himself stir in his gut and his groin. It had been a long time.

'You look older than you are,' she whispered against the rough sides of his hair.

'I got old suddenly,' he said. 'Overnight.'

'When you were a soldier?'

'Yes. That makes you old.'

'Are you going to kiss me properly.'

'I was going to but we got to talking.'

'Do it now.'

'Sure, I'll try and remember how it goes.'

He kissed her fully as she had asked. She began tugging at him, pulling him to the sand. He eased her down gently. Where they lay there was the bole of a felled palm tree. She was exploring his face, touching her fingers over its contours. 'I love your skin,' she said.

'Try not to poke my eye out,' he said gently. They were al-

106

most lying against the trunk of the fallen palm. 'This could be a giant's leg,' he suggested, touching it with his arm. 'He's been washed up from the ocean and he's stretched out here but nobody notices him because he's too big.'

'Like Gulliver,' she said. 'Do you like telling stories?'

'Well it's been a secret ambition of mine, you know, a story-teller. I'd be great in one of those Eastern market places. But up to now I haven't had much scope. You've got to have someone to tell the stories *to*. It's no good telling yourself because you've always heard the goddamn things.'

Gabby stretched herself along his whole body. His shirt was only fastened with one button. It came away as she tried to undo it. 'The shirt's going rotten,' he said. 'It's the air down here.'

'I'll buy a new one,' she promised. 'A button I mean.'

She lay her young cheek against his rough chest and he felt her plentiful hair cascading around his neck and across his shoulder. 'Once upon a time,' he began, 'there was a giant who carelessly lost a leg on Miami Beach. And along came two people and found that leg ...'

Gabby began to ease his trousers from his hips.

'What's this, they thought when they saw the leg.' His voice was controlled with difficulty because she was rubbing his stomach with her fingers and then she began to slide them down. They felt slim and luxurious on the enclosed parts of his body, but he continued with his story, closing his eyes. 'When they realized it was a giant's leg, they right away set out to find a giant with only one left leg, left leg ... leg left ...'

Now she had stripped him. He could feel the sand against his back and his buttocks. He still remained with his eyes closed. He could feel her taking off her clothes. She kneeled up, away from him, but now sitting astride his loins. His hands searched and went at once to her naked breasts. The touch went like a shock through him. The first finger and thumb of each hand carefully squeezed the nipples. He opened his eyes and saw what she was like. 'Jesus Christ,' he breathed. 'What a beautiful sight.'

His hands stroked her shoulders, went below her armpits

and ran down her hip bones. They made a hollow on each side and he rested his hands there. 'What happened next?' she asked. 'In the story?'

'Sorry, I got distracted,' he said. His eyes were held on hers now. Her hands were laid flat against his chest. 'You're sitting on my penis,' he mentioned.

'I wondered what it was,' she said throatily. She slowly descended across his body and lay on top of him, their toes meeting, their knees side by side, their thighs against each other. She put her hand down to him and brought him into her. In no time the tiredness had gone from his face. He was smiling and so was she. They lay together for some minutes, the sea and the traffic on Ocean Drive sounded.

'I ran away from St Pete's because of an older guy,' she said thoughtfully.

'You said,' he said. 'You mentioned it.'

'Sure. He was married and a big executive and that stuff. He still says he's quitting everything and coming down here to get me. He sends me letters.'

'That's thoughtful. If he gets down here will you go?'

'I don't know,' she shrugged. 'I guess I will.'

'Oh. We're keeping this from Bruce, okay?'

'Yes, we'll keep it a secret. It's more fun like that.'

They fell more silent than the immediate night. Then he said, 'What are we going to do with the old folks – the gang?'

She smiled in the dimness. 'Kidnapping,' she said slowly. 'I've a feeling maybe we should try kidnapping.'

Miami Beach's Hotel De Luxe Mon Desir sits with ponderous magnificence on a narrow neck of sand and land between the ocean and the narrow waters of the Intra-Coastal Waterway. From its fine and enormous main swimming pool a jetty runs over the sundeck and extends for a hundred feet into the sunny Atlantic.

At ten o'clock in the morning Gabby with Ossie and Bruce on either flank lounged on sun-beds beside the pool, along with a scattering of other early sunbathers, and casually watched the double glass doors issuing from the hotel. At five minutes past ten they opened and through them came an elderly man in a wheeled chair but wearing a bathing costume. He was propelled by a tall, claylike figure in the uniform of a chauffeur. The pair were Mr Cyril M. Hoffner, a millionaire from the Mid-West, and Landers, his personal servant and bodyguard.

The trio watched carefully as Landers pushed his employer towards the sundeck and then ran the wheeled carriage up a wooden ramp and on to the jetty. At a strong but measured stride the servant pushed the old man towards the open ocean. Bruce raised himself on his elbow. The others eased themselves up so they could see also.

At the end of the jetty Landers halted and then, after the briefest pause, he tightened his grasp on the vehicle, lifted, and emptied the old man into the sea.

Gabby, Bruce and Ossie observed this with amazement. A woman reeking of coconut oil sun lotion, who had watched the same performance, saw their consternation and laughed. 'He does that every day, she said. 'I thought he was trying to drown the old guy too. But he's just going for his swim. He's some character.'

'Certainly seems to be,' acknowledged Gabby. The woman leaned back on her sun-bed and began to anoint herself with a further libation of oil. She pulled her large sunglasses over her face. The trio watched the ocean and saw Cyril M. Hoffner swimming through the easy waves to a point on the sundeck where Landers had taken the chair. The big servant knelt and eased the old man from the water with no trouble. He wrapped him in a bath robe and sedately turned and wheeled him back towards the hotel.

The Sweetheart Bar in the Hotel De Luxe Mon Desir is casually lit, the bartenders are discreet and watchful; it is a place of illicit couplings of various sorts and where they mix a famous Vodka Collins. The bar is in the shape of a heart.

The Hotel De Luxe Mon Desir itself is one of the largest and most ornate on Miami Beach with fifteen hundred bedrooms, shops, hair and beauty salons, three swimming pools, a lifesaver, a golf professional, a gourmet restaurant, and a dwindling clientele. It was built in the late nineteen forties when Miami suddenly burgeoned after the war. It sought to remain obtrusively select by refusing to display its name.

It was the vacation haunt of the very wealthy who felt at home among its golden chandeliers, heavily draped curtains and pseudo-Louis furniture. Many came down from the wintry north in their private cruisers, voyaging from New York City, or even further north, in ease along the Intra-Coastal Waterway, travelling into the gradual sunshine, waiting politely for the many cantilever bridges to be opened to allow them to pass, and eventually tying up only a hundred yards from the main door of the Hotel De Luxe Mon Desir. For many of the visitors the most hazardous and uncomfortable part of the entire journey was traversing the six lanes of the highway that divides the hotel from the waterway. Special staff were on duty to escort the elderly or the nervous to the door of the hotel.

Cyril M. Hoffner was an annual migratory visitor. He was the man whose youthful brainchild had been the Hoffner Widespread Manure Distributor, a device which had given many of America's farmers cause for gratitude and had, of course, made Mr Hoffner one of the richest men in the Mid-West. Every year he would travel in January to New York to visit his sixth wife and then board his fine cruiser *Marilyn Monroe VII* (Mr Hoffner tended to get through a lot of cruisers and lots of wives) for his pilgrimage to Miami Beach and the De Luxe Mon Desir. Although Mr Hoffner had taken to travelling about in a wheeled chair, there was nothing crippling him, but he was seventy-three and had become obsessively lazy.

Ossie, Gabby and Bruce stood at the Sweetheart Bar and observed Mr Cyril M. Hoffner as Landers propelled him across the great ornate lobby of the hotel in the early evening. He was on his way for his daily perusal of the Dow Jones tape. It had not given him cause for anxiety for years but he liked to think he was still in contact with the market. He was a man of sullen temper on occasion, although in his offguard moments he had been heard to sing to himself snatches of traditional western songs. His words to the propelling Landers usually came singly. 'Forward.' 'Stop.' 'Back,' as if the servant was a human gear box, and Landers never spoke at all unless it could not be avoided. Bruce observed the massive, brooding man, six foot three from his boots to his scowl, with shoulders spread wide like the wings of a Boeing.

'Who's going to look after the ape?' asked Bruce quietly as they sat at the Sweetheart Bar.

'I thought maybe you could handle him,' smiled Ossie. 'Tough kid like you.'

'I never went to war,' said Bruce. 'You did.'

'He'll be easier to handle than a war,' replied Ossie.

'It'll be over quicker too,' said Gabby enigmatically.

Hoffner and Landers had gone from their view into the Dow Jones corner. They knew he would be back in less than two minutes. On cue the invalid chair with the great pushing servant reappeared around one of the hotel's famous bogus classical columns.

'Shit,' muttered Loose Bruce hiding behind his glass. 'That guy gets bigger with every step. Maybe Ari the Greek can handle him. At least Ari can run.'

'Once we've got the boss, the rest will be no trouble,' said Gabby quietly. The two bartenders were down at the pointed end of the bar, out of hearing. 'We just need the hostage,' she continued. 'That's what hi-jacking is all about. Power through persuasion.'

'There's three crew on the boat,' said Ossie. 'Brothers.'

'It gets better,' grumbled Bruce. 'All the time it gets better.' Gabby and Ossie continued drinking and watching Mr Hoffner being trundled across the lobby.

'The beauty of it is,' whispered Gabby, 'we won't need to hustle him or carry him to his boat. We can just wheel him there.'

'It will need to be about this time of the evening,' said Ossie looking at his watch. 'Seven. When he's going to look at the stock market report. We can count on him doing that. And there'll be just enough daylight to get the boat away from the dock, down the waterway and out into the sea before it's dark.'

Bruce looked apprehensive. 'Can you handle a boat like that, Ossie?' he asked. 'I couldn't. Anyway I get to feeling sick.'

'I thought you might,' mentioned Gabby.

'The crew will handle the boat,' said Ossie. 'We just press them.'

The map showed the eastern tail of the Florida coastline, curling down from Boca Raton to Palm Beach and finally into the long dotted tail of islands terminating at the humid old city of Key West. Ossie was taking the briefing. The members of the Ocean Drive Delinquent Society sat attentively. Molly Mandy leaned forward and pointed to Boca Raton. 'My sister-in-law lives at Boca,' she announced, smiling around as if it were an attainment.

'And it's real nice there at Boca,' said Katy. 'M-M-My cousin gets there every season.'

'No,' put in Ossie firmly. 'No ladies, Molly's sister-in-law has *not* met Katy's cousin. Can we take that as understood? Please ladies, we're trying to plan a hi-jacking, not play happy families.'

'Sorry,' muttered Katy. 'We just like a little social chit-chat.'

'Where would we be without it?' agreed Molly.

'Later, later,' said Ossie.

'Yes, please ladies, cut it out,' said Gabby.

'You didn't know your great aunt at Boca,' said Molly, determined to get the final throw.

'No, okay. You must tell me some other year, grandma. Right. Ossie, get back to it before they start again.'

'On Wednesday 16 February, at 7.05 p.m. we will abduct Mr Cyril M. Hoffner, one of America's wealthiest men, from the lobby of the Hotel De Luxe Mon Desir, Miami Beach. Mr Hoffner spends most of his time in a wheeled chair pushed by a man called Landers who looks as though he might be a buddy of Tarzan. However, we will eliminate Mr Landers. I'll give you the details later. Mr Hoffner will be persuaded at gunpoint to keep quiet until he is taken across the street, still in the wheeled chair of course, to his cruiser, *Marilyn Monroe VII*, which is moored directly across from the hotel. Right?'

'Right,' they all echoed. Their faces were beginning to shine.

'Steps will have been taken to make sure the boat is ready for sea as soon as we get the old guy aboard. We will get away as soon as possible, within two or three minutes. Landers, incidentally, will be taking the trip with us, so there's no reason for anybody at the De Luxe Mon Desir to suspect anything's wrong.'

'How does the old guy travel?' asked Sidewalk. He drew on a thin cheroot. 'Does he stay in his chair?'

'Good question,' nodded Ossie. 'He has a special ramp so the carriage can be wheeled on to the deck of the boat, and the saloon and his cabin have been designed so that he can run the chair right through. There is also a special kind of rack on the deck and another on the roof of the cabin. The wheels of the carriage can be locked into either of these so that on a fine day he can sit out in the sun.'

'Why is the p-p-poor man in this chair?' asked Katy, her habitual kindness surfacing. 'We won't do him any harm, will we? Carrying him off like this?'

'Our information,' put in Gabby, 'is that there's nothing at all wrong with him. He's elderly but he's strong.'

'He's just a lazy old bum,' put in Bruce. The others looked sharply at him and he bit his lip. 'I mean ... devil,' he said. The elderly folk nodded, acknowledging the apology, and returned their attention to Ossie and the map.

'Look,' he said. 'We'll take any further questions later. Just now I want to go on to what happens once we get the cruiser to sea. Using Mr Cyril M. Hoffner as our hostage we will see to it that the crew head south, then south-west, down along the Florida Keys to this point here.' He indicated an inlet on the map. 'That's Dove Key, a small island at present unoccupied, although there are a couple of vacation houses on it. It has a good dock and we can get the boat in there easily. It should be safe there for maybe twenty-four hours before the coastguard or anyone else takes an interest. By that time we – and Mr Hoffner – will be safely back in South Miami Beach.'

'Back here?' asked Ari speaking for them all. 'Jeez, what's the use of sailing all the way down *there*, just to come back *here*?'

'Exactly, that's the idea, Ari. Katy and Lou will take two cars down to the Keys and they will wait for us on the Intra-Ocean Highway at Marathon, just along the coast here from Dove Key. Marathon is one of the few places along the coast where it is possible to hide an automobile. The rest of the highway is too narrow – just a road going from island to island with no turnings. But Marathon is a fatter kind of place. We can have the cars waiting there without making people suspicious. The road itself passes directly through Dove Key so that won't be any problem. We get Cyril M. from the cruiser, immobilize the crew and our pal Landers, then we drive back to Miami. When the coastguard, or whoever it is, finds the boat it will be concluded that we've gone somewhere further down the Keys, probably to Key West, and that that's where we've got him hidden away. But we will be right back here where we started, with Mr Hoffner a guest right in this hotel.'

'He's not coming in my room,' said Molly Mandy immediately and firmly. 'There's no man spending the night in my room. My late Melford wouldn't like that at all.' She paused. 'No man of seventy-three anyway.'

'He's going to stay in Bruce's room,' smiled Ossie. He watched Bruce's eyebrows shooting up.

'Shit and corruption, why me?' protested the young man. 'There's no goddamn room in there as it is! God, I have to go outside to scratch.' He looked pleadingly at Ossie and Gabby. 'There's just no room for a wheeled chair,' he mumbled. 'Honest.'

'Okay, we'll take a rain check on that,' agreed Ossie. 'Maybe he could go in the bathroom at Katy's.' He smiled at Katy.

'I would do my best,' said the old chorus girl. 'I s-s-surely would. But it w-w-would be pretty difficult when I wanted to use the bathroom.'

'I don't agree with it,' said Lou solidly. He glowered at Ossie and flexed his fingers.

Gabby said firmly: 'Here we are, right on schedule again. Getting nowhere. For the present never mind where we'll keep him. Let's plan how we're going to *get* him.'

Her grandmother raised a frail, compelling hand. 'I would like to ask one, little-bitty question, dear,' she said gently. 'How much are we going to ask for him, this rich Mr Cyril M. Hoffner? I don't think we ought to be too greedy.'

'A million dollars,' said Ossie as convincingly as he could.

'But we'll settle for a hundred bucks and trading stamps,' grumbled Sidewalk. 'If things go like they always do.'

'Okay, okay,' conceded Gabby. 'So it hasn't worked out so far. But this time it will. I just know it.' She paused and regarded them carefully. 'We want a million dollars,' she said.

At seven in the evening it was what they called the Happy Hour in the Sweetheart Bar. A bulging black man loomed over the piano, producing some mellifluous sounds both from the keyboard and from his throat, the latter an amazingly high pitch coming from such a deep source.

The place was redolent with widows. They sat around, in their vivid, unsuitable gowns; pastel predators, their hair and faces of many hues, eyeing each other and any male who entered the bar whether escorting a lady or not. Bruce had been sitting for half an hour alone, observing the movements around in the hotel, and had already been on the end of many widows' winks, knowing nudges, and the blunt offer of a free vacation in Honolulu if he cared to take it in the company of a lady with ice-blue hair, several years older than his mother.

Gabby and Ossie appeared immediately on seven. 'We've secured the boat,' said Ossie quietly to Bruce. 'It'll be ready to sail in ten minutes from now.'

'Now we've got to get the man,' said Bruce. 'The quicker the better. These old women are monsters, man.'

At seven-five precisely Cyril M. Hoffner, wheeled by the mountainous Landers, appeared on the main concourse of the De Luxe Mon Desir's lobby. The hoary millionaire wore his customary sour expression, enhanced by the extreme lighting of the surroundings. He looked grey and belligerent as the blunt-faced servant pushed him towards the Dow Jones Averages.

Bruce left the bar with a tentative farewell wave to the clutch of widows. 'A whole *month* in Honolulu!' the one who had made the promise called shamelessly after him. 'All for free.' He shuddered when he thought of the cost. He began to walk towards the door. The pale-blue haired lady lapsed into a sulk and barked at the barman for another rye and dry.

Bruce's eyes followed the slow progress of Mr Hoffner over the large concourse of the lobby. The place was placid, the clerks at their reception desk around the corner, the shops now closed, the guests changing for dinner. Bruce saw Ossie and Gabby leave their bar stools and stroll towards the corner where the tape machine clacked out its fortunes. He eyed the small side door to the garden. He moved closer behind Landers.

Gabby made her move then. She approached seductively and confronted Cyril M. Hoffner with a smile and a gun.

'Please Mr Hoffner,' she said, 'make no sound. I don't want to have to use this.'

To her consternation an enormous grin slashed across his face. 'God, oh God,' he breathed delightedly. 'Don't tell me I'm being hi-jacked.'

'You are,' said Ossie from behind, his Russian pistol pushed into the massive ribs of Landers. The expression on the great face scarcely changed. 'Please don't cause any trouble.'

'Goddamn it,' said Mr Hoffner, enormously pleased, 'I don't fucking well intend to. It's not every day a guy gets hi-jacked in his wheeled chair. Shit almighty – I'll be all over the papers.'

Bruce on the other side of Landers felt a chill sensation enter his stomach. Why didn't things ever work out right?

The crew of the *Marilyn Monroe VII* consisted of three brothers known to their friends as Ding, Dong and Belle. When their employer was wheeled on to the deck via the special ramp, they were lined up against the wall of the saloon, rigid with enjoyable horror, covered by guns held in the hands of hooded figures.

'We resisted, Mr Hoffner, we *resisted*,' Ding called out as Ossie manoeuvred the old man's chair aboard. They had crossed the six lane highway without trouble, two younger people kindly pushing an old invalid across the road, with Landers like an out-size doctor in attendance. There had been no difficulty, in fact Cyril M. Hoffner had chortled enthusiastically all the way from the hotel. Ossie was glad when they reached the deck.

'Resisted?' echoed Mr Hoffner glaring at Ding. 'If you did, son, it's the first goddamn time ever.'

Dong, who was the tallest and darkest of the three brothers, eyed Ossie speculatively. 'I ought to warn you that this is piracy,' he whispered primly. 'For this you can be put in irons.'

'Gee, can you?' said his brother Belle, his eyes shining. 'Gee, you don't say.'

'Is this vessel ready for sea?' asked Gabby glancing at the hooded figures of Sidewalk, Ari the Greek and Molly.

'We've wound the clockwork up,' volunteered Ding. 'Why have these guys got masks on and you don't?'

'They're real ugly,' said Ossie. 'We thought they might scare you. Now let's get this show on the road. Start the engine. Come on, get going.'

'Sure, get going,' said Mr Hoffner enthusiastically. 'Otherwise we'll be caught.'

Bruce took the chair and propelled it deeper into the saloon, the wheels running between the special guide rails. He bent and pushed over two steel clips which held the rims and kept the chair stable. 'What are you going to do with me?' inquired the hostage with beaming interest. 'Throw me to the sharks?'

'It depends,' said Bruce ominously. Mr Hoffner grinned.

The engine of the boat growled and then roared like a dog disturbed in the night. They all felt the vessel vibrate. 'We're asking a million bucks for you,' said Bruce, he hoped coolly. He went to the cabin hatch and stood watching the traffic curling along Collins Avenue.

The vessel eased from the mooring, Ding calling playfully: 'Cast off for'ard,' and 'Cast off behind.'

Cyril M. Hoffner laughed at Bruce until he coughed. 'Jesus Christ,' he said. 'A million! Who are you going to get to pay that kind of dough?'

'Your family,' said Bruce, trying to sound confident. 'Your business associates.'

'Boy, have you got it wrong,' gurgled the old man. 'My family! Christ, they'd *give* a million bucks to see me rubbed out.' He laughed outright. 'And my business associates, *they'd* pay two million!' He looked around them. 'I guess you just got yourself a liability,' he said. 'A real lulu.'

'We'll see,' put in Gabby with more sureness than she felt. 'I think you'll be worth something to somebody.'

'My momma liked me, but she ain't in a position to pay because she's dead,' reflected the old man. 'There may be a few others who want to keep me alive for reasons of their own.' He shook his head. 'But a million bucks. No way. Maybe five hundred, stretching to a thousand, but not a million.'

Gabby eyed Ossie and they went out on to the deck together. It was cool on the waterway with the cruiser going easily between the high buildings and streaming highway on one side and the low-slung houses of the more expensive people of Miami Beach on the other.

'Is he kidding?' asked Gabby.

'He's kidding,' said Ossie, attempting to sound convincing. 'He's just a wily old bastard who works out a situation like lightning. That's how he became who he is. No, he's worth ransom money. Maybe not a million. But money.'

The daylight was running away from Miami Beach now, going quickly from the shore and over the block buildings of the main city across the lagoons. Lights mixed with stars and the sea was glowing with its own peculiar iridescence. Later there would be a moon.

The *Marilyn Monroe VII* grunted eagerly towards the passage to the open ocean as though enjoying her role in the adventure. Ossie felt Gabby's shoulder but after touching his hand in return she whispered. 'Cut it out, we're working.'

Belle was at the wheel with the hooded Sidewalk alongside him.

'Which way, Mystery Man?' asked Belle lightly.

'Out through the ocean channel,' answered Sidewalk pointing to the water junction ahead. Belle rang to ease the vessel's speed.

'Never been kidnapped before,' said Belle conversationally. 'When it happened I'd always kinda hoped it would be an Arab.'

'We used to rub out guys like you in the old days in New York,' muttered Sidewalk, finding it difficult to cope with the situation. 'Beat 'em up and rub 'em out.'

'Why ever did they stop?' sighed Belle. 'Must be heaven. Incidentally, I love your spats.'

'Shut your mouth and drive the boat,' returned Sidewalk. He could already feel the large easing of the open sea. He felt his stomach give a warning lurch.

Belle felt the first wave too. 'Beautiful,' he said. 'Just beautiful. Sure looks like we're heading for a fun sea tonight.'

Below in the saloon Cyril M. Hoffner felt the hunting movement of the boat also. He grinned with anticipation. Molly Mandy and Ari were sitting one each side of him. Even through their hoods he could see their consternation. 'Going to blow a little, I guess,' he said easily. 'Maybe even more than a little.'

Ossie climbed back into the saloon. 'Where are we heading, son?' inquired Mr Hoffner. His mood appeared to become more buoyant with each rise of the bow.

'Towards the Keys,' said Ossie. There was no harm in telling him now.

'Ah, then we'll really be in for some excitement,' confirmed the captive with patent relish. 'When the wind's coming up from Dry Tortugas it whoops around them Keys. And I can feel it coming up. We'll be rattling like a trashcan soon.'

'The boat is safe I suppose?' The inquiry came from beneath the hood of Molly Mandy.

The hostage blinked in surprise. He bent forward and intently examined Molly through her eye-holes. 'Jeez, a woman,' he breathed. He leaned closer so that his eye-ball was almost on hers. 'I'm right, I know I'm right. It's an old gal. This gets better and better.'

'Mr Hoffner,' said Gabby coming from the hatch. 'Please sit still. And button up.'

'Don't get excited with me, young lady,' the captive replied affably enough. 'You're going to need me before the night is out.'

Ossie saw that Gabby already had spray on her face. She wiped it away. He could feel an unpleasant sheen of sweat on his forehead. The cabin was moving irregularly in the growling sea.

'If it gets real exciting will you let me go to the top?' requested Mr Hoffner like a boy. Ossie and Gabby stared at him.

'The top?' said Ossie. 'You mean on deck?'

'No. On the top of the cabin. On the roof. I always go to the roof if it blows,' he said eagerly. 'The crew think I'm crazy, but boy I love it. It's been the most exciting thing I've ever known. Until now anyway.'

'Maybe, maybe,' answered Ossie vaguely. He too felt the situation was taking on the only too familiar feel of failure. By now the victim should have been cowed and writing begging letters to his relatives. Instead Mr Hoffner was the only happy man in the cabin. The *Marilyn Monroe VII* rolled and added a lurch. Ossie moved prudently towards the door.

'Aw, come on son,' pleaded the captive. 'Just get me out on to the cabin roof now. Before it gets too bad for you to stand. I tell you what, I'll write a good ransom note for you then, I promise. To my nephew in Philadelphia – the one that likes me, I think. Is that a deal?'

Ossie looked at the old man strangely. Then he glanced sideways at Gabby. 'I'm going to take a look at the sea,' he said. 'There's no way we're going to put you out there and see you washed overboard. We need you, Mr Hoffner. We need you.'

'Like hell you need me,' the old man grinned. The contortion sat strangely on his face as if it were unaccustomed to being there. 'Sure son,' he ruminated. 'I'm the most important person on this vessel. Don't think I don't *know* that. You guys are going to look goddamn stupid without your hostage.'

Gabby and Ossie nodded together. 'We could have used

somebody smart like you on our side,' acknowledged Gabby. 'Okay, we'll get you on the deck if we can.'

Mr Hoffner pushed his grin even further. 'You've got to humour me,' he said with relish. 'Just keep on with the humouring.'

Gabby and Ossie went carefully out on to the deck. The moon had now cleared the horizon and was peering down at the sea as though searching for something it had lost. A sailor would have categorized the conditions as fair, with medium swell. The *Marilyn Monroe VII* was running up one side of the liquid hills and down the other, the bright moon lighting the oily flanks, the waves and the refined whiteness of the vessel's decks. Gabby held Ossie's arm, too tightly for it to be a mere romantic touch. 'Jesus,' she breathed. 'How far have we got to go like this?'

'Seventy miles,' he answered. 'Maybe it will calm soon. I don't care for it either.'

'Bruce is all yellow down there,' said Gabby nodding at the cabin. 'I can't tell with the others because of the hoods. But I bet they don't look any better without them. What are we going to do, Ossie?'

'Get me to the deck!' The voice, like an answer, came from the saloon. They looked back to see the extended neck of Mr Hoffner jutting out like that of a strangely wheeled tortoise. 'I want to be up top!' he shouted. 'I want to rule the sea!'

'Okay, okay, Mr Hoffner,' Ossie replied. His stomach seemed to be rising to his neck. 'You win.'

'I already know that!' the hostage called back triumphantly. 'Now do as I say or I won't be a good victim.' They heard him laugh wildly at his joke. 'The crew know how to put me up there.'

He put his fingers into the sides of his mouth and blew a shrieking whistle. Ding and Dong appeared obediently. 'Mr Hoffner wants to go up top,' said Ding flashing his eyelashes at Ossie. 'Is that all right, sailor?'

'Get him up,' growled Ossie.

With accustomed ease they manoeuvred the wheeled chair on to the deck, deftly fixed it to a lift platform and while

Gabby and Ossie watched, astonished, raised it to the level of the cabin roof. It was all done as if the ship were becalmed. Ossie watched with reluctant admiration while they slotted the wheeled chair into the retaining fitting on the cabin roof. Ding hurried below and reappeared with a reefer jacket which he proceeded to put on his employer. Then Dong, as though taking part in some well-rehearsed ritual, leapt lightly from the roof, using a vertical stanchion to swing himself round and down, and brought up from the cabin an unopened bottle of Scotch whisky. He and his brother strapped Mr Hoffner firmly into his invalid chair, placed the bottle of Scotch in his hands and, smartly saluting, jumped down to the deck again.

There was one further touch, one further embellishment to the extraordinary scene to bemuse Ossie and Gabby. The old man was now perched high and astride his boat like some ancient fighting king mounted upon a huge and armoured warhorse. The vessel plunged and heaved over the long regular waves and the hostage shouted with the sheer abandoned enjoyment of it. There was little wind now and in front of him, in any case, there was a protective glass shield. Mr Hoffner snorted with freedom and gladness. Then came the final touch. He reached and turned first one switch and then another. The first illuminated the entire vessel, lighting it like a flashing ghost as it charged across the empty sea of silver and purple. Then, at the second switch, there burst out a brilliantly amplified recording of *The Ride of the Valkyries* played by the Berlin Philharmonic Orchestra under Bruno Walter.

What a sight it was! Any wandering fishing boat that night would have seen the dipping, rising cruiser, vividly lit, with an old man strapped in a wheeled chair on its cabin roof, and that old man frantically conducting the flying music of Wagner as it issued over the heavy sea.

From the cabin, the sickly kidnappers, Bruce, Molly and Sidewalk, the latter pair now having abandoned their masks, looked out hollow-eyed, upwards to the amazing sight on the roof. Bruce closed his lids with despair and *mal de mer*. The others, yellow-gilled, stared and let their mouths drop into gapes.

'I think we've got a lulu here,' sighed Gabby.

At three in the morning the *Marilyn Monroe VII* struck a coral reef half a mile off-shore at Key Largo. By this time the kidnappers had all been rendered helpless by the passion of the sea. Mr Hoffner had shortly before been returned to the cabin and was sleeping soundly in his chair with the bottle of Scotch almost drained but held conqueringly in his fist. Ding and Dong were playing Monopoly for cents and Belle, brimming with bourbon, was at the wheel. Ossie, holding on to the wheelhouse just prior to the collision, could not bear to take one more look at the dipping and rising moon. He knew they had failed again.

'Get this thing inshore,' he muttered to Belle. 'This is where we quit. Where the hell are we anyway?'

Belle, breathing Jack Daniels everywhere, consulted the chart. 'Just there, baby,' he smiled angelically. 'I guess.'

'What d'you mean, you guess? Don't you know?'

Belle looked amiably, quizzically, at the chart. 'I really don't know this coast,' he said. 'But if we're on course that *could* be Key Largo.' He wiped the chart exaggeratedly with his hand. 'If it's a dead mosquito,' he said benignly, 'we're lost.'

'Stop screwing about and get us in,' said Ossie. 'Just get us to the land.'

Belle bent at the knees and took another swig at the bourbon bottle. 'Key Largo here we come,' he said, happily turning the wheel. 'And real fast. Real fast.' He put the engine into full ahead and with power to match her elegance the boat curved shorewards towards the single string of lights showing where the road strung itself across the islands of the Florida Keys.

'Steady, boy, steady,' said Belle as if the vessel were racing ahead of her own accord.

Ossie looked doubtfully at him. 'What about rocks and things?' he said.

'We haven't got an inshore chart for here,' beamed Belle, a camp smile. 'So I guess the quicker we get there the better. I don't think there's too much danger.'

At that moment *Marilyn Monroe VII* scuttled across the reef less than a fathom down and took a large slice out of her bottom boards. Everyone was thrown to the deck by the force. But the gallant vessel, like a horse jumping an injurious barrier, went on with its own force and skidded through a lagoon before hitting shallow sand a mile offshore.

'Abandon the goddamn ship!' bellowed the voice of Cyril M. Hoffner from the cabin. The *Marilyn Monroe VII* halted spectacularly as if baulking at a fence. Everyone aboard was thrown forwards, threshing about on the deck or the floor of the saloon. The steering wheel came off its mounting and Belle was left bemusedly holding it in his hands.

Ossie got to his feet and gained the rail. Then the nose of the vessel was dipping as though it had smelled something on the sea-bed. He judged the distance to the shore by the lights. Gabby staggered alongside him. 'Anything wrong?' she inquired laconically.

'Let's get the old man into a boat or we'll have a murder rap on our hands,' muttered Ossie. He need not have worried. The faithful Landers now appeared on the deck carrying Cyril M. Hoffner like a child. Ding, Dong and Belle followed in orderly and serene fashion, Ding and Dong carrying the wheeled chair between them, Belle with a fresh bottle of Scotch and a case containing the ship's papers.

Mr Hoffner was laughing uproariously as the waves bit into his luxury cruiser. 'Goodbye Marilyn Monroe the seventh!' he shouted. 'Hello Marilyn Monroe the eighth!' This struck him as an enormous joke because he broke up into further laughter, hooting like a funny baby in the enormous hands of Landers.

The crew did not bother to launch the small lifeboat. Instead, one after the other in an apparently well-timed and rehearsed act, they dropped into the sea, which, Ossie was relieved to observe, came only up to their armpits. They held the wheeled chair above their heads like African tribesmen carrying a chieftain's seat. And, like a chieftain, Cyril M. Hoffner was placed in the chair and borne in some majesty towards the shore.

'Let's get going,' said Gabby to Ossie. 'This hulk's going to turn over before too long.'

Ossie sighed. 'Could be that's the best thing that could

happen to us.' He turned and saw his woebegone gang assembled on the deck, sick-faced every one, eyeing each other and eyeing the dark washing sea. 'Okay, abandon ship,' he grunted.

'They'll have the cops waiting on shore,' put in Bruce dolefully.

'Let's get there first then,' said Ossie.

He put Molly Mandy on to his shoulders and climbed into the ocean. The others followed one at a time. They went into the water up to their necks, and began a sad, liquid tramp towards the island.

There was no chance of getting to the shore first. When eventually Ossie helped Molly Mandy up the gradual sand from the dim sea, Cyril M. Hoffner and his odd henchmen were arranged on the darkened and deserted beach in almost regal formation, the chair like a throne in the centre of the four attendants. The Ocean Drive Delinquent Society looked a sorry clique, its old members bent almost double on the beach, water running from their garments while Bruce, Ossie and Gabby stood despairingly like some hapless native subjects standing to ask a favour of a local potentate.

'Jesus,' said Cyril M. Hoffner after surveying them. 'You guys are the greatest collection of bums I've ever seen. Hi-jack! You couldn't low-jack.' He stared at Ossie as though demanding an answer.

'Things go wrong,' shrugged Ossie.

'All the time,' put in Bruce.

Mr Hoffner began to laugh. Polite grins appeared on the set faces of Ding, Dong and Belle, although Landers, even more menacing when wet, remained wooden-featured, the awful eyes glaring from beneath soaked and dripping eyebrows. Not a soul had come to the beach from Key Largo. Occasional cars drifted along the inter-island highway, their lights carving the darkness, but from the settlement came only muted sounds, the easy wind in the wires of docked boats, a dog calling, dimmed voices.

The strange inquisition on the beach continued. 'What were you bums hoping to get anyway?' asked Mr Hoffner, managing to still his laughter.

'Experience,' replied Gabby at once. 'We're hoping to gain experience, Mr Hoffner.'

'And boy, oh boy, do you sure need it,' the old man agreed. He glanced along the set piece again. It was like a scene in a classic tragedy. Molly had sunk to her knees on the shingle by the waterline. Ari was solicitously hovering over her but she sent him away saying she was fine. 'I just felt like praying,' she grunted.

Cyril M. Hoffner, victim turned victor, now paused as though considering judgement. 'Okay, okay,' he said at length. 'You gave me the greatest belly-laugh I've had in years. I've never seen such goddamn incompetence. It's made me feel years younger just to know that you kids can screw things up too. You ought to get the old folks to put you straight. Anyway, I guess I owe you that.'

He paused, the faces all on him. He was a natural winner. 'I was going to get a new boat anyway,' he said eventually. 'And she was insured. And nobody here is going to mention it wasn't an accident.' He looked at his henchmen with a confident scowl. Then he looked back at the gang. 'So beat it,' he said.

'Beat it?' said Ossie. 'You mean go?'

'I mean go,' said Mr Hoffner. 'Just go.'

They went. The younger members of the gang helped their elders, and they staggered up the beach towards the sparse lights of Key Largo. From far behind they heard a shout of triumphant mirth.

eight

Loose Bruce was moodily drinking a blackcurrant juice in the Ragtime Coffee Shop on Collins Avenue, when in the mirror behind the counter he saw Gabby come through the street door. He concluded that Ari the Greek must have told her he was there because she made directly for him and climbed on the next stool.

'Hi,' he said quietly. 'Want a blackcurrant juice?'

'Back to high school,' she said. Then she shrugged. 'Sure, why not. Maybe I could go back to school too.'

He asked the waitress for the same again and she brought the drinks in plastic containers. 'We all ought to go back to school,' said Bruce a little bitterly. 'The way we performed on our big hi-jacking. We've got a lot to learn, I guess.'

She touched his shoulder sympathetically and at once he felt it was more than just a touch. He glanced at her. She was smiling reflectively. 'Well at least we gave Cyril M. Hoffner a new lease of life,' she said. 'That should keep him laughing until the old bastard's a hundred years old.'

'I guess it's demoralized everybody,' said Bruce, drinking the dark liquid through his straw. 'If we decided to quit the entire business right now – as of this moment – then I can't see anybody arguing. It was just so *embarrassing*. There's no way you can run a criminal organization like that, Gabby.'

The girl touched his arm again, this time to warn him to keep his voice down, but Bruce was acutely conscious of the contact. 'Ossie gone off on his fishing?' he said.

'An hour ago,' she confirmed. 'He needs to be alone, he says. Just him and the sea and the stars. He's been really grouchy since the Hoffner thing.'

'But night fishing,' shrugged Bruce. 'I just don't understand any guy going out there to sea, on all that liquid, from choice. Shit, it was bad enough on that cruiser, but sitting in a row-boat all night. Man, that's not for me.'

'He enjoys his quiet times,' said Gabby. 'He's quite a contemplative guy really. I suppose he's older and he's seen a lot more than we have and when you get older you get more thoughtful.'

Bruce felt himself stir. For the first time since he rode with her on the motorcycle she had grouped herself with him. She had said 'we'. 'He sure has,' he nodded at her in the mirror. Her face looked very soft and relaxed in the lights of the coffee shop. He could see her eyes were looking at him in the glass. 'But if I wanted to be alone, and I don't,' he continued, 'I'd go off and sit in Flamingo Park or just go to my room.'

'Do you still work the air conditioning with your ass?' she laughed.

'Sure I do. It's not too difficult when you practise.' He waited. 'You like older guys, don't you, Gabby? I mean the sort ... well, okay, Ossie for example. You like the way they have things worked out, nice and wise and calm. You like the grey hair around the edges, don't you?'

She laughed again, quietly. 'That's me, Bruce. I was crazy about my dad. But he preferred my mom, which I guess is the way it has to be.'

'Was the guy in St Petersburg, the one who motivated you to come away, was he older? Like Ossie?'

'About the same age,' she agreed.

'Touch of grey hair?'

She nodded sadly now. 'Grey hair. The wholesome girl's daddy fantasy. You know, the knowing eyes, and the sure grin, and on his very *last* open sports car – and the big job and the wife and the kids. In other words – disaster.'

'You really felt strong for him, huh?'

She sighed. 'I don't know. I never know how strong you're supposed to feel about anybody. I've never worked out the measurements. All I know is the last time I saw rainbows was when I was eleven. I look for them now and listen hard for chimes but I don't see or hear anything. This guy was okay, I suppose. I felt for him and I was hurt, very deep too, when he threw me out. But I didn't cry the day after. Now he writes me to say that – guess what? – it was me after all he wanted and threatening to come down and take me back.'

Bruce's eyebrows ascended a little. 'You don't say? And what if he arrives?'

She shook her head. 'I'd tell him to go screw himself. At least I *think* I'd tell him to go screw himself. When it came to it I expect I'd swallow my pride and just get into the car and go.'

'I really wish I could help,' said Bruce looking directly at her in the glass. 'I'd honestly like to help you, Gabby.'

'Maybe we could help each other,' she said with a frank laugh. 'I feel like I need someone just now.'

'Right now?' he said, still not looking away from their reflections. 'Like right now, when you've finished that black-currant juice?'

'Pretty much right now,' she replied.

Bruce turned to her and grinned. 'Maybe I could get a hair colour spray and put a few patches of grey in this.' He ran his hand through his untidy fair hair.

Now they were facing each other on the stools. She put her fingers up to touch his face and smiled teasingly. 'The grey hair needs to be other places as well,' she said slyly. 'That's how it really turns me on.'

'Oh,' he nodded. 'I see. Well, I have to be a little careful spraying things in that region. I once sprayed on what I thought was deodorant and it turned out to be hair lacquer. That was a terrible experience, believe me.'

She laughed outright and they bent forward and kissed. 'You mustn't tell Ossie,' she said. 'Promise. I just wouldn't like him to know.'

'He won't,' said Bruce eagerly. He paused. 'Are you saying what I think you're saying?' he asked.

'You're slow for a young guy,' she smiled. 'Maybe that's a good thing. Sure, that's what I'm saying. I'm depressed and I'm hungry and I don't mean for a pizza either. Maybe you could show me how to work the air conditioning in your room.'

Bruce dropped the money on the floor as he was hurrying to pay the check. Gabby knelt to help him pick it up. 'Hurry Bruce,' she whispered in his ear. 'I may die of night starvation.'

'I'm hurrying,' he whispered back. 'My hands are just shaking, that's all.' He handed her the money. 'Here, you give it over the counter. I may drop it again. I can't believe this is happening.'

She paid and they went out on to the street. 'Let's run,' he said eagerly.

He took her hand and they began to run along the street. She laughed at the childishness of it.

'We won't go to my room,' he panted. 'The bed creaks and everybody hears it. I just have to scratch my ass and they all start banging on the walls.'

'We can't go to my place,' puffed Gabby, keeping pace with him. 'Grandma's at home.'

'Ossie's,' he said, out of breath. 'He'll be out all night, fishing, and his bed can't creak as bad as mine. Okay?'

'Okay. Ossie's,' she said.

They dropped to a prudent walk as they reached the block where the Sunny Gables was located. 'Go ahead,' said Bruce. 'I'll count to a hundred and follow you. It won't look so suspicious.'

'Right, I'll do that,' said Gabby, out of breath. 'You just take a rest. I don't want you to be exhausted before we make it.'

'I'll breathe oxygen,' he promised. 'I'll be right there with you, don't worry.'

She kissed him lightly and walked down the sidewalk. He watched her go under the evening lights and almost hugged himself with anticipation as her backside swayed sweetly. There was a brass plate on the railings by which he had halted. He looked at his reflection in it and showed his teeth. 'Lonely no more, man,' he muttered. He counted to seventy, which was as long as his patience would allow, and then walked after Gabby.

Miss Nissenbaum and Mrs Nissenbaum were having their evening confrontation on their respective front porches. 'I'm cutting my rates next week,' said the Sunny Gables Nissenbaum.

'So you cut the food last week,' rasped her sister-in-law.

'Evening ladies,' said Bruce breezily as he went eagerly up the steps. His Nissenbaum smiled and the other scowled. 'I bet he don't pay any rent,' she alleged. 'Or not much.'

'He pays,' Mrs Nissenbaum lied boastfully. 'Just beautifully.'

She turned grandly with the remark and left her rival standing outside. 'Punk,' snarled the sister-in-law. 'Punk.'

All the rooms at the Sunny Gables had keys but few of the locks worked. Mrs Nissenbaum said it was a good thing in its

130

way because with so many elderly residents there might be emergencies. Even the bathroom was unlockable, the users being advised to sing. Ossie's room was easily entered and Bruce walked in and right into the naked arms of Gabby.

He stared at her disbelievingly in the gloom. 'I considered there was no point in wasting time,' she said, smiling uncertainly at his expression.

'No point at all,' he whispered breathlessly. He was naked with her in ten seconds. As they went back on to the bed it emitted the most terrible iron creak that either had ever heard. They froze with apprehension, then Bruce said: 'The hell, who cares,' and they returned to their embrace.

Throughout the next ten minutes the old man in the room on the other side of the wall was bent almost double with his ear pressed to a drinking glass which in turn was pressed to the thin wall like a listening trumpet. The creaking and twanging of the springs were within a few inches of him, just the other side of the flimsy screen of wood and plaster. He leaned closer eagerly. His wife called him from the bed at the other end of their small room. She was in bed knitting a pair of socks.

'Hal, what are you doing listening against the wall?' she asked. 'What is going on in there?'

'The Flip Wilson show,' he lied brilliantly. 'They have the television right next to here. I can hear every word. It's real good, Annie, real good.'

The Miami office of Smileytime Tours was decorated with murals of large, good-time grins. Overpowering open lips and happy teeth looked down from the walls of the lobby as Zaharran waited. He selected each monstrous painting in turn and returned the grin with a grimace.

'Mr Burlestone, our tour director, will see you now, Mr Zaharran.' The voice interrupted a particularly rude face he was projecting towards the back of the lobby. The expression was still nailed to his face when he turned at the girl's voice. He removed it hurriedly.

'Oh, sure, good,' he said. The girl was sharp in a peppermint uniform, green and white stripes curved over her curves.

Zaharran sighed inwardly and tried to pat his hair flat. She turned her provocative backside on him and swayed off ahead of his haunted eyes.

'So he's tour director now, your Mr Burlestone?' he called after the girl. His shambling amble had already left him yards behind her incisive steps. Her legs were opening and closing like scissors.

'Sure he is,' she sang over her shoulder with the briefest turn of her head. 'Best one we ever had.'

Zaharran's luxuriant but ragged eyebrows often reacted to the strange ways of the world. They did so now, rising ponderously like twin hedgehogs at the thought of Larry K. Burlestone, the beleaguered guide on the Everglades bus first robbed by the masked gang, now being an executive of Smileytime Tours. The peppermint girl stopped almost reverently outside the panelled door marked with Mr Burlestone's name. Zaharran thought her fingers actually touched, caressed the gold lettering before closing into the delicate fist that knocked upon the panel.

'Larry K. Burlestone says come in,' came a jovial shout from within.

'What a guy,' breathed the girl.

'Sure, what a guy,' agreed Zaharran in a puzzled tone.

They went in. The girl's face sweetened into a beatific smile as she saw the fat young man behind the desk. It was a big desk; to Zaharran it looked as if he were driving it. He was wearing a shirt of the same design and material as her dress except that the stripes were crimson. He rolled his young, well-fed eyes at her and Zaharran, three feet away, felt her quiver. 'Mr Burlestone,' said the girl. 'This' – she abruptly shut off her smile and looked at Zaharran as she might have looked at a mangy camel – 'this is Mr Zaharran.'

'Thank you, thank you, Selina,' said Mr Burlestone, rising heavily from the desk. It was like a striped sun coming up. The girl made a little bob with her bottom and, after another disparaging look at Zaharran, left the room.

'Are there any tours I can go on with her?' asked Zaharran. 'Like on a bicycle?'

'Ha!' The laugh was sweaty. So was the hand that shook

Zaharran's. 'We aim to please at Smileytime.' Burlestone looked at the card which the visitor had sent ahead. 'And what service can we do for George Zaharran, Criminalistic Inquirer and Investigator?' he read. 'I guess it's about the bus hold-up, is it?'

'Sure,' nodded Zaharran. 'Unless there's some different crime you'd like to talk about. Something maybe I could solve for you. Something simple?'

Mr Burlestone indicated first one chair, then checking Zaharran's bulk, went through a half circle and offered another more suited to the load it would have to bear. Zaharran sat down gratefully. His back was beginning to ache. He had suffered with his back lately. Maybe he would have to lie down before too long. There was a pause, but Mr Burlestone was not going to speak first.

'I expected you to be in the basement, servicing the oil in the buses,' began Zaharran. 'Or showing the tourists how to walk through a snake pit. But instead you're Larry K. Burlestone, tour director no less. How come, Larry?'

'Just great business,' beamed Larry Burlestone with jovial frankness. 'Just great. Have to turn folks away all the time. Since the hold-up just everybody in the United States wants to travel on the same bus on the same route. They're just *dying* to be robbed, Mr Zaharran. That's how folks are.'

'I can understand that,' nodded Zaharran heavily.

'My God, I thought I'd be right out on my ass when the robbery happened. Goodbye Smileytime Tours. So did the bosses, including the bum who was sitting behind this desk. But when the news got around and the business rolled up, it just hit them that we'd struck gold. Extra buses, extra novelties. We call it the Hold-Up Trail now and we even have a staged robbery take place in the exact spot where the real crime was committed. We have the masked gang and the guns and every goddamn thing. Folks love it. It's put that fucking Indian and his weary fucking alligator right out of business, I can tell you. Who the hell wants to see a guy fighting an old 'gator when there's a fun robbery?'

The old, heavy detective shook his head solemnly. 'Maybe you could coordinate the Indian and the alligator in the robbery,' he suggested. 'Have him take it on to the bus and threaten to bite anybody who didn't hand over the loot.'

For a moment a spark lit Larry's face. Then it died. 'Shit no,' he said. 'Every goddamn fag in the Protection of Wildlife and the Preservation of the American Indian would go crazy. It's too much trouble. I guess we do pretty well right now. How are the police getting along with the investigation? Not too good, I guess or you wouldn't be here.'

'Not good at all,' Zaharran agreed. 'The same gang tried a burglary at a big house in Palm Beach, you probably read. They screwed that up too, but they sure caused a disturbance.'

'Right,' agreed Larry, looking suddenly sad. 'We tried to arrange with the people there, Van der Vatt or some fucking name, to have a Smileytime Tour around the damaged house. But they were pretty shitty about the idea. It was a pity.'

'They would be,' agreed Zaharran sagely. 'The Van der Vatts ain't bus tour sort of folk.'

Larry looked down at the card again. 'So the police have brought in outside help,' he said. 'George Zaharran, Criminalistic Inquirer and Investigator.' Zaharran did not disillusion him. Instead he handed him his other business cards.

'I also do mail order astrology, real estate and novelties,' mentioned Zaharran. 'Maybe we could do business some time. For example I could provide you with five thousand inch-high plastic dolls, each one dressed like a robber, you know, little masks, everything. You could give them to the customers as a kind of souvenir.'

'I like that,' said Larry seriously. 'You know, I really *like* that. Let me think about it. You cost it out. Give me some figures, huh?'

'Okay. But right now I'm a criminalistic investigator and inquirer right? What I came for was to just get you to go over the things that took place on that day, the day of the robbery.'

'Christ, I've been over it so many times I dream it,' protested Larry. 'What else can I tell you?'

'You ain't told *me* nothing,' pointed out Zaharran. 'Others, yes. But me, no. Maybe I find something different. Working with mailed astrology and novelties, not to mention real estate, sure keeps you fresh for criminalistic work if you understand me. Just go through it again for George Zaharran, will you?'

Larry Burlestone sighed but made no more protests. He leaned back heavily in the important chair, put his large hands across his young outsized stomach and closed his eyes as if he were about to tell a bedside story to himself.

Zaharran himself closed his eyes and the two large men sat like some dozing mystics exchanging the secrets of centuries. Burlestone described the events of the previous 27 January in a suppressed tourist guide voice, whilst the detective listened, only moving to manoeuvre his back into a less painful position.

Eventually Larry came to the end of his story and his trance and wiped his brow with a peppermint-striped handkerchief. 'And that, Mr Zaharran, was all there was to it. Like I said, it seemed like disaster at the time.'

Zaharran searched for something to wipe his brow. He did not have a handkerchief. Larry Burlestone saw his problem and obligingly handed his over. The detective gratefully accepted the gesture, wiping his face and his neck and then pocketing the handkerchief.

'It gets steamy in here,' agreed Larry. 'It's because the air conditioning's not functioning too well. We sacked the guy who looks after it and it looks like he took a few parts of the machinery as well. You can't trust any bastard, can you?'

'It's getting more difficult,' agreed Zaharran. 'Now I would be grateful if you could just think if anything else happened that day. Anything unusual at all. Apart from the stick-up.'

Larry thought. 'Nothing. It was just another boring Everglades tour.'

'Just go through what you remember, Larry. When you were at the Indian wrestling with the alligator. Anything different there?'

'Nothing. I'm sure of that. It all went to schedule. Those things are so in the groove, with the same dumb people, and the same dumb questions – you know: "Is it a rubber alligator?" and crap like that – that I'd have noticed if anything different had gone on. No, nothing.'

'I take it the bus was on time.'

'All but a couple of minutes. We were minimally late leaving the reservation because some little old lady was in the wigwam.'

'What's the wigwam? The john?'

'Yes. There's a comfort station shaped like a wigwam. We have to remember to call it a wigwam not a teepee! But there's another wigwam that has the public telephone. She was making a call and we had to keep the bus waiting for her.'

Zaharran sat up quickly but heavily. 'Making a call? Why would you want to make a call from the Everglades for Godsake?'

Larry shrugged. 'I don't know. But people do. That's why the phone is there. Maybe she was calling the ASPCA about the Indian being lousy to the alligator. People do you know, regularly.'

'Or she might just have been giving the starting signal to the gang,' said Zaharran.

'Oh come on, Zaharran,' said Burlestone with a look of boyish petulance. 'She was just a little old lady. I can see her now running for the bus. She looked like she could drop dead before she got there.'

'You don't remember her name by any chance?'

'Well no, but I could think of it. There's a group photograph of all the people on that tour, taken at the Monkey Jungle on the outgoing trip. I could pick her out on that. The police should have her address and other details. But Zaharran, you're not starting on the right foot. Believe me, brother.'

Zaharran shrugged with emphasized heaviness. 'There ain't any other foot I can start on,' he said. 'They used up all the feet. Anything else?'

He could see immediately there was. He always knew by instinct. 'What else?' he repeated. He leaned forward and felt his back stab him. 'What else have you got, Larry? Not anything you've been hiding is there? Come on, tell Uncle Zaharran – or I'll get you for withholding evidence.'

'Well,' hesitated Burlestone quietly. 'There *was* something and it's kinda been on my conscience, but nobody had any proof that it was anything to do with the armed robbery.

136

But anyway, maybe I ought to show you and get the record straight.'

'Sure, maybe you'd better.'

His big doleful eyes watched carefully as the fat young man went to a cupboard in the corner of the office. He returned with a white woollen glove and handed it to Zaharran. 'A glove,' he said as if Zaharran would not know what it was. 'It's just a glove.'

'Where did you get it?'

'It was found on the bus after the hold-up. It may have been one of the customers dropped it, but it's certainly unusual for people to wear woollen gloves in Florida.'

'You ought to have been a cop,' sniffed Zaharran. 'But apart from being a glove, Burlestone, it's withheld evidence.'

The young man glanced up, quick apprehension in his tubby eyes. 'Yes, sure, but we didn't know. I mean *I* didn't. It was just there. It could have been anything.'

'The gang were wearing gloves,' remembered Zaharran. 'And it wasn't to keep them warm either.'

'Fingerprints?' suggested Burlestone, hurrying to get on the right side again. 'They didn't want to leave fingerprints, huh?'

'You get cuter. Maybe also to hide their hands.'

'Why would they want to do that? Hide their hands?'

Zaharran did not answer. 'Withheld evidence,' he intoned, holding up the glove. 'Why did you keep it?' He could see he had scared Larry K. Burlestone. The young man ran his fingers over his lips.

'It didn't come to light right away after the robbery,' he pleaded. 'One of our couriers found it when he went out to the bus and he put it in his pocket thinking it belonged to one of the passengers. He's a blockhead.'

'But then you thought you'd keep it. Show it to the tourists. "This, ladies and gentlemen, is a real glove worn by one of the robbers." That kind of thing. Good business.'

Burlestone shrugged. 'We haven't done it yet. But we were thinking along those lines.' He looked miserably at the glove. 'I guess we should have turned it in to the police,' he mumbled.

But Zaharran seemed to have lost interest in his guilt. He

held the white glove delicately between a large dirty finger and a bulging thumb. 'That's a real neat glove,' he said, seemingly to himself. 'Real neat. This is not just machine-knitting or crap like that, you know. This is expert work. This is what they call crochet work. It's difficult to learn, you understand. And there's not too many people can do that sort of work today. There's no patience around, you know Burlestone, no interest in finer things.'

Burlestone was puzzled. 'Yes indeed,' he agreed doubtfully. 'I'm always saying that to myself. I tell the people around here all the time.'

'This is the sort of glove that a little old lady could make, but not too many other people. The lady who made the call from the wigwam. Now could it have belonged to her?'

Burlestone tried to show his eagerness to help. He was still worried about withholding evidence. 'I don't think so, Mr Zaharran. I mean I can't be exactly sure, but I don't think she was wearing gloves. I helped her on to the bus when we were leaving the Indian and alligator show and I'm sure I would have remembered if she'd had gloves. They're quite rare in these parts as I said before. People don't wear them.'

Zaharran sniffed. 'Yeah, sure,' he mumbled, 'I remember you saying that.'

Burlestone looked pleased he had remembered. He looked even more pleased when Zaharran rose painfully to leave. 'There won't be any trouble will there?' he asked. 'About the glove? I mean I did show it to you voluntarily. I could have held it back. All I want to do is help.'

'I'll tell lies for you,' promised Zaharran without enthusiasm. 'There's nothing else, is there? Not one thing? Nothing more you can suddenly remember, like one of the gang was your uncle?'

The fat face blanched and trembled before an uncertain smile secured it. 'Oh, you're funny too,' gushed Burlestone. 'Yes sir, you're funny.' His face dropped to seriousness. 'No, there's nothing else. On my honour.'

'I believe you,' said Zaharran flatly. 'Now I'll need to see the group photograph you mentioned and maybe you could pick out the old lady who used the wigwam.'

Burlestone pressed a button on his desk. 'That's easy,' he said, obviously relieved that something was. 'We can do that right now.' They waited after he had called for the photograph, then feeling he ought to say something, Burlestone said with his professional smile almost restored: 'If you'd ever like to take one of our tours, please tell me, Mr Zaharran. It will be with our compliments. Maybe you'd like to take a trip through the Everglades.'

Zaharran smiled his ghastly, creased smile. 'No thanks, son,' he said. 'I spend my life in the jungle.'

Detective Salvatore saw Zaharran stumble out of a bus on Biscayne Boulevard and make towards the main door of police headquarters. He howled to himself and hurried from his office to waylay him before he reached the elevator. In that building the elevators took their time and Salvatore was sure he could stop Zaharran before he entered the doors. However, when he reached the ground floor Zaharran was not waiting there. Salvatore ran up the stairs and arrived out of breath in his office to find the criminalistic inquirer and investigator sitting like a large untidy mole behind his desk.

'For Chrissake,' puffed Salvatore, 'get out from there! Beat it! Jesus Charles Christ, I don't want anybody to see you in this office. I want you away from here. Now get going.' He made to pull at the big man's arm.

Zaharran yawned and ponderously removed himself from the chair, coughed, and complained about his aching back. 'I just can't hide. There's no way I can hide in a whole city, let alone in a crummy office like this. You want me to get under the desk?'

'Get out,' said Salvatore uncompromisingly.

'I've got something,' said Zaharran rolling up his bushy eyebrows. 'A lead. Evidence.'

Salvatore stalled. 'No, I don't believe you,' he said.

Zaharran grinned. Salvatore said: 'Okay, let's get some coffee.'

The detective knew the policeman would not throw him out now. 'This gets too much,' he said, pleased. 'Can I have some French fries as well? I didn't get any breakfast.'

'You'd better not be fooling,' said Salvatore. 'Come on before the whole goddamn police department knows you're here.' He tugged at the large man's arm. It was like a mouse trying to pull a boulder. But Zaharran turned his large frame to the door and ambled towards it under his own motivation. Salvatore followed him agitatingly, giving him tentative pushes towards the landing and the elevator.

They went to a coffee shop three blocks away, which Salvatore hoped was far enough for him not to be observed. Zaharran was sweating when they reached there but he still said he wanted French fries. Salvatore sighed and ordered them with coffee. 'Okay, what have you got?' he demanded, as if the food and drink had to be repaid with information or at least reassurance.

'I've got a glove,' said Zaharran quietly. From a baggy pocket he produced the crochet-worked glove and dangled it like a ghostly hand before Salvatore. The policeman reached out to touch it but Zaharran eased it away. 'My evidence,' he pointed out. 'You forget, buddy, that if I don't crack this case, I don't get paid. Once I'm on a retainer, I'll start sharing the goodies.'

Salvatore looked flustered. He stared at the glove. 'Sure George,' he said. 'I'm real sorry. I'm going to try and fix something for you. I'll have to get it under the heading of expenses or maybe I can get something out of the welfare fund. After all, you are an ex-cop.'

'Thanks,' answered Zaharran heavily. The portion of French fries appeared in front of him and, cheered by their appearance, he handed the glove without further argument to Salvatore. The policeman examined it. 'Full of holes,' he said. 'Whoever made this thing kept dropping stitches.'

'It's meant to be like that,' sighed Zaharran through the French fries. 'It's goddamn crochet work. It's special work. It's like cheese. When it's full of holes it's special see? It's the same thing. That was made by an old lady. They don't make them like that anymore. It was found at the scene of one of your robberies.'

'You don't *know* that it belonged to one of the gang, though?'

'They wore gloves. Not many people wear gloves in Florida.'

'Fingerprints,' shrugged Salvatore. 'They didn't want to leave fingerprints.'

'Okay, detective. But that's a fancy glove for all that. Maybe they wore gloves to hide something else. Like they wore masks to hide their mugs.'

'Their hands? But why should they want to hide their hands?'

Zaharran poured coffee on top of the French fries in his mouth. 'Because they got veins and callouses and they're thin. Things like that maybe. Because they're *old* hands.'

'Old hands?' Salvatore's coffee cup was hinged to his lip.

'Right. And in more ways than one, Salvatore. My guess is that this is someone who has come out of retirement.'

'A dame too?' said Salvatore. He allowed the cup to tip over his lip. He wiped the coffee away from his chin with his hand. 'An old dame?'

'Guys and dolls,' said Zaharran. 'All over again. Remember the raid on the Van der Vatts' place during the benefit for old folks? And they had old folks there, right? Sort of demonstrating them. Showing people what old folks looked like and where their benefit money was going. And at the bus hold-up there was an old lady who had to make a phone call just before the bus left. My guess is she was tipping off the rest of the gang in ambush.'

'I'll get you expenses,' promised Salvatore eagerly, his eyes brighter than they had been for weeks. 'I'll also get a grant from the welfare fund.'

'Can I have some more French fries?' asked Zaharran.

'Sure, sure. And some more coffee?' said Salvatore eagerly. 'Waiter, more coffee and another portion of French fries for my friend.'

The waiter moved smoothly up the counter as if he were on wheels running along a rail. 'In general,' he said, 'we don't serve French fries on their own. They got to be with something. Like hamburger, hot dog, frankfurter. But not generally by themselves, you understand.'

'Frank, George?' asked Salvatore.

'Frank, Albert,' acknowledged Zaharran.

'Frank, Charlie,' said Salvatore to the waiter. 'And French fries.'

'Frank, Carlo,' called the waiter to the man who was doing the frying.

Zaharran said: 'Will you get somebody to check out the details that old lady gave when she came into headquarters from the robbery. Her name and address and everything. I've seen her in the group photograph. I take it they were photographed in the office too?'

'Sure they were,' said Salvatore. 'We had each one photographed while they were making their statements of complaint. I'll get them to you so you can pick her out. Then we'll make a check. Anything else?'

The waiter glided towards them with the coffee and frank and fries. Zaharran took a bite from the frank. 'This is living,' he said.

'Grants from welfare are limited,' said Salvatore, almost to himself. 'But I can get expenses for you, George. Jesus William Christ, we got men charging expenses for just breathing. I knew you would come up with something.'

Zaharran said heavily, 'I'd also like to take a look at the photographs taken at the benefit at Palm Beach. Not just the police photos, but all those taken by the society column craphounds. Can you fix that?'

'We've got the file in the office,' said Salvatore. His expression fell. 'But I think I'd better bring it around to your place. Having you around headquarters is not good for me. Nobody talks like a cop to a cop, you know that. They tell tales like old ladies.'

'I know, I know,' mumbled Zaharran. 'Just get the file. Bring it over to me on Washington. The place is difficult to find. But you'll find it. You're a detective.'

Salvatore went at his customary worried slouch along Washington Avenue sidewalk, dodging slowly in and out of the crowded life of that section of South Miami Beach. He had left his car three blocks away and now he was sorry. All over the pavement people were talking. Hot smells and voices came from the cooking shops along the route and there was a line fifteen yards long at a diner that sold half-price lunches after three-thirty. They also served early dinners before five-thirty. The two hours were the busiest of their day. Some people stayed and ate both meals. The afternoon sun was cutting directly down the avenue. Ladies blinked under antiquated straw bonnets, to which many had added a flower or two, and men sweated as they carried bags of groceries. Salvatore, carrying a folio under his arm, searched the shop fronts for the name of George Zaharran.

'Hi, honey,' called a fat lady with big lips from a bench in front of one of the peeling hotels. 'Want to swing?'

He stared at her, scarcely crediting what he thought he had heard. 'I'm looking for George Zaharran,' he said. 'He's above a salt beef bar. Know him?'

'No baby,' she replied as if she had learned the lines especially for the moment. 'But if you find him, bring him too. I got a nice friend.'

He smiled, still uncertain that he had got the right sense of it, and continued his passage. Some Cubans were discussing the world in a corner. There were a few coloured people in the street. But the faces all about him were the faces of retired white Americans. Some of them had dogs, and one man, much admired, had a parrot in a cage. A group of elderly folk were bent close to the bars because the man had mentioned that the parrot could sing. Salvatore paused in interest, because he liked parrots and sometimes went alone to the Parrot Jungle where they rode bicycles and roller skates. The man said he would only tell the parrot to sing if everyone donated a quarter to its upkeep. Within ten seconds he was alone in the street.

Eventually Salvatore saw the sign in the window of the salt beef bar, a cardboard square with the announcement: 'George Zaharran. Criminalistic Inquirer and Investigator. Formerly of the Police'.

At the door of the salt beef bar he was confronted with a steaming mass of customers besieging the counter for end-of-the range bargain sandwiches; those who had obtained their bargains were eating them violently and talking at the same time. It seemed to Salvatore that there had just been some emergency. But he was wrong. It was just the normal daily conversation in the establishment.

He elbowed his way through the crowd to a small steamy door at the extreme end. On this the title 'George Zaharran. Criminalistic Inquirer and Investigator', also appeared. It had been defaced in various ways by the customers of the salt beef bar, one of whom had written the unkind words 'He don't know nothing' under the name. At the deepest end of the place it seemed the customers were even thicker on the ground and even more vociferous. It was like forcing his way through a creek of Jewish crocodiles; all around him were gnashing jaws and feverish arguments. He had to diswedge several voluble men from behind the door before he could open it towards him and see that he had to climb a flight of hidden wooden stairs to the office of the old policeman.

At the top of the stairs was another door on which appeared several name plates. 'Zaharran Mailed Astrology', and 'Zaharran Real Estate'. 'Zaharran Paper Novelties', said another. 'George Zaharran, Criminalistic Inquirer and Investigator' was a more sober plate half way down the door. Salvatore knocked.

'Come on in for Chrissake,' croaked Zaharran's voice.

Salvatore pushed the door. It opened to reveal the enormous man lying flat on his back on a short length of carpet placed in front of a similarly large and untidy desk. He was aiming a pistol at the ceiling. As Salvatore entered he fired a sucker dart against the plaster. 'Got him,' he grunted with satisfaction.

'Who was it, Batman?' asked Salvatore without humour.

'A fly,' Zaharran told him. 'Flies make great target practice. They're real difficult to hit. You should get your boys trying it.'

'I can see the commissioner walking in on a dozen cops firing sucker darts at the headquarters ceiling,' said Salvatore sourly. 'I can just see it.'

'Cheaper than range practice,' said Zaharran, still making no attempt to get up from the floor. 'Save the taxpayers' money on bullets.'

'And then you have to spend the taxpayers' money on ceiling repairs,' argued Salvatore, who could always find a reason. 'Forget it. If we need any flies killed we'll call you. I've got those pictures you wanted to see. I had to smuggle them out.'

'Great. Did you check on the old lady's address? Mrs Molly Manders, remember?'

'I've got somebody checking it out,' said Salvatore sitting down. He stared at Zaharran bleakly. 'It's real difficult discussing things with you like this, George,' he complained. 'In that position, I mean. Can't you get up and sit behind the desk or somewhere.'

'Not even somewhere, pal. It's my back. It keeps going. It just goes. The only way I can get it into shape again is to lie on the floor like this. For an hour. And I've only been down here' – he looked at his watch – 'twenty-one minutes. If you want a normal discussion you'll have to wait or come back another time. I'm sorry, but that's the way the pisspot spills.'

Salvatore grimaced and argued no further. 'I'll call the bureau,' he said, reaching for the phone. 'Maybe they've got the information on the old lady by now.' He put the receiver to his long narrow ear, and began to dial. A look of querulous puzzlement took over his face. He shook the instrument. 'What's wrong with this thing?' he said.

'It ain't connected,' admitted Zaharran from the floor. 'I didn't pay. Things have been bad, captain, I told you that. It's just there as an ornament, a decoration, in case I get somebody come to call. It looks better if a private eye has got a phone.'

'You've got it right there,' sighed Salvatore. He put down the receiver. 'Okay, where do I phone?'

'Downstairs. If you can get through that rabble down there, you'll find a phone on the hook on the back wall. Next to the Jewish Racing Calendar.'

'Shit,' said Salvatore, with studied impatience. He looked down at the spreadeagled body and the prostrate face. 'If you crack this case and get the reward will you pay the bill and get the phone reconnected? You will won't you?'

'I promise,' nodded Zaharran eagerly. 'Right after I get the electricity and the water put back. Just now I have to read by candlelight after seven o'clock and I have to walk two blocks and cross the street to wash my hands. It's no pleasure for me, I can tell you, no pleasure at all. Maybe if I get the reward I'll be able to afford all sorts of goodies, like underwear and hot drinks.'

Salvatore was at the door. He went ill-temperedly down the uncovered wooden stairs into the crowd of the salt beef bar. As soon as he had gone Zaharran eased his body up as if it were on a strong hinge and reached for Salvatore's folio. He slipped the photographs out of the cover and quickly, his large thumbs and fingers moving like a shuttle, he went through them.

They were the photographs taken by the society photographer at Mrs Van der Vatt's party. There were duplicate prints of each. Swiftly his veined eyes went across the faces. He stopped suddenly and brought one photograph close up to his eye. His ragged smile appeared. He slid the photograph clear of the others and pushed it under the piece of carpet upon which he was sitting. Then he replaced the folio and lay tiredly back on the floor again.

Eventually Salvatore's stamping steps could be heard. He came in looking as though he had been brawling. 'That's my idea of Hebrew Hell,' he said nodding back fiercely down the stairs. 'I'm glad I ain't going where that lot are going. Jesus Jacob Christ, I didn't think you could get so many people into one lousy room. And they're all pushing and shoving and talking at the same time. Some bastard had his beard in my face the whole time I was on the phone.' He sat down and looked steadily at Zaharran. 'Okay,' he said. 'You were right. They've checked the address Molly Manders gave. It don't exist. There's no such street. I guess we should have checked them all out before, but it would have been a long job and there just didn't seem any need.'

'Fine, fine,' Zaharran nodded at him. 'That's not bad to go on. Now, how about these pictures?'

Salvatore took the folio and took out the prints. He handed

146

the whole batch to Zaharran who examined each one with the nape of his neck flat on the floor and the photographs held, each one at a time, over his head like a canopy.

'Swell occasion,' said Zaharran, staring up as if the picture was miles above him. 'Just look at all the rich ladies and gentlemen. They're the sort that get robbed. Just look at all of them. Ain't no good robbing poor people. And that's Mrs Van der Vatt, I recognize her. I always read the society columns when I pick up an old newspaper in the park. Ah, and these are the old folks they led around the ring by the noses, eh?'

'It was *for* them,' said Salvatore defensively. 'For old people's charity.'

'We need it,' agreed Zaharran. 'Gee, I wish I could have been there. Maybe there's a kind of list for these functions. Maybe there's some place where you can put your name down. Like a bureau. I should get down there and tell them I'm available.'

Salvatore looked uncomfortable. 'I'm sure to get you expenses,' he said doubtfully. 'If I have to go without myself I'll get something. Okay? Now do you see anything in the photographs.'

'Nothing,' lied Zaharran, 'except a lot of people having a good time.' He passed them up to Salvatore. 'I guess you'd better just leave me to get on with it, captain,' he said. 'Don't pull your detectives off the case or anything, I may fail.'

'There's no way I'm going to do that, so don't worry,' said Salvatore getting up from the chair. 'Not that they've turned up anything so far. If you get something big or even not-so-big, you'll put us on to it I guess.'

'Oh sure. Then you can have the reward for the police Christmas party,' said Zaharran.

'Okay, okay. But don't double-cross me, just don't double-cross me. I'll get a description circulated of this Molly Manders woman.'

Zaharran eased himself up on his hinge. An anxiety had taken over his vast face. He grinned pleadingly towards Salvatore, his teeth like the broken railings of a park. 'No, please

147

captain, give me a break too. Let it lie will you for a few days? Well, a couple of weeks. I need to work without a lot of hassle going on. I think I can find her.'

Salvatore stared at him. 'You mean that?'

'Right now I mean it,' Zaharran assured him. 'As true as I'm sitting on this floor.'

Salvatore looked doubtful. 'Okay. You turned her up. You can keep her. Just temporarily. But if there's any more raids or anything, I'm putting a warrant out for her. Got that?'

'Got that,' agreed Zaharran. 'And I also got a backache.'

Salvatore got to the door and with a silent nod went out.

Zaharran eased himself to the horizontal and waited until the footfalls had gone down the stairs. He heard the hubbub as the lower door opened. Nobody could come back up those stairs without his hearing. He rolled over like a walrus on to his side and withdrew the photograph he had taken from beneath the carpet. He held it above his eyes and grinned. 'Ari the Greek,' he muttered to himself. 'All these years and he's still got that same goddamn nose.'

Zaharran took a disintegrating suitcase with him and wandered with studied aimlessness along Ocean Drive going south. It was mid-afternoon and the sun filled the air with heat. Even the grass seemed to sag and the sea-grape trees hung their heads. The ocean was banded blue and green and frilled white. It was almost unattended, vacant as the sky. Three thousand old folks congregated on the humid grass bordering the beach for their unending convention. It never became too hot. The sun gave life and life was worth having.

The ex-policeman's normal appearance was such as to merge almost faultlessly with the background. He was wearing a large pair of multi-creased azure trousers and a Honolulu shirt he acquired long before Hawaii became the forty-ninth state. He sported a pair of moderately clean white shoes although his socks were of differing colours. His other clothes bulged like blisters from his split suitcase. Only one item had he added to his normal appearance. He now wore a dun-coloured wig, not as a disguise since even the most disinterested, distant and distorted eye could have immediately seen it for what it was, but because he had been given it by a dying well-wisher and until now had not had the opportunity to display it. The wig was not a particularly good fit and the perspiration on his head caused it to slip forward like a pancake on his forehead, but a mere faulty adornment like that was unlikely to cause comment in that region. Many people had wigs that did not fit.

Zaharran was looking for Ari the Greek. The Prohibition days when he had known him were now far distant, and the detective hoped that Ari's memory was not so active as his own. However, even with the beacon of his unique nose, Ari was no easy quarry amid the elderly thousands along Ocean Drive. Zaharran walked the length of the lawns and gardens first, keeping to the sidewalk, apparently meandering aimlessly, his suitcase banging from a pendulous arm which it seemed to stretch to twice the length of the other one. But from beneath the fringe of the slipping wig he watched as carefully as an Indian in the grass. The insistent heat of the Florida day began to broil him and he had to squat on a bench for a while. On the grass before him was a man playing a sorrowful cello while another attempted harmony on the musical spoons. It was a difficult combination but they had managed over months of experiment and rehearsal, so Zaharran imagined, to make a melody and form a descant and they applied themselves to this with deep concern. Outsized seagulls stood on the grass listening, heads cocked, and being soulful creatures, finding the rhythm to their liking.

Zaharran found it soothing too and his big shaggy head soon began to nod. A pleasant haze enveloped him and an infant snore wriggled from his lips. The sound of the snore was enough to bring him awake and he sat up with a start and looked about him quietly, as if ashamed at sleeping on duty. As he did so a squat figure in red vest and running shorts trotted towards him, spinning at apparently inspired intervals to perform a spasm of shadow boxing. Zaharran's hooded eyes shone quietly. He had found Ari the Greek.

The nose was unmistakable, bobbing away in front of its owner as though loosely hinged to his face. Zaharran three-quarters closed his eyes and hunched down as if in untroubled sleep. He felt the wig slide forward but this time he was grateful for its added concealment. From the crevices of his eyes and from beneath the thatch of the wig he observed Ari the Greek carefully.

Ari, he decided, looked good. There was no doubt about that. He had to be in his sixties now, thought Zaharran, but he seemed as active and as lithe as ever. The ex-policeman, who had once been boxing champion of his state force, felt a touch of envy to which his back added a twinge of pain.

Ari the Greek sparred by him, revolving on a complicated pattern of footwork in front of the men playing the cello and spoons. His feet obligingly danced to the time of their music for a moment but he did not look at them nor they at him. It was the same with the chess players and the Slavonic dancers along the same path. On South Miami Beach everyone did what the new generation liked to call 'their own thing' without interference from others. Among the old folks it was called courtesy.

Zaharran permitted his eyelids to lift a degree more to follow Ari's progress. He could not hope to follow him on foot, especially with the burden of the suitcase, and he was grateful as well as interested when he saw the Greek begin jogging on the spot while he conversed with two young men in denims who appeared through the screen of old people. Zaharran settled back and observed. It was quite rare to see young folks in this part, especially young folks who talked intently to old folk. He gave a little start when a striking girl in jeans and a white shirt with military chevrons just above her brown arm walked from the opposite direction and joined them.

He wished that the cello and spoons would quit for a while, so he might catch a fragment of what they were saying. It was a serious matter, he could see, for none was smiling. The girl kept pushing her glance around furtively as if keeping watch. The rendezvous lasted only a couple of minutes before the party split in three, Ari continuing on his jogging run towards the ocean, the girl and the older of the two men walking towards Ocean Drive and the youngest man sitting on the grass and gazing at the diminishing figures of the other two. His expression was moody. Zaharran could sense the old detective magic working. He had almost forgotten the feeling. Today was the day he was getting the breaks.

Loose Bruce sat for a while on the grass wondering if Ossie would notice if he took Gabby to Daytona Beach when they made some money out of a robbery. The sun seemed to concentrate on him and he succumbed to its drowsing touch. Zaharran was pleased to see him lie back on the tough grass and close his eyes. The young man was not prostrate for long. He sat up, blinked, and then removed the cowboy boots and socks. He set them on the grass beside him, wriggled his toes and then the rest of his feet in the sunshine and with a sigh settled back again to doze.

Zaharran could tell when a man was really sleeping and when he was only napping. He had been inside too many prisons and watched too many prisoners not to know. The deep breathing told you nothing, only the small movements of the eyelashes giving away whether a man is in sleep or only feigning or napping. Eventually Bruce's eyes began the tiny butterfly movement that told the detective that he would not be easily disturbed.

The cello man and the spoons player were having a sudden but acute dispute about some aspect of their duet. It became acrimonious. The spoons man raised his spoons threateningly and the cello man raised his cello, projecting the pointed end towards his fellow player. He looked like an aged knight with a fat lance. They paused two paces apart and then burst into mutual friendly laughter and shook hands. They settled down to play again and, as if he had been waiting for the cover of the music, Zaharran got up and moved largely but easily along the path towards the sleeping Bruce.

Although there were dozens of people all around, they were so occupied with their various activities, whether it was bridge, reading, talking, dancing or listening to a transistor radio held against the ear, that no one noticed him. He approached Bruce and almost without pausing in his walk and by means of the merest stoop he bent and stole the young man's boots.

*

Loose Bruce wandered fooloose, barefoot, disconsolate along the grass of Ocean Drive. His eyes searched ahead among the hundreds of sitters beneath the sun. His astonishment at finding, on waking from his grassy sleep, that his cowboy boots had vanished was only matched by his puzzlement that anyone in that old-fashioned region should even have considered the outrage.

Zaharran circled him patiently, like a threadbare shark, his shabby suitcase in one hand and the purloined boots in the other. He waited on his moment and then, smooth and casual, approached Bruce from behind. 'Hey there, son,' he said with gruff cheerfulness. 'You wouldn't be looking for these now, would you?' Bruce turned quickly and beamed as he saw Zaharran holding out the boots.

'Gee, yes, thanks,' said Bruce, the words tumbling out gratefully. 'Where did you find them?'

'Right down by the ocean,' lied Zaharran blithely. 'Standing there on the shore, their toes pointing to sea, just like they was thinking of walking in after whoever it was that usually has their feet in them. I figured the guy had gone for good. I made the sign of the cross, picked them up and brought them here. Then I saw you walking around like some barefoot boy. Here, take them.'

He handed Bruce the boots and watched paternally while the young man sat down and eased them on his feet. 'No socks with them?' inquired Bruce. 'The socks went too.'

'Not a sock,' confirmed Zaharran. 'Guess you'll have to say goodbye to the socks. They're probably floating to Cuba.'

'Thank God I got the boots,' said Bruce. 'I ain't got any others.' He stood up on the grass and looked down fondly at the boots as one would look at twins recently lost and found. Then he glanced at Zaharran and held out his hand. 'My name's Bruce,' he said. 'I'm sure grateful mister.'

'George,' said Zaharran. 'I'm George.'

'That's neat and easy,' returned Bruce. He glanced at the suitcase. 'What are you doing in these parts?'

'Travelling,' shrugged Zaharran. 'Just going south. But I guess there's not much more south left. Only the ocean.' He glanced around. 'I guess this is where I'm going, right here.'

152

The people were leaving the grass now because the afternoon was advanced, the sun slinking over the western buildings of Miami and the diners were offering their cut-rate meals to early eaters. They left the grass and the sea-grape trees in their droves, most of them carrying the little light chairs that were their badge of office and their physical and moral support.

'Got anywhere to stay?' asked Bruce. He sat on the bench and began to polish his boots fiercely with a piece of newspaper as though comforting them on their return. Zaharran smiled inwardly, grateful for the young man's making things easy for him.

'Not a single place,' he said. 'I was just considering that maybe I ought to start looking. It's just that I don't have much money. So I got to be careful. Can't stay at the Fontainbleu.'

'Nor me,' agreed Bruce. 'I stay right over there. See, under the trees.' He pointed under and up. 'See, Sunny Gables Hotel. It's okay. And the lady don't charge overmuch. You just have to smile at her.'

'A good Christian action,' suggested Zaharran.

'In her case no. Her name's Mrs Nissenbaum. You'll have to get your religions straightened out if you're considering moving in there.'

Zaharran tried to look as if the idea had never occurred to him. 'You think there might be a room?' he asked, thrusting forward eagerly. 'And the rent not too high?'

'Come along with me,' Bruce offered cheerfully. 'I can fix it for you, George.'

They shook hands solemnly and Bruce picked up the older man's suitcase and turned towards Sunny Gables. The wig slipped spectacularly over Zaharran's forehead and he pushed it back impatiently. It stuck out of centre. He did not care. He was always grateful if someone did his work for him. He stepped out heavily alongside Bruce.

'Where you from?' asked the young man. 'Where did you come from to go south?'

'Savannah,' replied Zaharran who had once been to Savannah. 'I been there for a couple of years. That's north from here, you know.'

'Sure,' nodded Bruce, thinking there was nothing strange in the remark. 'Generally speaking if you're heading south it's the north you come from. That's nearly always the case.'

The logic caused Zaharran's wig to slide again as he raised his bearish eyebrows. He moved it carefully this time to a safer location on his head and looked speculatively ahead as they crossed Ocean Drive. On the outside terrace of Sunny Gables sat a line of old folk, looking at the world like a jury, set eyes, set faces, apart from small movements of the jaw. There was not much movement or conversation, although one lady did rise to brush a fly from a potted plant. She knocked at it seven or eight times with a battered magazine as though it were a locust. The insect escaped but the plant was destroyed by the onslaught. She stared at it in dismay and tried to prop up the broken stems and leaves only to see them flop hopelessly again. She shrugged and manoeuvred the plant pot behind some others.

The faces in the chairs viewed Bruce's approach with a suitcase and a prospective guest with mixed reactions. 'No room,' croaked one man glaring at the following Zaharran like one bull seal objecting to the approach of another to his harem. 'All sold out. Full up.'

'There's room,' argued a lady next to him, smiling beguilingly at Zaharran.

'Yes, there's room,' echoed two others. 'Plenty of room.' They were visibly cheered by the advent of a new male.

Bruce paused at the top of the short flight of steps which led to the hotel. 'Ladies and gentlemen,' he said, setting the suitcase down on the stone. It had only just lasted the journey. 'This is George, from Savannah. He was heading south.'

'Then why don't he keep going?' asked the disgruntled man. 'There's no room. Just keep moving.'

'There's room,' snarled the grey lady at his elbow. 'You know darn well there's room. You're just jealous because he's ten years younger than you.'

'Hah!' snorted the man. 'His wig's ten years older. Hah!'

Bruce jerked his head towards the door and Zaharran walked after him towards the hotel lobby, raising his wig carefully as he departed from the terrace, an action which brought hoots of appreciation from the old ladies and further grumbles from the man. 'In the old days, I'd have beaten that guy to a pulp,' the man said, his trembling hands clutching his walking stick. But the fury passed quickly. He sat back and the dying sun touched his face and soon he was drifting into the sleep which occupied so much of his days and nights.

Lou Yen Lew's is a noted Kosher Chinese Restaurant on Washington Avenue, South Miami Beach. It is an ornate place, like a prayer house with cooking smells, with pictures of the Great Wall, Shanghai Harbour and former President Nixon on the walls, and ventilated by great sweeping old ceiling fans.

Some of the more well-off people eat there and others make it a place for commemorations and celebrations. One Jewish widow went there every year for ten years to mark the anniversary of her husband's death and every time wept copiously into her Kosher wun tun soup. The staff, from Cochin China, grew to know the date and placed a pile of clean napkins on the table, a kindly gesture typical of the Chinese Jew. In the eleventh year the widow did not arrive and they knew that she had gone to join her husband and would cry no more. It was just one of the small dramas that are to be found every day on South Miami Beach.

Sidewalk Joe and some of his acquaintances used to visit Lou Yen Lew's every Monday night for other reasons.

There would be eight or ten participants around the table. They would eat first, simply, cheaply and late, and then, when the other customers had gone from the restaurant and a look-out had been placed on the door, they would get down to the true business of the evening.

Each table was equipped with a turntable upon which were placed the various Chinese dishes. It was revolved by hand during the meal. But once the eating was finished this circulating top became the sort of gambling machine frowned on by the Miami authorities.

A simple arrow – usually a six inch nail – was placed on the table with the pointed end touching the rim. Bets were placed at the centre and the wheel was then spun.

Around the table the gamblers watched its whirl and the winner, who found the nail pointing at his chest at the end of the spin, would collect sometimes as much as ten dollars.

The sessions, like all gaming sequences, were performed with a seriousness bordering on the grim. The lights in the restaurant were diminished and the spinning wheel illuminated by a single beam which made the six inch nail shine like the blade of a silver sword. The faces all around the circle were set, the shadows trapped in the creases of the skin, and even the winner, by some unwritten but acknowledged rule, was only permitted to smile seriously.

On the day after the arrival at South Miami Beach of George Zaharran, Loose Bruce had sought out Sidewalk Joe in his daytime pitch by Ocean Drive where he played in the aged men's poker school and asked his permission to take his new friend to the secret wheel of fortune at Lou Yen Lew's. Zaharran hovered like a large shadow beneath a sea-grape tree some distance away and he nodded a grim greeting when he saw Sidewalk Joe turn his head towards him.

'Has the guy got any real dough?' asked Sidewalk, turning back to Bruce. 'I don't care to play for pennies.' He looked down at the paltry stakes of his poker school. 'I have to, but I don't care for it.'

'He's got a few bucks,' Bruce assured him. 'He's played at games in Savannah.'

'He ain't going to sing about it?' asked Joe doubtfully. He took another glance at the big, waiting figure beneath the branches. 'It's something we don't want any songs about.'

'Sure, I understand that,' said Bruce. 'He's to be trusted, Joe, I know he is. He's moved into the Sunny Gables. He's looking for some action at the table.' He leaned closer to Joe's old jagged ear. 'Ossie thinks maybe he could be some help with our other operation.'

Joe looked at him sharply. Throughout the conversation he had been dealing the cards with expert off-hand swiftness. His eyes reverted to the table. Bruce bent nearer and reassured him. 'Nobody's told him. Jesus, do you think we'd tell *anybody*? It's just that he might be useful. He's that sort of guy.'

'Bring him,' said Sidewalk out of the corner of his mouth, in the traditional gangster manner. 'Tonight. Mind he don't forget his dough. Or his tongue. Okay?'

'Okay, Sidewalk. Thanks.'

Joe was already pushing up the bets a quarter a time. Bruce saw that he had two kings, a queen and two aces and he'd only picked up one card. He went back to George, nodding the affirmative as he went. Zaharran smiled.

That night in Lou Yen Lew's the table was spinning. It was not the smooth revolution of the genuine gaming wheel, for there were little undulations and slower and faster places on the circular jogging journey of the Chinese roundabout and thus there were seats at the edge of the board which were more popular than others because of the increased odds in the pointing nail stopping there. So lots were drawn for the places at the table and it was a rule when, very rarely, a trusted newcomer was introduced, that he had to sit at the chair where the wheel was known to travel by with the most speed. That seat was left for Zaharran.

Loose Bruce introduced George around the table. Sidewalk, in grey waistcoated suit and mended shirt, inquired, during the interval in the game: 'And do you have another name to go with George, mister?'

'Seltzer,' replied Zaharran blandly. 'Like Alka Seltzer. That fizzy stuff.'

Nobody said anything. The wheel had begun to spin. Given a firm push the wheel would travel around for a minute or so before coming to its hesitant stop. The house was a big one for that school, a dollar a bet. The Chinese waiters, drawn by their inborn fascination for gambling, crowded at the back of the chairs. Often they split a fifty-fifty bet with the player sitting nearest to them.

Zaharran's head could descend into his body on occasions, in the manner of a ponderous, half-withdrawn turtle. It was almost as if its weight was too much for the neck, which contracted in coils to accommodate it.

Now from its low position it moved infinitesimally from side to side, the eyes following the pointing curved journey

157

of the nail but at the same time taking in the fixed faces around the rim of the table. Sitting immediately opposite was Ari the Greek, his nose making little pushing movements to urge the wheel. It was a nose like an extra hand. Gabby was to Ari's left. Zaharran noted her animated beauty appreciatively. Ossie was next to Gabby, his strong face watching the spin intently, his tough grey hair scattered untidily across his forehead. Bruce sat next to him, the sunburned expression full of naïve hope and the eyes innocently expectant. Zaharran took in Ossie and Bruce. Considered them carefully. He wondered which one slept with the girl.

There were other players but, unless Zaharran's policeman's instinct was awry, they were not the people he sought. They were old men with gnarled hands and dulled eyes. But at the far side, in the best seat, suspiciously watching even the Miami fly that alighted for a brief ride on the table, was Sidewalk. Zaharran knew a genuine, old New York gangster when he saw one.

The table slowed as though it had become weary performing for them. Zaharran saw the eyes of Sidewalk and Ari rise to him even before it had commenced its final three circuits, soon to be joined by the eyes of the other players as it slowed obediently and the nail came to rest pointing directly at Zaharran's breastbone. He reached out without hurry and took the money.

'This is a good game,' he smiled at Sidewalk.

'Beginner's luck,' said Bruce nervously. He looked tentatively at Sidewalk and then at Zaharran.

Gabby said: 'Grab it while you can.'

'Sure is beginner's luck,' nodded Zaharran, taking care not to look up from the money he had accumulated. He stuffed it into the pocket of the voluminous trousers and threw the final dollar into the centre of the wheel as his wager for the next game. 'Anybody want to change seats?' he inquired, looking about him with fat innocence. Nobody did.

Sidewalk fluttered his dollar into the centre and the others followed suit. Sidewalk spun the wheel as he always did.

Zaharran glanced at the embarrassed Bruce and smiled

diffidently at Gabby. 'I wonder can I do it again?' he said ingenuously. 'I just wonder?'

Twice more during the course of the evening he won and at the conclusion of the session he was thirty dollars richer. Sidewalk was last from the table. 'George,' he said, getting up elegantly. His shoes caught the light. 'We got another game we play. Like to take a chance?'

Ossie moved close to Sidewalk. 'Watch it, man,' he whispered. 'Don't make any trouble. Trouble makes trouble. Understand?'

'Sure,' said Sidewalk amiably. 'I don't have any trouble in mind.' He walked towards Zaharran and put his hand on the fat arm. There was no reaction but a guarded smile. 'It's a great game,' he said. 'And quick. We take the cards and we throw them up at the fan there.'

Zaharran looked up to where the huge old-fashioned fan cleft the air above their heads. 'And when they come down?' he asked.

'When they come down every guy catches a card while it's still flying, see? Whoever gets the highest card wins the loot. Okay?'

'I've got a better idea,' said Zaharran.

'I thought you could have,' said Sidewalk. 'What is it, friend?'

'Just you and me, Mr Sidewalk. We'll play the game. Twenty-five bucks we put down. Then we throw the cards into the fan.'

'Twenty-five bucks?' Everyone looked anxiously at Sidewalk. That was a lot of money on South Miami Beach. A grin broke unexpectedly on his face although it disappeared again quickly, as if it had no right to be there. 'Okay, you got a bet. What's twenty-five bucks anyway?'

The old men all looked at each other and shrugs were exchanged. 'What's twenty-five bucks, anyway?' they echoed to each other. 'What's twenty-five bucks?'

They gathered around the rivals. The Chinese waiters stood in one clutch as if ready collectively to defend themselves in trouble. Ossie and Bruce, sensing the tension, glanced unsurely at each other. Gabby wondered how much twenty-five dollars meant to Sidewalk. All of twenty-five dollars she guessed. Sidewalk pushed the pack of cards towards her. 'Okay,' he said. 'You throw, lady.'

'You sure you want to go through with this?' said Gabby. She hesitated. 'For twenty-five dollars?' She looked at Zaharran and then hard at Sidewalk. Sidewalk nodded and Zaharran said: 'Throw them, little lady.'

Gabby did. She shuffled and tidied the pack. Ari the Greek said: 'No need to shuffle them, Gabby. The fan shuffles 'em.' Then she threw them into the revolving blades of the fan. The cards seemed to hang in the close air for a moment and then the four blades caught them and flung them to all corners of the room. As they floated down Sidewalk grabbed a card in mid-air and so did Zaharran. Sidewalk immediately slapped his down on the table. 'Queen,' he said quietly. 'Of Spades.'

'Eight of Hearts,' sighed Zaharran, throwing his on the floor. He reached into his deep trousers and counted out twenty-five dollars for Sidewalk. Sidewalk laughed and so did everyone, including the relieved waiters. 'I'll buy you a beer, mister,' said Sidewalk shaking Zaharran by the hand.

'Thanks, I need one,' said Zaharran. He did too. It was not every day that he threw away a winning card, a King of Diamonds. If Salvatore ever paid his expenses he would make sure the twenty-five dollars was included.

Gabby lay naked in Ossie's arms in the beach tower which had for so long been the scene of his employment. She stirred uneasily and he looked questioningly at her in the diffuse moonlight.

'Something wrong?' he said. 'You don't seem too happy, Gabby.'

'Me? No, I'm okay, Ossie. I guess you can't expect to be as kookie as I am and be calm and happy all the time. It's a tough combination.'

'I *know*,' he guessed. 'You got another letter from Prince Charming in St Pete's. He's coming for you on his white horse with his shining lance in his hand.'

'Stop it,' she half-laughed. As she said it a droopy-faced

pelican dropped dozily on to the rail of the watchtower and sat there ridiculously, observing them with hooded eyes.

'Oh God,' said Gabby. 'Now we have an audience.'

'Beat it,' said Ossie to the pelican. The bird obeyed but was back within two minutes with two colleagues. They sat, their huge beaks hanging like pockets, each watching the naked humans with unembarrassed interest. Ossie clapped his hands at them but they only flew a few yards before returning.

Gabby laughed. 'Maybe they think we're a couple of big fish. Maybe they haven't seen naked people lying flat before. Maybe we'd better split.'

'Let's split,' agreed Ossie. 'We'll go to my room. If that's all right with you.'

Gabby only hesitated momentarily. They had never been together in his room. She had only been there with Loose Bruce. 'Okay,' she said. 'As long as you don't have a creaky bed.'

'It creaks,' he told her. 'But I've never seen a pelican in there. Let's go.'

He stood up and put his pants and shirt on. She put a brief dress around her body and pulled her panties up beneath it. 'Okay?' she said addressing the pelicans. 'The show's over. Hope you had a good time.'

As the humans went down the steps of the watchtower the birds croaked a little and flew away as if disappointed. Ossie took Gabby's hand and she felt his assurance flowing into her. They walked along the beach and then up over the lawns to Ocean Drive and separately into the Sunny Gables Hotel. It was late. The banjo player had gone, Mrs Nissenbaum was eating her supper, and the old man who cleaned up the place in return for his room was dusting the leaves of the rubber plant. He hardly noticed the two people. He was very intent on the leaves and he wiped each leaf carefully. Mrs Nissenbaum liked clean leaves.

They went swiftly to his room and stood together in the gloom. He undid the buttons of the dress and she pulled her panties to her knees with her hand and then the rest of the way with one foot. She took his shirt away and he let his pants fall to his ankles.

They were instinctive lovers and once they looked at each other in the dimness of the room they closed together with no further words, their bodies touching firmly and enjoyably all the way down. He moved his hands up her thighs to her hip bones and then to her small stomach and below.

Ossie smiled at her in the wan light and she returned the smile and put her lips to his hard chest. They shuffled one pace to the bed and he eased her on to it. There came a loud twang of old bed springs. They clutched each other, transfixed with it.

In the next room the old husband opened his eyes at the noise. He glanced quickly at his old wife. She snored softly. He left the bed and crept to his voyeur's position by the wall. All day he had been secretly at work with a chisel and had made a peep-hole through the plaster. Eagerly his eye went to it. He could see the dim figures on the bed a few feet away. He heard Gabby whisper: 'Take it easy now, darling, this bed's like a bell.'

They moved again and the twang resounded through the room. He looked at her anxiously in the dark. 'Maybe nobody will hear,' he whispered. 'Maybe they're all asleep.'

'They'll hear,' she forecast grimly. 'When it does that I feel like the Hunchback of Notre Dame.'

Holding each other's ribs they attempted a tentative roll across the mattress. There came some muted creaks and groans from the bed beneath their bodies but nothing major. Ossie smiled down at her in the half light. Gabby smiled back. Then, like some booby trap being sprung, the most resonant twang that ever issued from a bedspring vibrated through the room. They lay still, waiting.

There came a furious banging from beneath the floor as if someone were buried alive down there. Muffled shouts issued up. Ossie swore fluently.

'To hell with it,' he said to the girl. 'I pay for this room. At least, I'm going to pay for it when I get enough dough. And while I rent it, I do what I like in it.'

'Not if Mrs Nissenbaum finds out,' pointed out Gabby. Her body was hot and her eyes sleepy. 'Come on Ossie,' she said urgently, 'let's give it another pitch.'

'They're only jealous,' he whispered. Carefully he man-oeuvred himself to her, feeling her soft flesh on his, thigh mounting thigh. The bed remained quiet but they were not fooled by it. It was merely waiting in ambush.

Ossie and Gabby moved into each other, easily and softly as familiars do. They knew each other now, every hill and culvert of the lover's body. He kissed her face and she returned the kiss from beneath him. It was very hot in the room. Ossie felt full. He moved harder into her. Twang!

The bed emitted the loudest noise to date. It was as if one spring had been jammed below another and had been released by some movement of their lovemaking. Twang. It sounded again. That did it. From every side, it seemed, from above and particularly below, the elderly inhabitants of Sunny Gables Hotel set up a fusillade of protest. Banging, kicking, shouting. Except the room to the left, where the old man sat and waited and watched. He was not complaining.

'You bastards are spoiling the late, late show!' howled a denizen to the right.

'So what?' bellowed Ossie back. 'You're spoiling *my* late, late show. Fuck off the lot of you! You old bums!'

Gabby was somewhere below him howling with laughter. He put his hand gently over her mouth. 'I think we're going to have to finish this some other time, baby,' he said. 'Mrs Nissenbaum will be on her way up soon.'

Gabby nodded mirthful agreement. She rolled from the bed looking like a wet fish. She put her meagre clothes on and kissing him briefly went out of the door and down the stairs, just as the old folks were coming out of their doors all around. In their nightdresses, nightcaps and ancient pyjamas they converged on Ossie's door and there they were grouped, hammering with their bony fists, when Mrs Nissenbaum thumped her way up the stairs and made her way through them like a riot cop pushing aside a mob.

'That guy's disturbing us!' one man said, prodding Mrs Nissenbaum with a stick.

'He ruined the late, late show.'

'He does things in bed.'

'Disgraceful at this time of night.'

'Are you in there!' shouted Mrs Nissenbaum, rapping her knuckles on the door. 'Come on, young man, are you in there!' Her eyelash had fallen across her eye like a seal. She pushed it back into place. 'Answer me, mister!'

Ossie let out a huge echoing yawn. The bedspring harped again as he eased himself from his horizontal position. 'What's the racket?' he called towards the door. 'Who's making all the noise?'

'Open this door, please,' ordered Mrs Nissenbaum grimly. 'It's Mrs Nissenbaum. Come on, young man, open up.'

The door opened and Ossie appeared there, yawning, eyes blinking, naked with a long manilla envelope held in front of his private parts. 'Mrs Nissenbaum,' he inquired amid the gasps of the old ladies, 'why are you making all this noise.'

In the next room, the old husband left the hole in the wall and retreated to his bed and his old, snoring wife.

Sidewalk Joe said: 'Listen, just listen to me. We either got to get something going soon. Like quick. Or we'd just better forget the whole goddamn thing.'

Ossie nodded. 'You mean the confidence will disappear.'

'Jesus,' said Gabby. 'Since when did we have any confidence?'

'I've got a suggestion,' said Bruce. They were sitting in Flamingo Park under the Tree of Knowledge. It was a fine Florida day with no clouds, no wind and no waves. The sun had the sky to itself.

Bruce looked around, surprised that he was being given unusual hearing room. There were only four of them under the tree, for it was the morning most people went to collect their social security and there were always long lines at the office on Collins Avenue. Sidewalk, who retained some of his old privileges as a gang boss, had an arrangement whereby he could dispatch an emissary to collect his. He now smoked a cigar and looked with the others at Bruce, but with no great hope.

'What I want to say, to suggest, anyway, is that we bring in another guy. That guy George.'

A groan passed from one to another. 'We need another

hand in this outfit like we need fleas,' said Gabby. 'Jesus, we don't make enough dough to go round as it is.'

'One thing we've never had,' pursued Bruce, 'that's luck. Not once have we had a lucky break. It's always gone the other way. Now George, now there's a lucky man.'

'If we want a mascot why don't we get a black cat or something?' asked Ossie sourly. 'Or a tattoo on our ass?'

'Just a minute. Give me a break,' insisted Bruce. 'I know that guy. I've talked to him a lot since he came here. He *makes* his luck. He's not just hoping it will come along. The things that guy's done! New York, Philly, Savannah, all over. He's told me. He could be the one to turn it for us.' He paused and looked around at their doubting faces. 'And we sure need somebody.'

Zaharran made a massive sight sprawled on his narrow bed in the Sunny Gables Hotel. He was stripped to the waist, his chest hairy and his stomach enormous. He was smoking a dubious cigar and the smoke hung around him like rainclouds around a mountain. His instinct told him that he might be getting a caller and it was right. After he had been prone there for an hour, had rested his nagging back and smoked three evil cigars, there came a knock and Loose Bruce and Ossie walked in at his call.

'Hi,' he said, his huge head revolving towards them as if moved by a slow mechanism. 'What's this, a raid?'

'Kind of,' smiled Ossie. He was still not feeling sure about George.

'We just wanted to talk to you,' said Bruce, who was sure, but was worried that the others had already made him responsible for the results of the new man's recruitment to the gang. 'We got a proposition to make. If you're interested.'

'Oh God,' groaned Zaharran. He rolled his eyes. 'It's not work is it? I ain't fit to work, that's for sure, son. I ain't hardly fit enough to lie here. It's my back. I got agony all the way down from my neck to my ass.'

'No, no, it's not work, not exactly,' Ossie assured him. He looked around the close room. There was the customary small armchair and a stool. He pulled the armchair forward for the full three feet it would travel without colliding with anything and made to sit on it.

'The left hand leg at the front,' warned Zaharran, without moving. 'It's come off. You have to keep your weight towards the back. What do you guys want anyway?'

Bruce sat on the stool and pulled it nearer to the bed like a doctor with a patient. Ossie manoeuvred his backside into the armchair and eased his weight away from the left front corner. The chair wobbled but he managed a balance.

'It's like this,' Bruce began. He paused with uncertainty.

'Like what?' asked Zaharran. His retired policeman's heart was beating hopefully. He even glanced down in case its palpitations might be visible through the hair on his chest.

'Well, George, you seem like a guy who's got all his nuts and bolts. You've been around. New York, Savannah and places. And you've *done* things. Am I right?'

Zaharran turned his expression half an inch towards the young man.

'Sure,' he said. 'I've *done* things. Yesterday, for instance, I had a crap. What kind of things?'

'Crime,' Ossie put it bluntly. Bruce looked at him half grateful, half annoyed.

'Yes, like crime,' said Bruce. 'Remember, you told me, George.'

'Oh that,' smiled George. The smile wandered down his face like a trickle of water. 'Crime. Well, sure, I've tried my hand at everything including crime. But I did two years in South Carolina State Prison and that kinda cured me. It's quite a cure, believe me.'

'That was for the thing you did in Savannah,' prompted Bruce. 'You told me, remember?'

Zaharran dismissed the thought with a wave of the decomposed cigar. It curved through the air like a burning aeroplane. Its odour had reached both the younger men and they wiped their eyes. 'That's all gone and past,' said Zaharran. 'I didn't mean to bore you with those things, son. I was just passing the time of day. We seem to have plenty of that to pass down here.'

'That's just it,' said Ossie on cue. 'Some of the people down here have found they don't care just to hang about until they're dead. So they *do* something. They take *action*, George.'

Zaharran ordered his heart to stop banging. He eased himself up on his thick, pale elbows. His great sweaty face revolved from one to the other as if it were on oiled castors. 'What?' he asked. 'What do they do?'

Bruce glanced at Ossie. It was the signal for him to continue. 'So far, not much,' he said carefully. 'But we have a group of people down here who like to take part in a little excitement. A little robbery and that sort of thing.'

Zaharran erupted into outsized, convincing laughter. 'Ho! Oh, Jesus Christ!' He roared. 'That's the best yet! Robbery! The poor old bastards from around here?'

'Right,' said Ossie quietly.

'Right,' repeated Bruce more sharply. They felt hurt at his mirth. Zaharran looked at their serious faces and burst into a further peal. Bruce produced his Russian pistol and stuck it into his fleshy belly. Zaharran stopped laughing.

'No bullet would ever penetrate that, sonny,' he said seriously. 'Move it up to the ribs. Give it a fair chance.'

For some reason Bruce took the advice. He moved the gun up to the ribs. 'This is a Russian gun,' he said. 'A Muscof 43. It could make a hole in you as big as a plate.'

'That's if it was loaded,' sighed Zaharran. He pushed the muzzle of the gun away. 'Okay, so you're serious. I guessed you guys didn't just go around doing good works down here. And the chick also. So what's the plot, the scene like you say today. Yeah, what the hell's the scene?'

Bruce put the gun into his shirt. He was glad he had not misjudged the older man's nerve. 'We've got some associates,' he said carefully. 'Just a few. Already we've tried out some things and they worked, well almost. They would have worked even better if we'd had someone with experience and *luck*. We figure you could be that someone. The pickings are good George, real good.'

'I didn't like it in South Carolina State,' said George, shaking his large head. 'In fact, I really disliked it a great deal. I

167

don't reckon Florida State Penitentiary's any goddamn better. It's worse from what I understand.'

Ossie leaned forward and tipped over the chair. He ended on his knees by the bed. 'You don't have to pray,' observed Zaharran. 'Those measures are unnecessary.'

Embarrassed, Ossie got up and balanced himself on the chair again. 'If we get caught you could just say you're of unsound mind, you're mad. At your age it sounds plausible.'

The eyebrows, thick as twin moustaches, went up. 'Thanks a million,' Zaharran said. 'So I end up in the state asylum. That's a great consolation.' He paused, then thought he had gone far enough. 'Okay,' he said. 'What's in it?'

Boyish joy lit Bruce's face. He leaned forward eagerly. 'You mean you'll consider it? Oh, that's terrific.'

Zaharran sighed. 'Well, to tell you guys the truth, I was lying here, like when you knocked on the door of this salon, wondering what to do with the rest of my life. Maybe, I thought, I could go pearl-diving, or get out to Africa and catch lions and tigers and crap like that, or walk the tightrope in a circus. The possibilities were just endless. On the other hand, I thought there was quite a good chance I might just lie here and rot. And then they'd take me out and stuff me into a hole in the unholy ground and that would be that for good old George. So what you have proposed seems reasonable enough to me.'

'Great,' put in Ossie. 'Just great.' The chair overturned and he tumbled forward as he held out his hand. 'Everything will be great from now on, I know it will,' he said.

'Why from now on?' said Zaharran sagely. 'So far not so good?'

'Not so good,' Ossie admitted for Bruce. 'We've done three operations to date and we're showing a loss.'

'Oh, that *ain't* good,' agreed Zaharran. 'That ain't good at all. If there's anything that should pay, it's crime. What's the next thing you got in mind? Can you tell me?'

'Sure, but later,' said Ossie. 'We'd like the others to be there.'

'They're good,' Bruce assured him. 'They've had lousy luck, but believe me they're real good.'

'They sure sound like it,' said Zaharran scratching his belly.

Zaharran's fist, the size of a plucked chicken, indicated the plan pinned on Molly's wall right next to her photograph of her Melford and the Elks. 'The US National Trust Bank,' he said in his heavy voice, 'is located on Broward, right here on this corner of the block. At the rear of the bank is a narrow street and pretty much opposite the rear door of the bank is another door that gives into Meggison's Funeral Parlour.'

'That's where I'm going,' nodded Molly conversationally at Katy.

'Soon, if you don't button up,' said Ossie, but so nobody heard.

'Meggison's you'll know because it has a kinda slogan over the back door giving the name and the words: "Trust Us With Your Loved Ones".'

'That's why I'm going,' whispered Molly to Katy. 'I think that's so nice, don't you?'

Ossie kept his teeth firmly together and Gabby looked at him as though she hated him before cautioning her grandmother to be quiet. Molly pouted a little, but dropped obediently into silence.

Zaharran continued. 'Now I know, and I'm not telling anybody *how* I know, that every Tuesday morning at nine o'clock there's a consignment of cash, all used notes, that comes in from small banks in the country areas. Our aim is to ... er, obtain .. yes, obtain this money and transport it out of the area by means of one of Meggison's funeral hearses. We figure a slow but safe getaway.'

He watched the faces suddenly brightening around him. He was like a new general propounding strategy to a previously defeated and deflated army. Ari the Greek and Lou the Barbender looked at him with dawning admiration, Sidewalk Joe creased his eyes and nodded affirmatively over his thin cigar. Katy touched Molly's arm and whispered: 'You'll get to ride with Meggison's sooner than you thought.' Molly smiled appreciatively. Gabby and Ossie watched the reactions and

Bruce grinned all around with proprietorial smugness.

'Our colleague Ari the Greek, although I could not at the time enlighten him as to why, has contacted his young friend who is a hearse driver for Meggison's and has learned that next Tuesday morning a loaded hearse, if you'll pardon the expression, will be waiting in the Meggison garage to take a deceased body to the cemetery. That funeral is timed for eleven o'clock. We have to make sure we drive it out of there in plenty of time. There won't be anybody at Meggison's except a clerk who arrives about eight-thirty – and, of course, the deceased in the coffin which will be already loaded into the hearse. It will be necessary to make sure the clerk is immobilized, of course, so that we have time to get away with the funeral. But nothing violent. We only want one body.

'Our entry into the bank will be as follows ...'

On Monday evening Molly Mandy, suitably attired in faded coveralls and mop cap, arrived at the side door of the bank just behind the group of half-a-dozen cleaning women who regularly entered the bank at that time. 'Nearly late,' she confided to the security guard who let her in without a murmur. She went briskly to the third floor of the building and locked herself in an executive bathroom. She was equipped with sandwiches and a flask of coffee and she slept fitfully on the carpet. No one disturbed her and at seven o'clock the next morning she went casually down the stairs and put a gun in the back of the security guard on duty at the back of the building. At her suggestion he opened a rear door and into the bank came Bruce, Ossie, Gabby, Sidewalk and George. Katy with her resounding whistle was placed at a strategic point on the block as a look-out. Ari the Greek and Lou the Barbender, wearing boiler suits and carrying window-cleaners' buckets, were entering Meggison's Funeral parlour.

They found the hearse as expected, standing ready to leave, with the coffin already aboard. A second funeral car stood behind it. A man came towards them from an office in the corner of the garage and Ari produced his Russian pistol. The employee gaped. 'The bank's across the street,' he said hurriedly. 'You guys have got the wrong block.' They tied and gagged him neatly and put him back in his office. Then they took off their boiler suits and brushed down the decent black mourning clothes they wore underneath.

Bruce and Ossie entered the bank carrying the components of the Russian rocket launcher which had for so long been an adornment of Molly's sideboard. Wearing their hoods they went swiftly but quietly to the panelled office of the manager, Mr Walter J. Smithly, where they set up the weapon on the desk, its unpleasant mouth facing the door.

When the staff of the bank arrived at eight-thirty each one was admitted by the security guard and then accompanied to the safe-deposit room by the masked Gabby and Sidewalk, each holding a gun. Nobody argued.

At eight forty-five Mr Smithly himself arrived for the day's business and, upon entering his office, found himself confronted by a Soviet Dov Anti-Personnel Missile Launcher Mark III.

The weapon was intended to look much more threatening than a mere hand gun and it had the desired effect on Mr Smithly who was only a year from retirement. 'I have to tell you that if you do not obey our orders, this weapon can take your head off,' said Ossie quietly from below the mask. 'You understand that?'

'I really don't want that to happen,' Mr Smithly told them mildly. 'I'm playing golf this afternoon.'

Zaharran blinked in admiration below the mask. He wondered if they made bank managers like this anymore. Ossie motioned the man to sit down in a corner chair and Bruce turned the rocket firer a fraction to cover him. 'That's been outmoded these five years,' said the bank manager, nodding with interest at the weapon. 'It's amazing how this old hardware gets around.'

'It still shoots,' said Ossie briefly.

'Right. I bet it does. Be quite difficult to patch a guy up after a hit with one of those,' agreed Mr Smithly. He was a tanned, fit-looking man and he had not gone pale. He began to practise short-pitch golf shots in the chair, closing his knees together and making economical sweeping movements with his hands.

'I guess it's the ten o'clock Wells Fargo you're after,' he said. 'Sometimes they're late. They stop for coffee at the second bank. But they shouldn't be too long.'

Ossie said: 'You're pretty cool about this, mister.'

'Oh, I am,' said Mr Smithly. 'And why not? There's no way I'm going to have my head taken off by that thing. I'm due to retire to Boca Raton next year. I'm looking forward to uninterrupted golf. There's some real nice golf at Boca.'

'You don't say?'

'I do. And in any case, I'll certainly get some glory from this. It's not every bank manager gets robbed at the end of a rocket launcher. Pictures in the newspapers. My grandchildren will be tickled pink. And to think I thought this was going to be just another day at the bank.'

Mr Smithly chatted on amiably while they waited. He even produced some photographs of his grandchildren, which the masked Molly moved forward to view until Sidewalk ushered her back. He told them there was a coffee machine outside and gave Gabby a handful of quarters for the coffee. 'That's a nice hand for a bank robber,' he observed as she took the coins. Ossie bit his lip between his teeth beneath his hood.

But then, for once, things began to go right. The security van turned up promptly at ten and the cases of used bank notes were brought in through the side entrance. Gabby went to the safe deposit room and returned with Mr Smithly's bespectacled secretary. She sat staring into the bad end of the rocket launcher while her boss went into the outer office and calmly signed for the consignment of notes. One hundred thousand dollars.

'Looks like a real nice day, Mr Smithly,' said one of the visiting guards as the cases were checked.

'It usually is in these parts,' replied Mr Smithly easily. 'It seems you can't get used to Miami after Cleveland, John.'

'You're right, sir,' said John jovially. 'I wake every day expecting it to be snowing. But it never is.' He took the papers. 'Thanks Mr Smithly,' he said blithely. Smithly had written: 'We are being held at rocket point by robbers,' on the consignment sheet but the breezy John didn't notice. He put the papers in his pocket and went out into the shining street.

'Have a nice day,' he called over his shoulder.

Ossie looked down at the assembled boxes of money. His heart was rising. 'Mr Smithly,' he said, keeping his voice as level as the bank manager's had been, 'I want to tell you it's been a great pleasure. You're a nice man, and brave too. If I ever need some financial advice I'll come to you.'

'The US National Trust Bank is here to serve,' recited Mr Smithly with the trace of a smile. 'I'd like to shoot the lot of you, but since it's you who has the hardware there's no way I can do that. And I'm not risking any lives in this bank for the sake of a few thousand dollars. There's plenty of dollars around.'

'Very sound, very sensible,' put in Bruce.

'We are going, taking the money with us of course,' continued Ossie. 'Everybody is to remain in the safe deposit room downstairs for ten minutes. You are to stay here. I'm afraid we're going to have to take your secretary along with us to make sure this is done.'

The girl gave a frightened start and for the first time Mr Smithly reacted. 'What about me?' he said. 'Take me. I'm just as good a hostage.'

'No, we'll take her. But don't worry. She's not going to be hurt. Not if everything's kept quiet. We want ten minutes start, that's all, Mr Smithly. If nobody bugs us she'll be dropped on the Tuttle Causeway. You can have her picked up from there. If they do bug us you can pick her up from the harbour. Okay, let's go.'

The last words were directed at the gang. They moved swiftly, picking up the boxes and carrying them towards the rear door. Bruce stayed crouched behind the rocket launcher. Gabby took hold of the secretary's arm and silently led her towards the door of the office. When she reached it the secretary suddenly turned back and kissed Mr Smithly full on the mouth. He reacted with an amazement he had not shown throughout the entire drama. He looked at the masked Zaharran and raised his eyebrows with a touch of pleasurable anticipation.

'Goodbye Mr Smithly, darling,' said the girl when Gabby got her to the door again. 'I will always remember you.'

'Don't worry, Freda,' he said, wiping his mouth. 'You'll be back in no time. We won't call the police until we know you're safe. I'm sure these gentlemen will keep their word.'

Gabby took the girl out of the office, the gun a foot away from her girdle. When they were almost at the rear door and out of Mr Smithly's view, she abruptly turned her and made her go downstairs to where the rest of the staff were in the safe deposit room. Gabby opened the door and nudged her in with the rest.

Ossie nodded at Molly. She went out and into the street. Katy was on the other sidewalk. Molly waved and the wave was answered. The two old ladies went towards the rear door of Meggison's.

Ari the Greek and Lou the Barbender were standing in their funeral clothes beside the hearse and the second car in Meggison's Funeral Parlour when Molly and then Katy came carefully in through the side door.

'Gee, you look neat,' said Molly to the men. 'Real sad.'

Katy kissed Lou earnestly. 'You look like you're dressed for a wedding,' she whispered.

Lou blushed. 'One day, sweetheart,' he answered throatily.

The two ladies looked into the hearse at the bright coffin. 'Who is it?' whispered Katy. 'Anybody we know?'

'No names,' said Ari, shaking his nose. 'We don't want no sentiment entering into this. You'd better get a move on, girls.'

The feathery pair hurried away to a small ante-room and there, surrounded by vases of flowers and wreaths, they reversed their street clothes, the bright Miami colours turned to reveal black linings which became their mourning dresses. In two minutes they were sitting sedately and sombrely beside Ari and Lou in the rear seats of the car to follow the hearse. They waited expectantly. On time the side street door opened and Gabby, Ossie and Bruce came in, followed quickly by Sidewalk Joe and the lumbering Zaharran. Ossie and Bruce dismantled the missile projector and, casually lifting the coffin lid, placed it carefully alongside the body of the late citizen lying there. Ossie wondered if some archaeologist of the distant future might conjure some intriguing theories of how an old man came to be buried with such a lethal weapon beside him.

The money was in three canvas bags and these were put into the second funeral car, under the feet of the mourners. The gang were all now rid of their masks and they changed their clothes standing alongside the hearse, reversing anything and everything so that in a few minutes they were all rigid in burial black. They made the change smoothly and without hurry.

Bruce sat at the wheel of the hearse and, glancing at his watch, nodded. Sidewalk drove the second car. George operated the street door of the garage, got into the second car and the two vehicles slid reverently out into the Florida day.

The drove at a dead march pace, ten miles an hour, around a one-way street and past the front of the bank. With great caution nine pairs of eyes swivelled to take in the scene. The bank was silent. Nobody had moved to give the alarm.

The funeral sailed serenely by, hardly noticed by anyone on the sidewalk. Bruce steadied his hand on the wheel. He leaned over to Ossie.

'Listen pal, where are we heading? Is this a Jewish funeral or some other kind?'

'Jesus,' said Ossie. 'I forgot to ask.'

'Great,' muttered Gabby. 'Now what do we do?'

'Go to the Jewish cemetery,' said Lou almost below his breath. 'And if they don't expect us there, go to the other goddamn place.'

'I vote we leave this wagon train by the side of the road and beat it,' said Bruce. 'It ain't going to make any difference to the guy in the box.'

'We can't,' protested Katy. 'Not just leave the poor man.' But it was unconvincing. She added: 'Maybe we can ... but ... somewhere ... nice.'

They pulled to a stop in the car park of Miami's Hialeah Race Course. At that time of day the vast area was deserted. 'I promised we'd take them back,' said Ari. 'I told the guy. I said he could have them back in time for the funeral.'

'We'll pass him another hundred dollars,' said Ossie. 'The quicker we get clear the better. Okay?'

They left the hearse and its coffin parked decently and getting into the second funeral car they drove away. It was a big race afternoon at Hialeah and the coffin remained there until nightfall, the centre of interest and speculation for thousands.

'One hundred thousand bucks,' breathed Ossie. 'At last we got it right!'

The loot was piled on the table in Molly's room, like a haphazard wall, the notes in wrinkled bundles of a hundred. All around the members of the Ocean Drive Delinquent Society sat as if attending at some shrine.

'And it's all real,' said Bruce, easing forward to touch the notes. 'Every goddamn buck. And all ours.'

'More than ten thousand each,' breathed Katy. 'A girl could get married on that.' She rolled her eyes at Lou. He coughed and grinned sheepishly.

Gabby said: 'I suggest we deduct ten thousand dollars for expenses. For this and for future operations. Anyone object?'

No one did. 'Well, I guess we'd better start giving out the Christmas presents,' said Gabby. 'Ain't no good just looking at the stuff.' She broke a section from the wall of the notes and counted it into each lap, starting with Katy and ending with George. Only Molly seemed unsure. 'I still think it seems just a little dishonest,' she whispered to her granddaughter.

'Okay,' Gabby said decisively, 'we'll take yours and share it around evenly. Is that what you want, grandma?'

Molly closed her mouth and closed her hands about her ten thousand.

'Just one thing,' Ossie said, looking around warningly. 'Don't everybody go out splashing this stuff around. Sit on it for a while. Nobody buys a car or a mink. Okay? Just let the situation cool. If we don't, somebody's going to get wise. I vote we split up now. Just disperse quietly and say nothing. We'll have another operation for you before long.'

Zaharran remained after the others. He sat there, a large hunched figure, his ten thousand dollars in his lap. 'Well, George,' breathed Bruce gratefully, 'we're sure glad you joined. You brought us some know-how and some luck. I hope you feel the same about it.'

'Sure, sure,' answered Zaharran. His wig slipped forward as he nodded and, since his hands were full of money, he indicated to the young man that he would be glad of some assistance in putting the hairpiece back in place. Bruce obliged. 'I never had so much dough,' said the older man. 'And it was all so easy.'

He rose and went to his small suitcase which he had left in the room. He opened it and stowed the money carefully. Then, like some unkempt roadside salesman, he went out into the close, star-lit night. His mind was travelling like a round-about. Then he patted his little case reassuringly and laughed to himself all the way down Ocean Drive.

nine

Zaharran was asleep on the floor of his little office when Salvatore came in after knocking once. The knock was insufficient to wake the big man and the policeman stood looking down at him as God might look down from heaven upon an extinct volcano. The visitor however was not, at the best of times, given to poetic reflection and especially not today. He nudged Zaharran with first one foot and then the other.

One eye opened down there. 'I ain't no football,' said Zaharran. 'I don't like folks kicking me.' With heavy difficulty he levered himself up on to his elbows and worked his face about to try and settle it into its daytime creases. 'You're living dangerously, Salvatore,' he continued as he tried to get up from the floor. The policeman got his arm and helped him with a heave. 'Have a care with the back,' warned Zaharran. He did a cumbersome swivel movement and his backside closed with the chair. He sat down and looked at Salvatore.

'Living dangerously,' he repeated. 'You should know better than to creep up on a guy in my line of work when he's sleeping. I might have knocked you over with my forty-five.'

'With your snore, maybe,' sighed Salvatore. 'You heard the news? They did it again, the bastards. They robbed a bank this time.'

'Sure, I heard the radio before I went to sleep,' nodded Zaharran. 'They seem like they're getting better.'

'Jesus Alvin Christ,' said Salvatore. 'Is that the best you got for me? *They're getting better!* Do I need a detective to tell me they're getting better?'

'An elementary deduction,' admired Zaharran sagely. 'While I ain't retained on a financial basis, what do you expect? So what gives?'

'They took a girl, a secretary from the bank, to cover themselves. They said they would leave her on the Tuttle Causeway, but instead they just pushed her into the strongroom with all the rest of the staff.' Salvatore sighed deeply. 'And get this,' he said. 'They stole a funeral!' Zaharran's eyebrows ascended and he whistled. 'Yeah they hi-jacked a funeral,' said Salvatore. 'There's a funeral parlour right across the street from the bank and they got away in a hearse. They took it – with the guy in the coffin – to Hialeah.' He put his head in his hands. 'I need help, Zaharran. I was hoping you might have come up with something.'

'Not much,' lied Zaharran. This was it, he thought. From now on the die was cast. He'd never had ten thousand dollars in cash before. 'I've been circulating down on Ocean Drive. It's real nice down there on the beach. The ocean's kind of lazy and they have some funny pelicans and lots of ...'

'Stop!' howled Salvatore. 'I don't want a guided tour around the district! Fuck the pelicans!'

'That's an indictable offence, I shouldn't wonder,' said Zaharran. He leaned forward. 'Okay, listen Salvatore. It's no consolation to you, I know. But I'm watching. That's all I can tell you. I'm watching.'

'Great,' sighed Salvatore. 'I get a grant for you – a hundred and fifty dollars no less – from the pension fund and all you can tell me is you're watching. That's big dough for watching, Zaharran.'

'Did you bring the money with you?' asked Zaharran practically. 'I mean now?'

'No,' Salvatore snapped. 'It has to go through channels. You know that. Maybe it will get through by the end of the month.'

Zaharran sighed. 'By which time I am lying down there on the floor and when you come in and kick me, I don't move. And why don't I move? Because I'm lying dead, that's why.'

'I'm going,' said Salvatore. 'I really am. I come out of that crazy goddamn office, with everybody yelling on my head, and come here hoping to get some good news, or maybe even a little sympathy, and all you can tell me is that I might find you lying dead. A great big deal that would be. What sort of sympathy have you got? What sort, I ask you?'

Zaharran regarded him with a face crammed with sorrow. 'I'll tell you what I'll do, Salvatore,' he said. 'I'll sell my novelty business to you. And the astrology by mail, cheap. That could be a winner. All it needs is a little foresight. You could quit the force and put all your efforts into it.

Salvatore regarded him balefully. 'I'm going home,' he said. 'I'm going home to my wife and family. They don't love me either, but I got a roof and a door there. I'm protected.'

'Listen, pal,' said Zaharran. He was genuinely sorry for Salvatore, but he kept thinking that he had never seen ten thousand dollars before. 'Listen, I'm working on it, okay? That's the best news I've got for you.'

Loose Bruce and Gabby were sail-surfing off Key Biscayne, balanced with young grace on the fibreglass hulls while the fresh wind pushed into the vividly striped sails. They were half a mile out and the sea was vacant. Neither wore any clothes, his shorts and her bikini were tied each to the single masts of their craft. The wind and the sun whirled about them. Their browned bodies bent easily as they manoeuvred the sail-boats. They laughed with exhilaration.

'I'd like to get to know you better, lady,' called Bruce as he curled his craft closer to hers. He bent it away again before she had time to answer.

'Never better than you do,' she called after him. She watched him dip into the side of an ambitious wave and brace himself as the sail-board met the challenge and rose triumphantly.

'You're crazy,' she yelled happily. 'Mad!'

A long wild sand spit ventured out into the sea from Key Biscayne with a group of palms standing on it like marooned folk waiting for rescue. The white houses and other buildings on Key Biscayne, beyond the spit, were just visible among the greenery as they moved towards it and cars moved busily across the causeway and along the ocean front.

They both knew where they were heading. They shifted their weight and coaxed the single sails of their novel craft with the wind. Now with its strength right behind them they headed at speed for the beach. They both began to shout, feeling the naked exhilaration. Gabby's blue and white striped sail stretched taut beside her and over her head and Bruce's red diamond on a white sheet was in the full swell of the sea wind. They rode over the waves like two horsemen bearing banners.

The sail-boards sliced fast over the last remaining water and the pair turned them expertly at the optimum moment, so that they slid beautifully on to the low shelf of beach. They kept the momentum and tumbled ashore, rolling delightedly on to the easy white sand. Bruce turned and caught the girl in his brown arms and they rolled across the beach. They lay laughing at the end of it, covered with spray and with sand adhering to the spray. They kissed and parted laughing because their lips were sandy. Bruce rose and took the girl's hand. They went back to the fringe of the water and caught the sail-boards which were fidgeting in the low water, trying to free themselves from the beach. They pulled them clear, then bent and rolled into the sea again to wash away the sand.

They stood up in the shallow water and admired each other's nakedness. Her hand went out and caught hold of him. His head dropped forward when she touched him and he pushed his fair rough hair into the smooth vale between her large breasts. His hands went to their flanks and he pressed them to his cheeks. They looked up at each other and grinned now, the time for laughter having gone. 'I've been getting hungry for you, Gabby,' he said seriously.

He picked her up and put her across his hard shoulder, smacking her buttocks playfully as he did so. She giggled and returned the smack, hanging down his back like a large shining fish. 'No fighting,' he warned. 'If there's any fighting, I do it. Okay?'

'Okay,' she said. 'I'll go along with that.'

Bruce unloaded her none too gently on the sand. 'I've got sand all stuck to me again,' she whispered as he knelt over her.

'We're stuck with it,' he said. He kissed her on the face and then on the lips. 'Want to come on top?' he inquired.

'Sure. Today I want to be boss lady.'

'Right, start climbing,' said Bruce. He lay back into the warmth of the beach, feeling it across his shoulderblades and his backside and the backs of his legs. She climbed on him, an immediate dreaminess overcoming her so that her movements were at once slowed, her face taking on an uncertain smile as if she did not know what was to occur next, her eyes half closed. Bruce grinned with anticipation, his hands went about the deep indentations of her waist and he eased her into position. Her face broke into a series of small spasms as she settled on him. Then, when they were together, she fell carefully forward and rested her breasts against his tight chest and her thick hair against his face.

They lay on the beach and the sun lay on them. The considerate frond of a palm tree occasionally stretched itself in the breeze to give them some momentary shade. Its shadow fanned across their forms as they moved slowly. It was no time for passion. It was too hot. They took it easily and quietly like young people do who feel there might be many more times ahead. Gabby groaned as she rode him at a little under a canter. He lay easing himself up to her and down into the sand again in compliment to her movements. The whole time they did not alter their pace, not even hurrying, as so many do, towards the end. They came as they went, almost idly.

Afterwards they lay for several minutes, dopey against each

other, a few small movements coming from her in a lazy effort to gain another sensation. Their bodies were sweating, glistening like lizards. Their eyes remained closed, their skin relaxed.

It was while they were in this semi-embrace that they were spotted by a large Florida crab, staggering like an afternoon drunk along the usually deserted shoreline. He had little experience of humans and their habits, even less their sexual fashions, and the entangled limbs and adjacent trunks lying so quietly on the sand took his curiosity.

He advanced without fear or caution and upon reaching the side of the girl's thigh took a deep crablike breath and began to climb. Gabby, believing the touches came from Bruce's fingers, remained placid and it was only when the crab mounted the back of her thigh and was there resting that she demurred. 'Baby,' she whispered. 'You've just got to cut those fingernails.'

Bruce who had one hand on her naked backside and the other trailing idly in the sand moved both hands to her waist and half opened his eyes. 'Is that two hands you've got around my middle?' asked the girl half rising and waking rapidly. 'Two?'

'Two,' he confirmed, puzzled but unworried. 'Sorry about the fingernails.'

'Bruce, there's something on my leg,' she muttered. Her eyes widened and she looked backwards over her shoulder to see the crab's bright black eyes regarding her with the insolence of the conqueror. For a second she was immobilized, then she flung herself sideways from Bruce with a cry that set the gulls and pelicans wheeling in worried circles in the sky.

The crab, self-preservation rating higher even than curiosity in its priorities, slid from her leg like a sailor abandoning a ship. It scampered away to the familiarity of the sea. Gabby screamed again and Bruce, after sitting up in alarm, began hooting with laughter as the hind quarters of the crab scuttled away across the sand.

'This is station WAIA, Miami, serving the golden coast from the Palm Beaches to the Florida Keys. Here is the weather for *twenty-four hours to six p.m. tomorrow. It's getting hotter folks. Tonight there will be clear skies and a high of seventy-five degrees, a low of sixty-two, and a ten per cent chance of rain. Tomorrow a high of eighty-five and clear skies, little breeze and a calm sea. Today is April fourteenth and this is WAIA your music way ...'*

After Easter, in those latitudes, the sun gets hotter along the southern ocean coast, the humidity thickens and the wintering people go away. During the torrid summer the Florida beaches are left to the everyday inhabitants and those who cannot afford to move.

Along Ocean Drive in that month, competition among the retired people for a place in the shade of the sea-grape trees increased and there were occasional arguments and disputes in the vivid dialects that so many of the denizens could summon, sometimes even involving the use of fists and what force could be fired in the elderly breasts. It was not easy to keep a temper in that off-season heat.

Ari the Greek got up very early on those days for his run. The sun was just swelling from below the Atlantic when he trotted from the front porch of the Sunny Gables Hotel and went on his jogging journey along the amber beach and eventually along Ocean Drive and the streets back to the hotel. He was so early these mornings that the Washington Avenue store was not open when he passed it so he could not go in for a blood pressure test. He needed to make a special journey late in the day.

His blood pressure was all right but Ari's conscience was bothering him. He had not spent a cent of the illicit money that had come his way. It remained in a box hidden at the back of the cupboard in his room. It seemed to call in an increasing nagging voice, calling out that he had, at his age, committed a major felony. Bootlegging was different and it was so long ago.

He even confided these misgivings to Molly, who at that season took her metal detector to the beach as early as Ari went on his run. 'Maybe I'm old fashioned or crazy,' he sighed, 'but I get all that loot out and I say to myself, "Ari," I say, "who needs it!".'

Molly nodded, for she understood him well. Without looking

up but continuing to weave her curved patterns with her metal detector, even obliging Ari to move his sneaker-clad feet out of the way, she said: 'It didn't seem so bad when we were losing, if you get what I mean, Ari. When we made a hash of the jobs it seemed to be okay. Kinda square and fair. But I got to tell you I've been worried too. It ain't the thought of getting caught. I keep wondering if that poor guy at the bank got into trouble. The manager, I mean. He seemed such a nice man, just like my Melford, I thought, and he was just about due to retire.'

'Nearly one of us,' said Ari sadly.

'Not the sort at all we should have threatened with that rocket firer,' she continued pensively.

The machine she was using gave a whirr in her ears. Ari heard it and his face sharpened with interest. 'What is it, Molly?' he asked. 'Something big?'

'A quarter at the most,' she shrugged. 'Probably a dime. I can tell by the tone.' She produced a small garden fork and proceeded to prod and scrape the sand. Ari watched with interest. Eventually the now rising sun touched off a glint of silver and Molly bent and recovered a coin, a dime, from the sand.

'It ain't much,' she said, looking at it fondly, 'but at least it's lost – not stolen.'

Ari's face clouded and she looked up and saw he was troubled. 'I'd better be on my way,' he said. 'Once the sun gets up this running ain't so funny. 'Bye, Molly.'

' 'Bye, Ari. Have a nice day.' She smiled her motherly smile and Ari, after glancing at the sun as if it were particularly pursuing him, jogged away.

'Keep running,' she called, beginning to sweep the sand with the detector again. 'Just keep running, Ari.'

'Sure,' he called back over his shoulder. 'While I'm running I'm living.' He did a quick spasm of shadow boxing. 'It won't make me rich, but I'm living,' he said to himself. He wondered, once again, what the hell he was supposed to do with ten thousand dollars.

Lou the Barbender and K-K-K-Katy sat holding hands at the Parrot Jungle watching a bright cockatoo pedal a tiny cycle along a tightrope. 'That's so cute,' sighed K-K-K-Katy. 'Makes you feel you want children of your own.'

'I hope they don't look like parrots,' put in Lou gently. 'I'm allergic to feathers.'

She laughed her silvery girl's laugh and nudged him. 'I mean seeing all the children enjoying this,' she said. 'I didn't mean they would *be* like the parrots.'

'I liked the little one on the roller skates best,' said Lou. 'The parrot. That's real neat.'

They watched the remainder of the novel performance and then went unhurriedly from the amphitheatre to walk around the tropical gardens alive with shouting birds. Lou bought two ice-creams and they sat admiring a row of exquisitely-hued cockatoos, large as chickens, who perched and posed for round-eyed photographers and cackled: 'Watch the birdie.'

'I know we won't have children,' said Katy, patting his hand and speaking carefully. 'We're just a little too late. But if we did I wouldn't want them to know their parents robbed a bank.'

She was looking at his big cheek, his strong nose and his suntanned forehead. His eyes remained forward, staring as if he was trying to identify one cockatoo especially. 'Nor me, honey,' he said gruffly. 'I'd like them to tell the other kids that their daddy was the strongest man in America and their mommy had the prettiest legs. But not that we robbed a bank. No, I don't go for that.'

'It don't seem right getting married on stolen money either, Lou,' she whispered. Now she wanted to get it all off her conscience. 'It won't help us to be happy. We'll always have to live with it.'

He nodded ponderously, still considering the coloured birds. 'Maybe God will strike me dead on our wedding night,' he forecast gloomily. 'Dead like stone – and then you'll have my share to worry about as well. Twenty thousand bucks on your conscience, Katy. I couldn't leave you with that sort of legacy.'

'I wouldn't want it,' she sighed. 'Gee, I want to get married, Lou. More than anybody knows. But it's not the way to finance it. I want us to save up what we get legally. We could save enough in a year. We don't need much.'

Lou shrugged in agreement. 'A year now ain't going to make

any difference, honey,' he said, apparently addressing a huge turquoise and yellow bird which was leaning forward, intent on every word. 'We're not going to get any older in a year.'

'That's right!' exclaimed the bird. 'That's right! That's right, buddy! That's right!' He rocked to and fro with the excitement of what he had said and let loose a huge screech to emphasize the point. Katy laughed and Lou nodded his head in slow wisdom.

'He seems to agree,' said Katy, squeezing Lou's arm. They had finished the ice cream and now they went, her delicate hand in his big paw, towards the exit to the park where their excursion bus was waiting. Other people were going the same way. Katy bent her head against Lou's shoulder. 'It's not that I don't enjoy doing it, baby,' she said. A young couple walking the same way and two feet from them both turned and registered surprise. 'I love every second of it,' continued Katy, oblivious of the attention she was getting. 'It's the most exciting thing ever. But it's the consequences. When I open the box and see all those little faces looking at me ... so accusingly.'

The young couple swallowed jointly and hurried ahead. 'Jesus, what d'you know,' breathed the boy. 'And *we're* supposed to be the kookie generation.'

Molly Mandy, her best hat on her head and determination in her elderly heart, left the front door of the Sunny Gables Hotel and headed for the post office on Washington Avenue. She was carrying a supermarket shopping bag and in the bag, parcelled with the utmost care, was a package containing ten thousand dollars. It was addressed to the manager of the United States National Trust Bank on Broward Boulevard, Miami, and one contained a note which said:

Dear Manager,
I am sending this money back to you because I can't sleep for it. It's more than I have ever seen in my life before but I was brought up not to steal, even from those who have plenty, and so I am sending it back to you with my compliments. This is only my share of the money taken from your bank in the raid but I am sure you will be glad to see it back safely.
Yours faithfully,
A Robber

Her heart banged like a gong all the way along Washington Avenue. She was sure she would meet some other member of the Ocean Drive Delinquent Society and her guilt would show. But the street was much as it always was, hot on one side, shaded on the other. The hot side was very hot, for it was afternoon and the sun was striking along its whole length, but she braved the discomfort in exchange for fewer people. She reached the post office and went in gratefully. The clerk took the parcel and weighed it. His eyebrows went up. 'That packet is going to cost a packet, lady,' he said.

'It's worth it, mister,' she said mysteriously. 'Every cent.'

Five minutes later she came out of the building feeling years younger and pounds lighter. She chose the shaded side of the street and walked like a girl in springtime, swinging her hips, a smile gracing her face and her hat at a jaunty angle. She said 'Hi!' and 'Good afternoon,' and 'Great to see you,' to people she did not even know.

One person she did not see had watched her walk to the post office and had followed in her wake, had sat on a seat opposite while she deposited the parcel, and had observed her lighthearted exit from the building and her sunny progress down the street once more.

It was Zaharran. He was smiling a knowing smile.

The riverboat *Florida King* left Fort Lauderdale every afternoon at two for a cruise along the green-banked miles of the inland waterways. It was built like the Mississippi paddle steamers of older days, with many decks, brightly painted bows and superstructure. It carried three hundred passengers seated in rows along the decks one above the other. As it made its two hour voyage it looked, from the banks, like a giant sandwich, with the tourists as the filling.

It was a popular excursion because what the area lacked in geographical variety and history it made up for in opulence. Immediately the steamer left Fort Lauderdale pier and headed for the creeks and canals it voyaged on tranquil green water cushioned by the lawns and trees and glaring white houses of the very rich indeed.

The tourists, fortunate enough to be able to visit this last leg of the United States when it was winter elsewhere in the land, gazed with a mixture of interest and envy as the homes of the wealthy slid by. Sometimes a person was to be seen in a deck chair on a lawn, the ship's guide would announce his or her household name over the loudspeaker and the entire three hundred trippers would wave and call.

Sometimes the household name would wave wearily back and the tourists could then go home to Wisconsin and Ohio and say they had exchanged greetings with a multi-millionaire.

Overhanging the water were willows and palms, hibiscus and brilliant tulip trees, giving it a hybrid aspect, part temperate, part tropical. Each pure white house had a landing stage or a boat dock and the slender and luxurious craft, tethered like pets, moved, idle and rich, in the wash of the large riverboat.

'On your left, folks – look left, not right, sir – just below that big, beautiful tree, the one that touches the water, is the lovely home of George C. Peckin, President of the United Whisky Importers and a dozen other corporations. That house – believe it or not – is called Scotch Corner.' The guide had recited it a hundred times over the microphone but he tried to sound lively.

An appreciative titter drifted over the packed rows on the paddle-steamer, but too many were staring at the shaded luxury being indicated to appreciate the joke. Ossie, Gabby, Bruce and Sidewalk sat on one row. K-K-K-Katy, Lou the Barbender, Ari and Molly, and Zaharran sat in the row behind. Their heads, like the rest of the two hundred and ninety heads on the vessel, moved obediently from one side of the waterway to the other, as if following some slow and travelling tennis game.

'These wonderful homes have been built by famous industrialists and politicians and some by film stars. Not *all* the stars are in California, folks. The house coming up on the left is the home of Miss Tottie di Milo ... that house just on the strip of land projecting into the waterway, with the luxury cabin cruiser moored there. I wonder who can be visiting today ... ?'

The mansion was still a hundred yards ahead but many of the eager sightseers could not wait so they stood and leaned this way and that trying to get a view around the screening trees and perhaps catch a glimpse of the famous movie star and her visitors.

'You remember the movie *Where the Boys Are*, folks?' A chorus of vague assent came from the sandwiched decks. 'Well that was one movie made right here in Fort Lauderdale. And the boys are still here, and the girls I'm glad to say ...'

The ponderous showboat had now drawn abreast of the house of Tottie di Milo. As it eased along the waterway, it cleared the trees and the dazzling white home unrolled before the thrilled eyes of the tourists. 'Wow, what a shack, ladies and gentlemen,' enthused the guide who said it twice a day. 'A lovely home. Miss Tottie is resting after making a movie. And when you're a big girl like Tottie di Milo you sure need your rest!'

The tourists sniggered dutifully. The guide continued to shout. 'Next week she is throwing a great big bonanza party for all the society people and the show people who happen to be in Florida right now. I sure would like to get a pass to that, wouldn't you? What a bullfight that is going to be!'

An envious buzz of assent rose from the decks. 'One thing that's truly unique about the house,' went on the man indestructibly. 'It has a river – yes, people, you heard right, a real, wet river – running right through the salon. It empties into the waterway just by the boat dock. There's not too many houses, even in wonderful Florida, that have a genuine one hundred per cent river going through them.'

The chorus of amazement at the news was overcome by an even louder emission as the people spotted a bikini-clad figure issuing from the widespread reflecting doors of the house. The glass flashed in the sunlight as she came out. Right on cue. 'And my goodness, are we in luck!' the commentator gabbled. 'Wow! It's Miss Tottie di Milo herself!'

There was such a rush to the left hand side of the ship it seemed to wallow and list that way. 'Steady, steady,' came the warning. 'Don't capsize the boat. It's all we have.'

'I'll capsize it if that broad rescues me,' said Ari the Greek ruminatively. Zaharran sniffed heavily and moved to the other side of the boat as if hoping that his weight would counterbalance the list.

'Miss Tottie has come out to say hello,' announced the commentator excitedly. 'Give her a wave, folks. Show her we love her!'

There was multiple waving and the riverboat lurched sluggishly. The goddess, posed and poised on the bank, waved a bandana and flashed her famous teeth in the sun. She was joined by two obediently playful dogs and then by a long, loping figure in shorts wearing a hawser of gold chain around his neck.

'Gee and look who's here!' bellowed the commentator. 'None other than Herb Specter, folks. I guess you've all seen the movie *Skin and Skin*. Mr Specter was the star of that movie.'

Excitement aboard the *Florida King* was reaching the proportions of a mutiny. Molly and K-K-K-Katy urgently joined the mass hoping to see Herb Specter, Molly standing unceremoniously on Ossie's lap to do so. He struggled painfully but patiently.

'Only this morning, folks, I read that Herb had left his wife back in Hollywood, California, and was entering a new romance. Well now we know who it is don't we? We have it exclusive!'

A huge chorus of satisfaction and acclaim rose from the crammed tourists. They waved with renewed fury and Tottie and Herb waved back with dignified movements, like royalty, from the lawns that sloped to the water. Eventually the boat eased itself further away and reluctantly and raggedly the people sat down. The hull righted itself.

'Could you ask the captain if we could get real close on the way back?' a lady called to the guide. 'I'd sure like to take a picture.'

The commentator smiled grimly. He said below his breath, 'We'll beach the fucking ship and you can get an autograph.' He waved to her, indicating that they would do their best.

Molly sat down again, perspiring with the efforts she had made to gain a vantage point. 'It's just great to see the greats, isn't it just?' she said to her granddaughter. Gabby rolled her eyes and patted her grandmother's hand.

Zaharran, still on the far side of the deck, was confronted

by a big, flowered lady who demanded the restoration of her seat. 'I was just keeping the boat upright,' he grunted and lumbered back to the opposite rail. He looked down at Ossie and Ossie saw an expression in his bulbous eye. The big man leaned over the rail and consulted the water as if he were sounding the fathoms. Ossie got up and stood beside him.

'You found what we came for?' asked Ossie quietly.

'Ah,' said Zaharran lazily. 'I was just thinking what a great coincidence it is that the lady over there ... in the house ... with the boobs and the ape ...'

'Tottie di Milo,' said Ossie. 'What were the thoughts?'

'Yeah, that's her. What a coincidence that she should be having a big, big party next week, with all the society and all the stars and suchlike, and there's us looking for another operation.'

'How do we get in?' asked Ossie quietly. 'The place is bound to have security all around it. She's that sort of star.'

'Well, she's got a living river running through the place,' sniffed Zaharran. He smiled through the sniff. 'That ain't too bad for a start.'

ten

They sat in a silent, shadowy circle in Molly Mandy's room, the central light falling on the plan that Ossie had spread over the table. Already there was a suppressed excitement about them, the faces inching forward, alive with anticipation and interest. For the Ocean Drive Delinquent Society there was no source of adrenalin like the plotting of another raid.

'Obviously the river that goes through the salon of Old Creek House is not much more than a stream,' said Ossie pointing to the appropriate part of the plan. 'It is no Mississippi.'

An elderly audible smile came from those around. K-K-K-Katy reached and found Lou's hand, Ari exchanged some sort of left-hand jabs with an invisible opponent, Zaharran sat like a pile of wet cement, small ripples of movement going over his large body, but his eyes steady and intent. Gabby looked at the composed Ossie and then at the youthful Bruce, his brown face like copper in the subdued light. Inwardly she shrugged.

'The river,' Ossie went on, 'is in fact ten feet wide and four deep. But that's a constant depth. It's got a square concrete base even if it's been planted with various reeds and stuff like that. It runs almost down the centre of the main room and out through an arched tunnel into the waterway. That's the way we are going in.'

He drew a small circle on the map with his fingers. 'Just here, almost at the back of the room, where the faucet feeds the water into the river there is a kind of round ornamental pool with fish and this is kept separate from the river itself by a removable metal grille. That grille we will use as a mooring for the boat. Okay?'

Doubtfully Ossie looked around the circle. 'I take it you've all at least seen pictures of an Everglades fan-boat. Maybe you've seen a real one, or on television. It's a flat-bottomed skiff, designed for use in the swamps where there's no great depth of water and where there's a lot of weed and other crud that would catch in the propellers of any other type of craft. It can be used in as little as five inches of water, so we should have depth to spare. It's propelled by a fan mounted on the stern, an outsized version of one of the desk fans you see in people's offices or homes.

'We've had a long talk about this, Gabby and Bruce and myself, and we think that this fan-boat is just about right for our requirements. It's narrow enough to get through the tunnel from the river to the house and it has no draught to speak of so we'll have plenty of water below the hull. There's one disadvantage. At the most it will carry six people.' He glanced at the large Zaharran. 'Five if we take George,' he said. He smiled apologetically but Zaharran merely nodded acknowledgement. 'We also need a look-out,' went on Ossie. 'And two people to have the getaway cars ready – in the right place at the right time.'

He paused and then said: 'Personally I'm sorry about this because it's George's brainchild, but if he wouldn't mind ...'

'Don't worry about me, son,' said Zaharran shaking his head in slow motion. 'I'll fix the cars. I'll be there when you get ashore.'

'Great. Thanks. We need six for the operation, I think. Would Katy mind being the look-out? She's really good at that.'

'I don't mind, dear,' said Katy. 'I can wh-wh-whistle.'

Molly clasped her hands in front of her face with excitement. 'Oh good, goody, good,' she said. Then her face clouded. 'I made a mess of my mask,' she confessed. 'I was trying to drink coffee when I was wearing it. Just kinda practising, you understand. And you can't drink it like that. I'll have to send it to the valet service.'

Gabby, among others, closed her eyes. 'I wouldn't do that, grandma,' she advised. 'They may get a little suspicious having a mask and a hood in at the valet service.'

'You're darn right,' said Molly emphatically. 'I'm sure glad you mentioned it, dear. Okay, I'll get the coffee out myself.' She looked up benignly oblivious of the defeated looks she was getting. 'What's next?' she asked brightly.

Ossie coughed. He said slowly: 'Yes, well, next ... You really won't take the mask to the valet service, will you, Molly ... ? No, good. Just try and remember. It might be like taking the guns to the pawn shop, if you understand what I mean.'

'Sure I see,' nodded Molly blandly. 'I'm not completely crazy.'

'Good, good,' said Ossie. 'That's very reassuring. Now, there's the small matter of obtaining the fan-boat. Our good friend and colleague Sidewalk here knows where they keep the fan-boats at night and he and Ari are going to borrow one for a while.'

'It's a yard where they renovate them,' said Sidewalk Joe.

'It ain't too difficult. And it ain't that far away either, so that will make it easier. I've always wanted to drive one of them things.'

Ossie nodded at him. 'Fine. Now the details will be worked out between Gabby, Bruce and myself, as usual. Maybe George wouldn't mind remaining behind as well. His know-how was pretty useful last time.' George's head nodded. 'I guess that's all, ladies and gentlemen,' said Ossie. 'Don't talk about it, even among yourselves. You never know who's got ears that may be functioning even in South Miami.' He smiled at the joke, but they didn't smile back.

Molly leaned over to Ari and said: 'What did he say?'

'I don't know,' said Ari. 'I didn't hear.'

'Wednesday,' said Ossie a little more loudly. 'Assemble here at nine. We plan to enter the house at ten-thirty and be out with the profits by ten-forty. Any further questions?'

There were none. The old gang went out singly to their small rooms. Gabby, Ossie and Bruce said goodnight to each one. Zaharran moved towards the table. He was going to be in charge of the getaway cars. The perfect trap. Now he had them. If he wanted them.

Tottie di Milo had experienced some little difficulty in getting together enough fun people for her party, because Fort Lauderdale at that time of the year was not the place where the fun people gathered. She was saved, however, by the surprising advent of Frankie Moon, the popular singer, who had come down from New York to give an in-person concert in Miami. He had with him various members of his travelling world, his dumb wife, his two dumb mistresses and his children by various alliances and marriages. His musicians were the famous Billy Bolon group and they had their various affiliates, and there were some supporting singers and a progressive comedian. She asked them all to her party and they all accepted, there not being a great deal of excitement in Miami out of season.

She also invited neighbours of Old Creek House who happened to be in residence, including George C. Peckin, the

194

president of United Whisky Importers, who had a group of business associates and their wives as his guests at his water-way home.

Miss di Milo was busy completing her late guest list a few days before the party when there was a telephone call from the Miami Police Department.

'I've done nothing,' she said immediately in her famous film voice. At any time of the day or evening, even if she had been awake for hours, it was the voice of a voluptuous woman just roused from sleep. The voice of a long-haired lovely, speaking with her eyes closed.

'Oh,' she sighed. 'You're *not* going to arrest me? Oh I'm so glad, captain, so glad.'

Captain Salvatore on the receiving end of this honey per-mitted himself to enjoy the sensation. Betty, his wife, had just nagged him for ten minutes on that same phone. 'No, Miss di Milo,' he breathed. 'We're not arresting you, much as we would appreciate your company. The area of this bureau could do with a little glamour.'

'You're just *so* kind,' she breathed. 'I'm afraid I don't look very glamorous just now. I'm just in an old pink silk robe. Nothing else at all. Not one little thing.'

Salvatore bit his lip fiercely at the thought. He returned to business. 'Miss di Milo, you're having a society party, so I understand, in a few days.'

'News travels,' she whispered. 'Just a hundred little people. All close friends.'

'Sure, sure. I bet you've got more than that too. It's just that I'd appreciate it if I could come over and take up some of your time discussing your security arrangements.'

'Security?' She seemed to wake up at the word. 'Why? What's wrong with my security, captain? I have a little guard at the gate all the time.'

'I know, Miss di Milo, I know. But you may know from the newspapers that we've had a gang operating in the Miami area over the past few weeks. They already made one raid on a party at a home in Palm Beach. So we're just keeping a surveillance on social events like the one you're proposing

195

to have on Wednesday. And especially social gatherings that are mentioned in the newspapers. There was an item in the *Miami News* about your party last night.'

'A gang?' she resumed her wondrous, embedded voice. 'A gang of robbers?'

'Masked robbers,' confirmed Salvatore.

'Masked? But, oh, that's terrifying. I'm shaking all over, captain. Somehow I've just got to calm down.'

Salvatore blinked at the phone he was holding. 'It's just a precaution, Miss di Milo. Don't let it bother you. All we want to do is have the house watched. A patrol car or maybe two on the streets leading to the property. Perhaps I could just call and familiarize you with the plans.'

'Any time,' she breathed. 'I'd just love to be familiarized.'

Salvatore put the phone down and, standing up quickly as if hoping to catch his reflection by surprise, looked in the mirror on the wall. Without much hope he tried to arrange his sparse hair so that it covered more of his scalp. He smiled courageously and brushed his teeth with his finger. Then he picked up the intercom phone. 'Detective Cook,' he said. 'Are you solving big crimes?'

'No, captain. I'm looking in the newspaper to see what's on TV tonight.'

'Well get off your ass, Cookie. We're going to see a lovely lady. Well I am. You can sit in the car.'

Tottie di Milo wondered what she should do while she waited for the policeman. She had bathed luxuriously and attended to the ritual of her make-up. She thought perhaps she ought to put some clothes on and this she did, although she often felt better without. But when she had dressed the detective had still not arrived. Habitually she found it difficult to fill in vacuous moments and she sat down and stood up again several times in front of a full length mirror, each time adopting a different pose, trying urgently to decide which did the most for her.

Then she brightened because she had an idea and generally they came slowly. She went down to the main salon of her beautiful house, to where the living river flowed through the floor. At the ornamental pool at the top end of the huge semi-circular room she took a bowl of freshly cut meat and began to feed the new acquisitions that would, she was sure, be the sensation of the party. Two Everglades alligators.

The gang left the two cars on a short jetty near Fort Lauder-dale Bridge, one of the series of cantilever bridges which opened to allow large vessels to progress along the Intra-Coastal Waterway, the operation being worked by a man in a small wheelhouse on the beach side.

Zaharran and Lou the Barbender stayed with the cars. K-K-K-Katy had already taken up her look-out post in a telephone booth in the street leading to Tottie di Milo's house. Around the corner out of Katy's view, and Katy out of theirs, Detective Cook and two policemen sat in a car beneath some trees. Another patrol car was two hundred yards away.

The remaining members of the Ocean Drive Delinquent Society embarked on the fan-boat which Ari and Sidewalk had casually stolen and brought to the jetty. It was ten o'clock on a thundery night and the waterway was shaded although the lights of the district shone all around and the bridge was busy with cars. The robbers arranged themselves carefully, three on each side of the slight craft. Ossie and Bruce in the bow, Gabby and Molly next to Sidewalk and Ari behind them. Nobody was hooded yet. Molly held her hood like a present to be opened at Christmas. Her lively eyes were brimming with excitement and apprehension, and they widened even further when a touch from Sidewalk on the starter of the boat sent the fan whirring softly and the boat moving through the dark, silky water.

Sidewalk kept as close as was prudent to the right-hand bank, easing the odd vessel along with all the quiet he could manage. A few disturbed waterbirds croaked as they passed but there were no other alarms. Like commandos the gang crouched on the slight deck. They were approaching the neck of the waterway where the lights of Old Creek House could be seen filtering through the trees. Music, which travels well across water, floated to them. Bruce turned and gave a shadow of a nod to the others. Unhurriedly they began to put on their hoods. Bruce and Ossie mounted a useless Russian mortar in the bow of the boat. They eased its barrel down to the horizontal because it looked more menacing like that. Then Molly Mandy, in the excitement of putting on her hood, fumbled and dropped it into the water.

'Oh dear,' she whispered. 'Mine's gone over the side.'

Ossie turned around with Bruce. Both immediately turned to the front again and uttered swearwords. Gabby looked helpless. 'We've got to get it,' she said. 'She'll be recognized if we don't.'

'And I *do* want to wear it,' pleaded Molly. 'I *do* so.'

Tight-faced, Sidewalk turned the shallow boat around in as brief a circle as he could. They found the missing hood floating towards them but it had gone by before anyone could grab it, so they had to circle again and chase it up river. Eventually Ari fished it from the waterway and handed it silently to Molly. 'I'll wring it out,' she said brightly.

'I'll wring her out if she does it again,' said Ossie to Bruce under his breath.

Gabby leaned forward in whispered anger. 'Drop dead,' she muttered. 'If you take old people on a goddamn picnic you expect jam to be spilt.'

'Okay, okay,' sighed Ossie. 'Do what you can. We're behind the schedule.'

'You always were,' said Gabby rudely. She helped her grandmother to twist the water from the hood. They were now moving slowly towards the lawns of the house. The music issued more firmly through the trees. They could recognize the tune. Ossie leaned back and handed a hood to Molly. 'Better wear this,' he said without looking at her. 'Otherwise you'll get pneumonia.'

'That's mine,' protested Bruce.

'You're young,' said Ossie. 'You wear the wet hood.'

'I'll get neuralgia,' complained Bruce. 'Or toothache. I suffer hell from toothache.'

He took the wet hood from Molly nevertheless and pulled it over his head. Ossie looked around. He could see they were as ready as they would ever be.

'Okay?' he whispered.

The hooded heads nodded.

'Right,' he said. 'Get ready. We're going in.'

It was beginning to look like a good party. Tottie di Milo in her most angelic gown held the hand of her new lover, Herb Specter, and beamed around at all her guests as if she knew and loved them all.

The wide semi-circle of the salon made an excellent place for such a function, particularly on a night, such as this, of gathering off-season thunder. People did not enjoy being out of doors on lawns and patios in threatening weather and the living river flowing through the huge room lent it an added and welcome coolness.

Tottie's new alligators had naturally been a great attraction, with the guests gathering around the pool at the headwaters of the river, so to speak, laughing at them and cajoling them from the safety of the low barrier rail. The alligators, for their parts, bared their teeth hungrily, never having seen so many people at one time.

'It must be like looking at the greatest feast you ever saw – and not being able to touch a morsel,' philosophized Captain Salvatore. He spoke to himself, and possibly the alligators, for Miss di Milo apart, he had never met anyone in the room before and nobody had bothered to introduce him. When she had invited him as her guest he was flattered and delighted. But now he wondered whether he should have been there. It did not feel comfortable. He also realized that his gun was making a bulge in the coat of his best suit.

Hidden music eased its way through the room, glasses and laughter sounded. The singer Frankie Moon with his dumb wife, his dumb mistresses, his tribe of musicians, dancers, whoo-whoo singers, agents, managers and paid admirers, arrived late, to plan. They were in their normal extravagant mood and infused the party with a lot of noise. Frankie Moon himself got a lot of laughs by pouring a glass of bourbon down the yawning throat of one of the Everglades alligators as it came up and glared from the pool.

'Gee,' shouted Mr George C. Peckin of United Whisky, 'I'm real glad that was only bourbon, Mr Moon. If it had been our imported Scotch that 'gator would have been out of that darned pool looking for more!'

It got a laugh as such inanities get laughs at parties. Salvatore abruptly found himself in conversation with Tottie and trying desperately not to look down the front of her dress. Its angelic folds fell away unangelically from the shoulders revealing the twin hills of which Miss di Milo was so proud and which had gone a considerable way to making her famous.

'I feel really safe with you around, Captain Salvatore,' she said with a sigh that expanded her bosom even more spectacularly and had Salvatore's eyes desperately swinging for somewhere else to look. Her skin was like coffee cream, swollen and sweet with the material of the dress only just making an horizon below which, he knew, oh he knew, hid the loveliest pink buds in the world. God, he would have given half his pension, *fuck it, all his pension*, just to see them and perhaps touch them and a few other things for a couple of hours. After that he could die, he wouldn't care. Her suntan went zooming right down her cleavage. Jesus Bernard Christ, she must sunbathe in the skin. God, if only he could get a view of them.

'It's certainly kind of you to invite me,' he managed to say through all his imaginings. 'I don't think we need worry too much about any interruptions. But just in case, I have two patrol cars on surveillance, one at each end of the street. Everyone who comes in and out is checked.'

'Is there something wrong with your arm, Captain Salvatore?' she suddenly inquired solicitously. 'Why does it stand away from your body like that? Is it a wound of some sort?'

Salvatore blushed. 'It's my gun,' he explained. 'It don't really fit this suit.'

'Your gun?' she said in a thrilled voice. 'You have your gun with you?' She descended to a conspiratorial whisper. 'Guns turn me on so.'

Salvatore smiled like he hoped a television cop would smile. 'Always have this baby with me, Miss di Milo.' He patted the weapon and grimaced as it dug uncomfortably into his chest.

'Tottie,' she invited. He felt sure she let her dress slip forward. 'Please call me Tottie, Captain.'

Salvatore felt a warmth coming up like steam from his boots. Jesus Henry Christ, maybe this sort of woman liked beleaguered police officers with sparse hair and ill-fitting suits. 'Albert,' he whispered.

He looked around. Herb Specter, a big bastard there was no doubt, was sprawled on a couch with one of Frankie Moon's dumb mistresses. Maybe it was one of those parties he had heard about. He felt the gun moving with his deepening breaths and the strong beat of his heart.

'I'm calling you Captain,' she smiled. 'It sounds so much braver. And I want to try on your little gun.'

'My gun?' Salvatore stared at her bosom. 'But it's in a shoulder holster Miss di ... I mean Tottie. Here, I'll show you.' With theatrical secrecy he quickly opened his coat and revealed the gun in its holster. He could feel his own eyes shining and a warmth rushing through his veins. All at once his head seemed thick with hair.

'Gee, that's neat,' she said. 'Come on, Captain, let me try it. Please – just once.' Unbelievably she pulled away the front of her dress at one side revealing a whole flank of exquisite bosom. 'There's room down there,' she said plaintively. 'Plenty of room for a little gun like that. Let me get you another drink.'

She poured a huge glass of champagne. 'It's difficult,' he said with difficulty. 'Difficult to get the holster off ... and on. Maybe you'd just like to see the gun.'

Inwardly he cursed himself for being a timid fool but he quickly retrieved the situation. The champagne had given him daring. 'Oh no, maybe you could just get the holster to fit,' he said. 'But I don't want to take it off here. It's too public – and against police regulations, you understand.'

'Of course I understand, Captain dear,' she whispered like a conspirator. 'And I'm not one to tangle with regulations, truly.'

'If there's a room where I could take my harness off,' he suggested, his confidence growing wild, 'then you could go to your room and try it. It might be difficult to get it on without er ... some ... adjustments ...'

She winked at him hugely. 'We'll both go,' she decided to his explosive delight. 'We're both in this together.' She glanced quickly at Herb Specter who had now sunk deeper into the couch and almost deeper into the red-haired dumb mistress. 'Herb's having one of his celibate nights,' she said. 'He won't object. Come on, Honey Captain.'

Honey Captain blushed all down his chest. He knew it wasn't happening but, God almighty, she was holding his hand. He thought he needed another drink to keep the vision steady but she was insistent. 'I have some champagne in my room,' she said. 'We can drink while we're adjusting.'

Tottie flitted slightly ahead of him towards one of the distant doors around the circular wall. He glanced quickly around and went at a policeman's creep after her. Nobody seemed to notice. Salvatore thought his heart was going to spoil everything by leaping like an idiot clean out of his chest. He had a fleeting 'if the boys could see me now' thought, went through the door as if he were raiding a cat-house, and followed her through a series of snaking passages until they were at a door which opened at the touch of her fingers.

Salvatore had never seen a beautiful film star's bedroom before. She stood there on the thick carpet, her luxury body suddenly enfolded by the voluptuousness of the room. Salvatore felt so full he wanted to cry.

'Honey Captain,' she said in a voice no weightier than a sigh. The bedroom seemed to have an effect on her also. She suddenly became dreamy, wafty, and she moved over the carpet, her feet below her gown hardly seemed to brush the floor. Nor did Salvatore's.

'Honey Captain,' she repeated, 'you must sit on my bed.'

'Bed?' he answered hollowly. '*Your* bed?'

'Yes,' she said firmly, pointing to the high altar of the room. Pink, heart-shaped, with silks and frills and pillows like ice cream. Salvatore stared at it as if it were the electric chair at Sing Sing and he had been invited to sit in it.

'But *your* bed?' he said hoarsely. 'Are you certain?'

'Sure – I only let people I really love get on to my little

bed – even just to sit on it,' she said with sudden coyness. Salvatore knew he was going to wake up in one of his own cells on a charge of drunken fantasy, if there were such a charge. Jesus Bill Christ, she was pouring them more champagne. This was easy, easier than screwing his Betty in the back of his car all those years ago. Betty had kicked like hell. This vision was pouring champagne. She floated towards him, a glass in each hand; the glasses floated before her. He took one, hardly able to stand the devastation of her eyes. He almost missed his mouth when he tried to drink. With a playful push she sat him on the bed. He saw his own knees lock together like a virgin's and he pulled them forcibly apart. 'Now about this little gun,' she said, moving so close her perfume and her warmth added to his giddiness.

'The gun, yes, surely, the gun,' he gabbled, blowing little bubbles of champagne from the top of the glass. 'You wanted to see ... to fit my gun.'

'That's why we came, didn't we?' she smiled overwhelmingly. 'I only invite gentlemen in here for very special reasons.'

Salvatore thought if there was any more of this he would end up a jabbering lunatic. He tried to reach for the gun with the same hand as held the champagne glass. She laughed like a little bell. 'Crazy man,' she said, taking the glass from him. 'You can't reach it like that. You're getting a little confused ...' She leaned towards him and blatantly kissed him on the brow. 'I can't think why you're getting confused.'

'I'll have ... have to take my coat off,' drooled Salvatore. 'If that's all right with you ... in here.'

'There's no better place,' she whispered. 'Just wait a moment, don't go away.'

For a terrible moment he thought she was leaving because she got up and went towards the door. But, to his suffocating delight, it was only to turn the key. She turned across the room and smiled that internationally famous smile. Her bosom seemed halfway to him. 'There,' she said. 'Now you can take your coat off, Honey Captain.'

He struggled out of the stiff best suit coat and sat there in his trousers, his white shirt and gun. 'Oh, I'd really like to wear that, please. It would turn me right on.'

His fingers rushed to the buckle and, fumble though he did, he got the harness from around his body in quick time. He took hold of the gun in the holster and handed it to her like a knight surrendering his sword to a noble lady. 'Is it loaded?' she asked.

'Yes ... no. I can't remember,' he confessed. 'All that seems so long ago Miss di Milo ... Tottie. I guess it's not. Yes, I remember it clearly – it is. So please be careful.'

'It's you who's loaded,' she joked, silkily kissing him again, this time on the cheek and then on the edge of the mouth which he moved swiftly sideways to catch the kiss. Her full breast lolled across his shoulder. If he died later that night he would not have given a damn.

With a long, delighted, deepening smile she held the harness like the coils of a delicate dead snake. He watched her fine cream fingers run along its length and imagined them doing the same along his backbone. Then she got to the holster, bulging and polished. She removed the gun and set it aside with careful casualness. Then she began to massage the holster with her pink nails, running them over the worn, soft leather, and then, turning the palm sensually, revolving over the leather bulge at the end. Salvatore watched every movement of her fingers as though they were caressing his skin. His eyes grew wider and wider until they hurt.

'Beautiful,' she said throbbingly, still fondling the holster. 'So sexy, Honey Captain.' Her eyes came up like slowly moving moons and glowed at him. He could actually feel them on the skin of his face. He gulped at the champagne as a man in a desert might gulp at saving water. There was nothing left in the glass but he was unable to notice.

'You want another drink?' she said, noticing. His hand went to her urgently. 'No, no thanks, Tottie. Just don't move. Don't go away. You may never come back ...'

She laughed in a whisper. 'The little thing you put the gun into really sways me, darling,' she said. 'It turns me on just like nothing's ever going to be able to turn me off again.'

'Would you ... would you care to ... er, try it on?' he inquired like a lingerie salesman with a speech impediment. 'I'll help – it's kinda difficult.'

'Sure, please,' answered Tottie. There were some noises coming from the party but they were two corridors and many ages away as far as Salvatore was concerned. He would have shot anyone who had come into the room just now and would have stood a fair chance with a plea of self defence. She eased her lovely body and picked up the gun. 'And this,' she breathed, 'is beautiful, really beautiful. It double turns me on. Yes ... double.'

She held the police revolver in both hands, abandoning the holster and the harness like used toys. She rubbed it in her hands and closed her eyes with the feel of it. Salvatore with exquisite alarm saw her breasts heaving more quickly than ever. Jesus Cyril Christ, it was all going to happen; he *knew* it was going to happen. Why couldn't the boys from the precinct see him now? He'd show them! He'd show Betty! He'd show her! By God, he would.

'It fits,' she murmured, her eyes half hinging towards him. She had picked up the harness from the bed again and had slipped the gun into the holster. 'So snug,' she said. She began to move it with blatant sensuousness in and out, in and out, up and down, up and down.

This was more than a police captain of twenty years' involuntary blamelessness could stand. Salvatore's hands, trembling on the ends of his shaking arms, went out to touch her. They homed on to the right, blatant breast. He hovered like a man seeking a landing place in a planet and then sumptuously closing on to the flesh and holding on to it, soft and warm and vibrant. Tottie did not seem to notice. Men frequently had their hands on her bosom. 'I want to put the gun on,' she said in her normal voice. 'Will you help, darling?'

Salvatore was beyond words. He withdrew his hands with enormous difficulty, as if they were metal on a magnet, but was immediately rewarded because she bent and kissed his thumbs, left then right, as they were reluctantly moving back towards him. Then, with the merest easing of those laden eyes towards him, she slipped out of the top of the dress and pushed away the encumbrance of the lace bra. There she was, beautifully spread out and displayed, yards of bulging cream skin, it seemed, and large rosy nipples. 'Okay God, you can come and get me now,' challenged Salvatore.

'God's seen them already,' she said a little primly. 'Do you like them, Captain Honey?'

It was the most fatuous question Salvatore had ever heard. 'Big,' he managed to mutter. 'Big and ... big.'

'Thirty-nine inches at the last count,' she said, smiling fondly down at them. Like a careful housewife she brushed an imaginary piece of dust from the surface. Salvatore reached out and obligingly did the same. She continued to smile.

'Just tidying up,' he explained lamely. Then he reached out again and deliberately pressed one nipple and then the other with his bell-ringing finger. That was it. With a sob he abruptly collapsed forward on to all the magnificence and buried his face and even his ears deeply into it.

'Poor Captain,' said Tottie, stroking the sparse tundra hair at the back of his neck. 'Poor, poor Captain.'

Salvatore emerged, because he urgently needed to breathe. She leaned forward and kissed his wet face. 'It was real nice in there Tottie,' he shuddered. 'Real cosy. Like ... like ... home.'

'Did you find what you were looking for?' she inquired with a familiar laugh. She abruptly moved a yard further away from him. 'Now I want to get this gun belt thing on. You help, Honey Captain.'

He did not care a damn what he did now. Haplessly he lifted the gun from the holster and put it on the silken bed. Her fingers went to it and caressed it fondly. He took the harness and, never for a moment able to take his tormented eyes from her bosom, he fumbled with buckles and straps and eventually got the contraption undone. 'Excuse me, Tottie,' he said, leaning towards her. 'This has to go round your ... er, top.'

'Put it round then, baby,' she droned. 'Just hang it on me.'

From the eerie distant past he could hear the voice of his instructor at the police academy calling out the instructions necessary for the fixing of a shoulder holster. The voice echoed from the days when he was a clean-faced kid, all eager to serve the people and the law of the country. How things had changed. Jesus Willard Christ.

'I'll need to get very close to get this on you, Tottie,' he mentioned nervously. 'Very, very close, indeed.'

'Be my guest,' she said, moving forward the yard she had previously retreated. 'Honey Captain.'

He passed the main strap around her back, leaning against those lovely human pillows as he did so. Then came the strap around the front. He failed twice. 'I'll have to kinda ... hold these two still,' he said and put his hand firmly below her right breast before she had time to do it herself. He got the strap below that and then held the left breast still while he did the same that side. It was like holding a pound of warm jelly. Clumsily he buckled the straps and then fitted the revolver holster below the armpit so the side wall of the splendid gland decorating that side was lying snugly against it.

'That seems to be safe,' he said, professionally patting the holster into place and then arranging the breast more comfortably. 'I don't think that will move.'

'Now ... put the gun in, please,' she requested. Her voice was a husky drone. Her opaque eyes were on the holster. Trembling he picked up the gun. He checked the safety catch. 'We don't want any accidents now do we, please?' he murmured. 'Not in that locality.'

He slotted the weapon into the leather container. Her eyes closed. 'That's dreamy,' she whispered. 'Oh God, that's dreamy.' She began to rub her hands over the gun, the holster and the harness and then massage her nipples with her palms. 'I really like it, Captain,' she said as though she had forgotten him but then suddenly remembered he was there. 'I honestly do. It's so good. So very good.'

It's time, thought Salvatore. Now go and get it, you jerk. He made himself move forward, but she slid from beneath him with an unhurried agility born of extended practice. Suddenly the wonderful body was heading towards the door. Salvatore sat shipwrecked on the bed, his arms going beseechingly towards her as she went. At the handle she called back. 'I must show this to Herb, darling. It'll really turn him on too.'

She unlocked the door and was gone into the corridor and towards the crowded party in the salon. Salvatore sobbed with frustration. He rose hopelessly from the bed and sadly ran his hand down the luxurious quilt. Then he hitched himself together and went, a figure of disappointment and despondency, towards the door. He could hear the sounds of excitement coming from the main room. What an entrance she must have made.

Salvatore followed. He got to the main room just as Tottie di Milo was displaying the gun, and much more besides, to a group of entranced guests at one side of the room. Her lover Herb's eyes were wide with anticipation. Other guests were moving over to see what there was to see. Male shouts and exclamations of appreciation, like those from a football crowd, and some startled envious cries from the ladies filled the room.

Then there came a new diversion. Through the tunnel leading from the waterway came a humming that abruptly filled both the tunnel and the room. It was as though a creature from another world had made its arrival. All the people turned. Even the vision of Tottie di Milo was unable to hold them. Through the tunnel and into the living river of that extraordinary room roared the sharp little fan-boat and aboard it, armed and amazing, were the hooded members of the Ocean Drive Delinquent Society.

Salvatore, eyes unbelieving, mouth like granite, reached for the gun he didn't have.

Naturally at first the guests thought it was all part of the entertainment, especially when Tottie herself suddenly opened wild fire with the police revolver she had been so lovingly displaying. Certain that the bullets were blanks, everyone laughed when she began shooting, but the laughter curdled when one of the wild shots brought a large oriental vase in fragments to the floor. Herb managed to stand up from beneath the nerve-wracked wreckage of Frankie Moon's dumb mistress and attempted to take the gun from the trembling Tottie. She refused to be parted from it.

The hooded Gabby, stepping ashore from the fan-boat, pushed her Russian pistol into Tottie's slim waist to make the point. Tottie dropped the gun. Gabby checked it, saw it was empty, and kicked it aside.

'Okay, everybody, just listen,' ordered Ossie loudly. 'If nobody fools about anymore we can get this over with nice and quick and you can get on with the party.'

The gang were deployed three one side of the artificial living river and two the other. Bruce remained aboard the fan-boat, the propeller now idling to a standstill. He lay behind the fierce horizontal barrel of the unloaded Soviet mortar. The guests, collectively shaking, had backed towards the semi-circular walls of the room, which was where they were wanted. Around the walls they formed a nervous half-moon.

'Please take it from me, folks,' continued Ossie, waving his pistol like a rich man waves a cigar, 'we've come on business. Anybody who tries to stop us doing business will have only seconds to regret it. Okay?'

There was a mumbled obligatory assent from the guests. Ossie glared at them through the slits in his hood. So did Gabby. 'Okay?' Gabby shouted. 'Let's hear you!'

'Okay,' 'Yes.' 'Surely.' The words tumbled from the crowd to be followed by stares and mumbles towards Gabby, now that they realized it was a woman below the mask.

Gabby nodded towards Ossie. 'Right,' he ordered. 'This is how we play the game.' He was enjoying himself. It was going right. 'Everybody empties their wallets, their pocketbooks, purses, pockets, right on to the floor in front of them. All the way along there, see. Then everybody takes off watches, jewellery and anything else of value and places it – get me – *places* it, so it stays undamaged, in the same spot. Our collectors will be circulating.'

Salvatore felt he had to do something. 'And if we don't?' he said bravely, Tottie standing just in the corner of his eye.

It was Gabby who answered. She took a step towards him and nodded backwards at Bruce behind the menacing mortar. 'If you don't we blast everybody,' she said quietly.

'Ball brain!' Tottie called at Salvatore. He bit his lip with hurt.

'Okay,' he mumbled, stepping back. 'I only asked.'

'No more questions,' said Ossie. 'It's not a debate. Right, empty the goodies. Come on – move.'

Bruce in the bow swung the mortar first to one side and then the other. Its grim barrel and wide mouth made it a serious sight. Sidewalk, Ari and Molly began to prod the captives on their side of the river and Ossie and Gabby encouraged them on the other. The people reached for their movable wealth from pockets and wrists and fingers. They placed the valuables on the floor until on each side of the room there was a high-tide mark of glittering trinkets, cash, and leather wallets and pocketbooks. On her bank of the river Molly took a canvas bag and began to scoop the loot into it. Gabby did likewise on her side. A sniffling woman complained to Molly: 'Please don't rob me. I'm just a little old lady.'

'So am I,' said the voice behind the mask.

It was all accomplished speedily. 'Now,' called Ossie. 'Has anybody forgotten anything? I bet there *is* somebody.' He leaned forward and took a fat wallet from the coat of a stiff-faced man. 'Personal things,' said the man. 'Private things.'

'Stand over there,' ordered Ossie, looking fiercely into the man's eyes. 'We're going to shoot you.'

The words brought a fresh avalanche of wallets and other valuables piling on the floor. From both sides of the room they appeared. Salvatore's police badge was with them. Ossie picked it up and felt himself go pale inside. He felt for the policeman's gun. 'It's not there,' said Salvatore resignedly. 'The broad had it, remember. The broad who called me ball brain.'

A cop in the house spurred Ossie to get it over with now. He gave a low whistle and the members of the gang backed towards the captive river and their slim craft. 'Sidewalk,' whispered Ossie.

'Okay, I'm going,' came the return whisper. Sidewalk Joe climbed aboard and started the fan. It whirred softly and the boat fidgeted. They knew they would have to reverse through the tunnel. That would be the tricky part of the operation.

'We're going out ass-first,' Ossie called to the white-faced crowd on either side of the room. He pointed to the mortar. 'But just take it from me folks, that weapon will be pointing straight back into this room. If we hear a pin drop before we're clear we'll fire it. If the ladies present don't know what a piece of hardware like that does, maybe their husbands would just whisper it to them.'

He was about to signal the other members of the gang to step carefully aboard the fan-boat when he heard Sidewalk's soft curses. He half looked round. 'The reverse ain't working,' muttered Sidewalk. 'It can't make it.' Ossie swore but still calmly. 'It was in the repair yard,' Sidewalk reminded him.

'Never mind why,' snapped Ossie. He looked up. The semi-circular crowd could see there was something wrong. 'Stand still!' he bawled. He waved his pistol and Bruce swung the mortar from side to side. The guests stood still.

Gabby leaned to Sidewalk. 'Turn the boat in the pond,' she said, nodding at the circular oriental pool. 'You can get it around in there.'

'Good girl,' said Ossie. He whispered to Sidewalk who nodded. Gabby edged towards the metal grille gate that separated the pond from the river. It had a removable bolt. She took it out and with Ari holding the other side of the grille eased it up and out of its housing.

'Watch the alligators,' laughed Tottie di Milo suddenly. 'They haven't been fed.'

'Button up,' barked Gabby. 'Or I'll shoot you where you're biggest.' She was feeling the strain.

'Tell the alligators to button up,' giggled Tottie.

They did not believe her. The 'gators were lying at the bottom of the pool away from the lights and it was only when Sidewalk and Bruce, temporarily forsaking the mortar, began to push the fan-boat around the pond, just big enough for the manoeuvre, that the truth surfaced. The wooden mouth of a large and hungry Everglades alligator suddenly appeared at the low edge of the boat within inches of Bruce's hand. Then another long, jagged jaw surfaced alongside the first.

The creatures were jostling each other to get to the most obtainable man they had seen for some time.

'Oh Christ!' exclaimed Bruce. 'She's right!'

Sidewalk stepped ashore smartly. Bruce was quickly after him. Ossie was staring at the vertical jaws. But Gabby was still aware. 'Turn it round,' she said sharply. 'Get it out of there.'

Gingerly the young man and the old gangster returned to the deck and eased the craft around in a full circle. The alligators had a snap or two at the smooth hull but could get a hold of nothing. Then the bow was pointing the right way again, out towards the waterway. 'Get the gate back,' said Ossie to Ari and Gabby. 'We don't want those bastards following us.' The pair slotted the gate into its housing. Sidewalk pressed the starter button and the fan whirred. With relief and with their loot the gang boarded the small craft. The robbed guests were still standing against the walls. Then at the moment Ossie was about to say. 'Let's go,' Tottie broke drunkenly away from the protective arms of Herb and recklessly running forward plunged up to her lovely armpits in the river, blocking the river and their exit. 'Nobody ain't going from here,' she howled extravagantly. 'You bastards!'

The gang stared horrified. Salvatore, Herb and some of the more gallant were about to advance to her. Gabby turned her gun and shouted at them to get back.

The boozy Tottie was a different problem. She floated magnificently on the river, her great breasts like life preservers, bobbing on the water. 'Nobody leaves,' she shouted. 'It's over my dead body.'

'Okay,' shouted Gabby decisively. 'Let the 'gators out.'

Everybody's eyebrows, inside and outside of masks, shot up. But the girl was serious. 'Let them loose!' she called again. Ari, his nose pale and trembling beneath the hood, climbed from the boat to the shore. He pulled the pin from the grating and lifted the grille. The alligators, now awake and aware, made a move for the open river. Herb and Salvatore made a dash towards the floating Tottie again, but Tottie was no fool. With a wet howl she got herself from the living river and staggered into the embracing arms of her guests and admirers.

'Give it the lot,' said Ossie to Sidewalk. He did. The fan screamed and the small narrow boat shot forward and into the tunnel almost leaving its crew behind. They hung on by inches. Through the tunnel they roared and out into the concealing dark of the Intra-Coastal Waterway. The alligators, hardly able to believe their luck, slid out after them.

Screams and cries filled the house behind them. Women fainted on both banks of the artificial river. Salvatore made a run for the telephone.

eleven

'Yes, for Chrissake!' shouted Salvatore into the phone. 'A fan-boat. That's what I said. I know, I saw them. Listen they can only go two ways, up the waterway or down the waterway ... Oh, okay, okay, or across the waterway ... We got two cars right here. Get Cook to pick me up and send Stewart south along US One. We'll go north. Right, let's move ...'

He made for the door and then returned to get his gun and the holster from Tottie who was letting off small screams in a corner surrounded by numerous well-wishers and spectators. (It was not often you could see a famous actress virtually nude to the waist apart from a gun-belt, letting off small screams.)

'I just need to have my gun, honey,' said Salvatore briskly. He somehow felt better now. More assured. He was not a great policeman but he was a better policeman than a lover. At least he understood the basics. 'My gun please, Miss di Milo,' he repeated. 'I need to have my gun.'

'Take your fucking gun,' said the lady ungraciously. 'Causing all this trouble.'

He was tempted to argue the point but he knew there was no time. He took the gun and was pushed out of the way by the sanctimoniously concerned Herb who retrieved the belt from Tottie's bosom region and handed it scornfully to him. Salvatore strapped it on right away, enjoying the brief quasi-heroic moment, before turning for the door. The bell outside was chiming urgently. That would be Cook.

'Goodbye,' he called gallantly like a knight errant leaving on a mission.

'Fuck off,' Tottie called after him. 'I'll sue you, you bastard. You've lost my alligators.' This last thought, which had apparently just occurred to her, prompted a new spasm of longer wails and hysterical half-sentences. Salvatore went.

Cook was waiting outside. 'Why no all-cars call?' he asked desperately as they hurried towards the patrol car. 'We could have picked them up by now.'

'This is personal,' muttered Salvatore getting into the front seat. The two bemused patrolmen sat in the back. 'I want to get those bastards myself.' Cook started to move towards the gates. 'Go north on US One,' ordered Salvatore. 'Follow the waterway. If they're going north we should be able to hear that fan a mile away. Never mind the siren.'

The look-out, Katy, watched the patrol car pull away and put her hand to her mouth. It was too late to whistle now. But she tried it. She put her fingers to her mouth and let forth a tremendous hoot. Then – according to orders – she walked swiftly from the scene and got a bus back to South Miami Beach.

Cook rushed the car along the streets parallel with the waterway, every now and then pulling up by some private jetty or landing stage so that Salvatore could run eagerly to the edge and listen into the night. At the third pause he heard them. The unique whirr of the fan-boat's propeller. Exultantly he jumped back into the patrol car. 'We got them!' he shouted. 'Half-a-mile up-river. Come on Cookie, for Chrissake!'

Zaharran and Lou the Barbender were waiting with the cars at the planned place between Fort Lauderdale and Pompano Beach. It was an anxious time and Zaharran was grateful that Lou was inclined to fill in the elongated minutes by telling him some of the astonishing feats of strength he had performed in his prime years.

Eventually the droning of Lou's narrative was overtaken

by another drone. Zaharran, whose ears were in better shape than almost any other part of his ill-used body, sat up and quietened the strong man. 'They're coming,' he whispered. 'They're on their way.' He looked at his enormous watch around his enormous wrist. 'They're late.'

The two large men jumped with identical awkwardness from the car and Lou went to the wheel of the second vehicle parked twenty yards away. They watched the dark, limp canal intensely. Then like a moth in the gloom they saw the fan-boat approaching. They started the engines of the cars, then went back to the wooden landing stage to help their fellow conspirators ashore.

The fan-boat edged nearer. Even from the shore Zaharran and Lou could see the dim approaching smiles. 'You made it,' whispered Zaharran.

'Sure,' answered Ossie. 'We made it. But we've got to move quick now.'

The loot bags were carefully handed ashore. The fan had been stilled by Sidewalk and the frail boat fidgeted alongside the jetty. They put the bags into the front car and then helped everybody ashore.

'Let's beat it,' said Gabby. 'They're feeling sore back there. And there was that cop. He'll know what to do.'

'There was a cop?' asked Zaharran.

'Sure, he was at the party.'

Zaharran whistled.

Ossie, Bruce and Gabby jumped in the first car with Zaharran at the wheel. Sidewalk, Ari and Molly were in the second with Lou driving.

'I sure hope Katy's clear,' said Lou.

'She'll have taken off quick, don't worry,' said Ari. 'She'll be back at Sunny Gables by now.'

They started off quickly through the quiet street. Another ten seconds and they would have been clear and into the main road traffic of US One, indistinguishable from any other car, but while they were still running along the waterside street, Salvatore's police car turned from a side junction. Each knew who the other was.

'Cops,' breathed Ossie. 'Go like shit.' Zaharran put his foot down. He heard the car behind begin to rush after them.

'It's them!' Salvatore shouted triumphantly to Cook, so loudly that Cook winced and pulled his ear away. 'Go for them, Cookie, let's get the bastards.'

Cook had to perform a difficult manoeuvre at the junction to get the police car pointing the right way. He tried going on to the sidewalk, but misjudged the distance and had to back down again to avoid hitting a street lamp. Salvatore cursed him vividly.

But they knew what the cars looked like now. 'Why not call all cars?' pleaded Cook, ramming the car's nose along the street. 'We got them, boss. We can sew them up.'

'Shut your ass,' said Salvatore rudely. 'I'm getting these babies by myself. I know what I'm doing, Cookie boy, you just drive and fast. I'll show that Betty.'

They were half a mile behind, siren now going, when Zaharran turned on to the highway leading to the cantilever bridge at Pompano Beach. Lou's car was a yard behind them. Zaharran swerved out so he could see the police in his driving mirror. His driving skill caused Ossie and Bruce to glance at each other. He flashed his brake lights and Lou swerved inside and came level. 'Beat it over the bridge,' Zaharran shouted to Lou. He was giving the orders. 'Wait the other side.'

Now everyone was staring at the fat man. He grunted. 'I know what I'm doing.' Again Ossie's eyebrows went up. Gabby stared at Ossie then at Bruce. Zaharran turned. 'I know,' he repeated. 'Gabby – get over there to the bridge house. Stick a gun in the guy's ribs and get the bridge up. Do it!'

She reacted quickly to his tone. She jumped from the car. 'Then take off,' said Zaharran. 'Anywhere.'

The girl ran through the traffic to the far side of the highway. Zaharran started the car over the bridge. The police siren was getting nearer through the traffic at the back. 'Who are you anyway?' said Ossie.

'A friend,' Zaharran answered coolly. 'A friend who maybe will get you out of this situation. The cops will have an "all cars" alert out now, so hold tight.' He drove the car over the

216

bump of the cantilever. Behind them they could hear the drawbridge warning clanging.

Gabby, her hood down, her Russian automatic in the back of the trembling operator, watched the cantilever arms of the bridge rising like a man making a slow surrender. The bell was sounding and the barrier was down, the red lights flashing. The traffic stopped. Above the bell she could hear the nearing irritable sound of the police siren. She judged it as well as she could. 'Now buddy,' she said, 'just keep that bridge up there for as long as you can. Okay?'

'Okay, young lady,' said the bridge operator. 'I don't want to die. It's my birthday.'

'Happy birthday,' said Gabby. The bridge was almost up now, its fingers seeming to point to something in the sky. She heard the police car stop. She backed out, put the gun away and ran easily down a narrow street into the anonymous darkness. As she went she began wondering about Zaharran.

Salvatore was spitting with rage. 'That fucking bridge!' he kept shouting. 'That goddamn fucking bridge!' He sent one of the patrolmen running to the bridge house. He glared at Cook as if it were his fault.

'All cars?' suggested Cook blandly. 'Want to make the call?'

'No! I'll give the orders!' Salvatore howled. Oh God, he couldn't lose them now. What lousy goddamn luck. 'Get Stewart,' he grunted. 'And quick.'

Cook got the other patrol car on the radio. Salvatore grabbed the instrument. 'Where are you?' demanded Salvatore.

'Going south on US One,' he said. 'We're at Hollywood Beach.'

'Okay, turn around. Go across the bridge at Lauderdale. Suspects now on ocean side US A-One-A heading north or south. I don't know. They've fucked us at Pompano Bridge. Okay?'

'Okay, we're going,' answered Stewart. 'Why not make it all cars, chief?'

'Do what I say!' howled Salvatore. 'I'm doing this!'

The Pompano Bridge before them was now descending, the

patrolman having persuaded the frightened bridge keeper that it was the right thing to do, and that he was personally safe. The policeman ran as he saw the patrol car moving around the waiting traffic and jumped into the rear just as it was accelerating towards the falling arm of the bridge. 'A woman,' he said breathlessly closing the door. 'She stuck a gun into the guy and told him to put the bridge up.'

Salvatore cursed. Even as he did so Stewart, to the south, was crossing the Fort Lauderdale drawbridge towards the ocean. As he did so the policeman beside him called a warning and along the opposite lane, going in the other direction, roared the two fugitive cars. As Stewart braked and reached the summit of the bridge, it began to yawn open, horrifying the police crew. The car went nose-first down an ever-steepening hill. Bruce, a gun in the ribs of the bridge keeper, watched it coolly, then stepped back and ran into the shadows. Stewart's car came down the incline and slewed around in the road. Then Salvatore's car arrived. Now both cars were on the same side of the bridge.

Salvatore stared unbelievingly at the other police car. 'It's the Keystone fucking cops!' he bawled. He began to use his radio, swore again, and leaned out of the window. 'Stewart, you jerk. Where are they?'

'On the other side of the bridge,' answered Stewart. 'Shall I call all cars?'

Salvatore blasphemed again. Jesus Malcolm Christ, why couldn't they get anything right? 'Stay there,' he shouted. 'Wait till the goddamn bridge is down then get over it. Go north on US One, okay?'

He guessed right for once. He shouted at Cook loud enough to frighten that officer and Cook turned their own car north along Collins and towards the bridge at Boca Raton. They reached the bridge and mounting the middle reservation, skimmed by the traffic. Like Stewart on the previous draw-bridge they had just reached the summit when the road began to lift under their wheels. Salvatore went crazy. He knew what was going to happen and it did. The fugitive cars came in the opposite direction and the police car, passing them, had no alternative but to run down the ever increasing angle of the slope on to the wrong bank of the waterway. As they arrived on the other side so Stewart's car turned the corner at the end of the street. Stewart saw what had happened and grinned with mean satisfaction.

'Serve the bastard right,' he said to himself.

Salvatore ran to the bridge house himself. The Boca Raton bridge operator was ashen-faced, leaning on his little desk. He saw the policeman with enormous relief. 'A guy with a mask ... and a gun,' he mumbled. 'He had a *real* gun.' It was too late to look into the shadows now. Salvatore decided on one last throw. He ordered both cars south down the ocean side of the waterway. He sent Stewart over Pompano Bridge and his own car ran on to the cantilever at Fort Lauderdale. To his astonishment parked casually by the side of the bridge house was one of the runaway cars.

Salvatore ran over, his still unloaded gun waving, and followed by his panting policemen. Sitting in the driving seat, reading the *Miami News*, was Zaharran. He turned and gave Salvatore a huge creased smile.

Salvatore felt sick. 'Oh God,' he said, almost like a prayer. 'What the fuck is this guy doing here?'

'This guy,' said Zaharran slowly, 'is reading the sports page of the paper, because this guy just might as well occupy himself doing that because this guy just had a month's work screwed up by some cops.'

Leaning wearily against the hull of the car Salvatore said: 'You had them? You got them?'

'Sure I had them,' said Zaharran just as wearily. 'Right here. I was among them. I was right in there. I was ready to spring the trap. I even had the loot, Salvatore, right here in this automobile. But suddenly we get ambushed by the cops and suddenly I try to stall the car and suddenly they think maybe I'm working for the cops and suddenly they put a big Russian gun in my ear. I'm lucky to be sitting here with my entire head.'

'Okay, okay,' said Salvatore more eagerly. 'But you got them. You got descriptions?'

'Sure. Every face was the same. Covered with a hood with two eye slits. That any good to you? I never saw them without masks. After tonight I would have been all right with them. They would have trusted me. But you blew it, Captain Salvatore, you blew it.'

'How the fuck could we know?' demanded Salvatore angrily. 'You didn't tell us nothing.'

'Okay, you didn't blow it. It just got blown.' He folded the newspaper deliberately. 'There's a chance I might get the loot back,' he suggested. Salvatore's face brightened. 'And most of the dough from the bank,' added Zaharran.

'You can? You can do that?' Stewart's car arrived on their side of the bridge but Salvatore waved him away impatiently.

'Maybe, but I have to be left alone. Already I got some of the cash sent back to the bank. Ten thousand bucks in a package by post. Right?'

'Right,' said Salvatore. 'That was you then?'

'Who else? Santa Claus? But don't bug me. I got to do it my way. And only *I* know about my way.' He turned a slow old eye to Salvatore. 'For the reward.'

'For the entire bank haul there's ten thousand bucks,' said Salvatore. 'You know that.'

'What about tonight's? Will there be something for receiving that?'

'Well not yet. Jesus Harold Christ, it only just happened an hour ago. But I guess there will be. I guess that can be arranged. You can really get the stuff back?'

'I think so. But on my *own*. Okay Salvatore?'

'Okay, if that's what you want.'

'That's just what I want,' said Zaharran. 'I don't want any official screwing up of this. Maybe you'll let me know tomorrow about the reward for tonight's stuff. I'm already running at a deficit on this case.'

Salvatore nodded. 'Maybe next time we'll get the bastards,' he said. 'I got a feeling we will. Where did they come from Zaharran?'

'Philadelphia,' lied Zaharran easily. 'They came down from Philly.'

'I might have guessed,' said Salvatore seriously.

'And they won't be operating in the Miami area again,' continued Zaharran. 'They're splitting.'

'That's the best news so far. Where are they splitting to? Back to Philly?'

'Alaska,' sniffed Zaharran. 'Alaska, I heard.'

'Wouldn't you just know,' said Salvatore.

'Okay Mr Zaharran,' said Gabby. 'So you came to find us. Why didn't you find us?'

Zaharran sat in Bruce's room facing the three young ones. Bruce farted and restarted the air conditioning which had been faltering. Zaharran looked at him appreciatively. 'A short-term discomfort for long-term benefits,' he said quizzically. He looked around at them. 'I don't know,' he said, going back to the question. 'I came to find you, but somehow I didn't. I guess I got kinda fond of the older folks. I'm an old folk myself, see. I sympathize because I have the same problems. I get lonely and bored and frustrated like hell. I guess you could say I'm an old folk first and a retired cop second. And I never did have ten thousand bucks in cash before. That was too much of a temptation for a poor man.'

'You've sent that back too?' said Bruce.

'Sure. I didn't get a choice. Not after I'd collected all the rest from you. The bank got its cash back. It's a real nice deal for them. And Miss Tottie di Milo's friends got all their trinkets back and a story to tell their friends. And nobody is going to be any the wiser about you. As far as the cops are concerned you've taken off. For Alaska. So I guess everybody's more or less happy.'

'What about you?' asked Ossie. 'You pick up the rewards?'

'Sure I do. I've been working, remember. This is my profession. I have to live don't I?' They agreed that he had to live. 'You'll be moving out I guess,' he said, eyeing them suggestively. 'Somewhere not too near. Like China.'

'That direction,' nodded Ossie. 'We're just going, right now. We came to say goodbye.'

Solemnly Zaharran shook hands with each of them and they went out leaving him sitting in the room. He released wind to try and start the air conditioning. It didn't work. He was getting old.

Ossie, Bruce and Gabby walked down the stairs with their

respective meagre belongings. Suddenly they felt a yawning awkwardness between them. Nobody spoke. They went outside the Sunny Gables Hotel and stood on the uncomfortably hot sidewalk. Nobody seemed to want to make the first move. Then a new model Cadillac cruised along Ocean Drive and stopped right there by them. A bronzed, middle-aged man was at the wheel. Bruce and Ossie realized, with sinking hearts, who he was. He smiled handsomely and opened the door. Gabby quickly kissed Bruce and then Ossie and while they stood speechless stepped into the car and embraced the man. Then she leaned out of the automobile and dropped something into Ossie's hand. He looked down at it. 'It's the bullet we never used,' said Gabby. 'Maybe it was as well. It's a dud.' The car eased itself along the street and turned a corner towards Washington Avenue.

'Jesus help me,' said Bruce at last. 'And I thought she was crazy about me.'

'And me,' shrugged Ossie.

If the pelican cruising along from the Keys towards Fort Lauderdale that May day had cared to note - and pelicans, being forever lost in thought, are not, as a general rule, observant birds - it would have seen small changes along South Miami Beach. There were fewer people sitting under the seagrape trees along Ocean Drive, the terraces of the larger hotels, a few blocks to the north, were less populated and those that sat were off-season people. The waves were too dull for the surfers and the day too hot to encourage the rich widows to display themselves in their bikinis and pink boots. No students blew bubble gum at Hallendale. The voice of Station WAIA was hung with weariness.

What can I say folks you don't already know. South Florida is having the hottest day of the year so far. Phew! At noon the pointer got to ninety-eight degrees and the humidity is way, way up. Roll on November we say, don't you? WAIA your music way, serving the golden coast from the Palm Beaches to Key West ...'

Lou the Barbender and K-K-Katy were practising for their wedding, sitting in her humid, gown-hung room, he perspiring in his tailed coat and stiff collar, she wearing her unused wedding dress. On the following day they were to be married. Sidewalk Joe, playing poker now beneath the sea-grape trees, was to be their special guest.

Ari the Greek waited until evening before he took his run. As he left Sunny Gables Hotel, which would be his home forever, the rival Nissenbaums came out, arms folded, for their evening confrontation. The sun had dipped dramatically, gorged and red, grinning after a day's demonstration of its prowess. A small, apologetic breeze arrived late from the Atlantic and fussed around like an inadequate rescue team trying to alleviate a large disaster. Ocean Drive was still warm under foot but once he had crossed the street towards the ocean Ari felt the little touch of the zephyr on his great nose and was grateful. He made a brief shadow-boxing turn and then began to jog towards the beach. He went very easily, at not much more than walking pace, but before he had cleared the sea-grape trees there was a sheen of sweat across his old brow. The concrete calendar on Ocean Drive showed it was 17 July, eight-fifteen p.m. and still seventy-four degrees. Ari poked his tongue out at it as he passed.

He was not surprised to see Molly Mandy on the beach, her metal detector performing its habitual concentric circles.

He approached from behind and noted how, in the reduced light, the big earphones clamped to her small head gave her the silhouette of Minnie Mouse. He smiled at the image.

Thoughtfully he made a detour, still jogging, so that he did not startle her. He was a dozen yards to her right when she saw him from the corner of her intent eyes.

'Hi, Ari,' she called.

'Hi there, Molly, hot day.'

'Sure was. You still running?'

'Still running,' he confirmed, increasing the pace of his jogging on the spot just to demonstrate the point. 'While I'm running I'm living.'

She nodded, acknowledging the philosophy. 'And I'm still looking,' she said, staring at the darkening sand at her feet. ''Bye, Ari.'

''Bye, Molly,' he answered. He slipped into gear and jogged

away from her. She looked up from her search and watched him go. On impulse she called after him. 'Ari – you and me ought to go into business sometime.'

He slowed and jogged on the spot, half turned and then continued. 'Teeth,' he shouted back. 'Now there's a real *good* business. Teeth.'